Enchanted

First Published in Great Britain in 2019 by
LOVE AFRICA PRESS
103 Reaver House, 12 East Street, Epsom KT17 1HX
www.loveafricapress.com

The right of Bambo Deen, Fiske Nyirongo, Karo Oforofuo and Kiru Taye to be identified as authors of this work has been asserted by them in accordance with the Copyright, Design and Patents Act, 1988

ISBN: 978-1-9161546-6-7
Also available as ebook

BLURB:

Be enchanted. These handpicked tales of African deities and daemons, shamans and shape-shifters will keep you spellbound page after page.

Featured stories and authors:
Daemon Trapped by Bambo Deen
Finding Love in Betrayal by Fiske Nyirongo
Dream Seductor by Karo Oforofuo
Haunted by Kiru Taye

Daemon Trapped

BAMBO DEEN

BLURB

When long-suffering daemon Leonidas is trapped in Besidas' hotel, she is drawn into a world of curious and strange creatures. Stranded after a cruel attempt on his life, Leon has spent decades trying and failing to return home. Besi evokes emotions within him that he did not think were possible for his kind and for the first time he's enjoying Earth. But can Leon protect Besi when a dangerous entity from Leon's past comes for revenge?

PROLOGUE

The Forest had appointed four guards to preside over the four entrances that led to the home of different kinds of daemons and all sorts of creatures—both good and evil.

One day, the Western Guard fell into a trap specially set for him. What had started as a stroll to his post from his home ended with him looking up at the sky from a hole deep in the earth. He had not seen it coming.

He landed in the trap with his tools, his wand—a wooden figurine crafted for him by the Forest itself—in his hand. He could fly out of the hole with its help. However, with each attempt at escape, he felt the power of his life force draining out from him.

Truly in a bind, he had no other choice but to call for help. He screamed 'til his throat was sore.

When the familiar face of the Southern Guard appeared above him, relief flooded through him.

"Help me out of here," he called up.

To his surprise, the Southern Guard sneered. "Since you love humans so much, why don't you live among them?"

The Southern Guard waved his own wand, and the earth started shaking. The loose dirt beneath the Western Guard's feet slipped.

"The Forest pardoned me," the Western Guard shouted, but his colleague had disappeared.

His legs sank deeper into the hole, and glancing down, he saw what looked like another sky opening up below him.

He fell through the hole that became the sky and landed with a earth-shattering crash.

CHAPTER ONE

Besida Agbajor wasn't one for late nights in the office. But with her new bosses currently on vacation in Samoa during the week of their scheduled monthly meetings, she had little choice. She tilted her right ear to meet her shoulder as she scanned through the financials again.

"They aren't going to like this," she said to her empty office.

She had set jazz to play over the speakers an hour ago, and it did nothing to calm her nerves. She abruptly stopped the music and pushed her swivel chair away from her desk and laptop.

Rising to her bare feet—she had kicked off her heels a while back—she walked towards the window. Through the firmly shut sliding glass windows and the insect-proof netting, she counted three cars in parking lot of Gazania Hotels. The crowd that had stormed through the doors following the drama two weeks ago was thinning out.

Besi had to admit to herself that she had done a poor job of containing that scandal involving the former governor turned senator's wife and her lovers. After a blogger had put photos of the location online in a post that painted their establishment as a den of orgies, things had worsened. Gazania promised a secluded, private environment for anyone looking for a mindful retreat, so seeing their name and address plastered all over the Internet had been a huge blow.

Closing her eyes, she inhaled deeply. She held that breath for a beat and then let it go, imagining all her nervousness slipping away. Her laptop started dinging behind her, letting her know a call was coming through.

She squared her shoulders as she spun and returned to her desk. Somehow, it was less nerve-racking managing millions of dollars for seed companies than it was managing just one branch of her parents' business.

"Good evening," she greeted her parents.

William and Lolade Agbajor were seated in what could have been a generic room if not for the azure waters glimpsed from the open windows behind them.

"Good evening, Besi," Lolade replied. "We've had a chance to look through the files you sent last night."

It would have been surprising but not unwelcome if her parents had started with small talk about her personal life. Besi had not spoken to them outside business in months. Still, she went full swing into the details they required. In the middle of expounding on the figures from the recently opened pan-Asian restaurant that had been her idea, a small knock came on the door.

She glanced up—she had given express instructions not to be disturbed.

"As I was saying ..." she attempted to continue.

The knocking stopped, but now, her phone started vibrating loudly against the wooden surface of her desk.

She shot a quick look at her phone—Miranda, her operations manager who should know better than to disturb her. She hit the red button.

"Don't you want to answer that?" William asked.

"Not right now," she replied, shifting in her chair. Her phone began vibrating again. "It's from the hotel ..."

"And you would ignore it?" Lolade's voice dripped with disapproval.

Besi groaned inwardly at yet another faux pas.

"Excuse me then," she said and hastily rescheduled the call before calling Miranda.

"Hello, Miranda." She tried her best not to sound irritated.

"Sorry to disturb you, ma," Miranda said, clearly excited. "I am outside your office."

"Come in," she said before hanging up.

From the door, she immediately sensed something was up. Miranda rushed in, and when she was close enough, Besi saw her eyes were sparkling.

"What's the matter?"

"We have another situation." Miranda had whispered the last word.

"A what?" Besi jumped to her feet.

"Like the one with the senator's wife." Miranda let the implication hang in the air.

Cold dread washed over Besi, and she fell back into her chair.

"How bad is it? Who knows?"

"No one but me," Miranda replied confidently. "I heard someone shouting for help and rushed to investigate."

"You're sure no one heard this?" Besi asked again. She looked at her laptop to confirm its lid was down.

"I'm sure. You said it before, 'Don't raise any alarm, don't let anyone know that anything is out of the ordinary'."

"Great job, Miranda. Let's go."

Besi followed Miranda out her office. The door creaked closed behind them as they walked down the hallway. She was only a couple of months into this position and this town, so on any given day, she made sure she took the time out to appreciate the fact that this building was built in the colonial style.

Years ago when she had still been in New York, her parents had bought and transformed the house into this ten-room boutique hotel. However, as Miranda continued sharing the sparing details she knew of the current situation, Besi's entire body thrummed with impatience. Several images of what could have gone wrong swiped through her mind.

By the time they reached the door of the double room in the eastern wing, her stomach was rolling.

***

Leonidas' arms hurt, suspended as they were above his head, held in place by a pair of fluffy pink handcuffs. He shifted to lean his head, pressing it against the cool, tiled bathroom wall.

On any other day, he'd admire the details reminiscent of a Moroccan hammam. Frankly, every detail about this hotel had stood out to him from as early as when he'd driven past the gates artfully shielded with creeping vines. He would have savoured every detail if he hadn't been accosted in such an unseemly manner.

For the umpteenth time, he'd been bested. When he thought about it, this was less dangerous than other situations he had been in. Handcuffed to the shower in a fancy hotel, mostly naked. Becca and Razaq had taken pictures before they had left him, and Leon imagined those images would soon be online somewhere. What would the headlines say? Now that he couldn't picture, thanks to Rike—everything that came up on the Internet about him boasted about his brilliance and success.

"The brilliant woodworker bringing life to the homes of celebrities"

"We are collectively swooning over Leonidas Okpe"

"30 under 30: The designer, Leonidas Okpe"

The last one made him chuckle. *30 under 30* indeed—he had way more years than that under his belt.

He held back a yelp as his back muscles clamped down hard. He had done enough of that to know help was on the way. He gazed at the key resting on the edge of the washbasin.

Levitating was out of the question; that had never been his speciality. He had tried to disappear and will himself back home, but that had been unsuccessful. His energy levels were low, and after spending hours in this situation, he now suspected he had been drugged. He knew betrayal intimately, but at least, Becca and Razaq hadn't tried to kill him and inadvertently sent him to another universe. He shook his head and let it hang heavy, waiting for help.

"Excuse me," a soft voice drifted from the bathroom door. "Good evening, I am Besi Agbajor, General Manager of Gazania."

"Good evening," he grunted in reply.

"I'll be coming in now," she announced.

It sounded like she was struggling to get the door open. He heard one push and then another before the door gave way. His head swam at the sight of Besi, and he was immediately drawn to her angelic eyes set in a heart-shaped face accentuated by long braids. She was stunning.

***

Besi gasped. The first thing she saw was the broad expanse of his chest emphasised by the thick, strong arms that were suspended. His hips were lean in his black boxers that didn't leave anything to the imagination. She had never read *Fifty Shades of Grey*, but something about this bound man sent shivers straight between her legs.

He sent a lopsided smile at her, and goose bumps broke over her skin.

"The keys are on the basin," he said, pointing with his chin.

Those words snapped her out of whatever the hell that had been. She squared her shoulders and looked at the direction he indicated. Whoever had cuffed him there had left the keys.

A thousand and one questions ran through her mind, but the man looked tired, his face pale and drawn. She grabbed the keys and approached the bathtub. She looked up—she wasn't short, but she would need to tap into her yoga lessons to reach the shower head he was anchored to.

"Excuse me." She lifted one leg then the other to the rim of the bathtub, and she now stood face to face with him, looking into his eyes.

Besi swayed slightly. She looked up and scolded herself into concentration. Stretching one arm up, she sought the handcuffs with the keys. The other hand held the rail as she tried to insert the key into the tiny lock. She could feel the heat of his body and the light flutter of his breath. The lock resisted before giving way, and just as it clicked, she slipped.

It was a short fall, wouldn't have been anything serious if she had tipped backwards. But she'd slipped forward, her body gliding against the man she had just freed. She felt his arms try to hold her and fail. Embarrassment coursed through her veins, and it took all of her pride to hold her head high as she stepped out of the tub and away from him.

"Thank you," he said, stepping out of the tub, too. "This feels good, I ..."

She reached out as the man swayed on his feet. His weight strained on her, and she called over to Miranda for help. Together, they placed him on the bed.

"Do we need a doctor?" Miranda worried her bottom lip.

"Probably." Besi looked down at him. "Who knows how long he's been hanging there."

"But which doctor will come at this time? What if he dies? You know who he is, don't you?"

"Not going to happen," she hushed Miranda. "I think I can call someone."

In her haste to get here, she had left her phone in her office. She rushed towards the door, but his voice stopped her. As she looked over her shoulder, her eyes widened at the sight of him sitting up. He was calmly wearing his clothes as if he had not been in handcuffs for hours. As if he had no lost consciousness.

"Excuse me, Mister ..." she started.

"Just call me Leon," he said, before clearing his throat. "There is no need for a doctor."

"Are you sure you're all right?" She had to search through her brain for the appropriate words.

"I am," he replied, and incredulously, he winked at her. "I can't find my phone. Is there any I can borrow?"

"Mine," Miranda said, her phone in her hands.

Besi waited until Miranda had made the call to Leon's personal assistant and then entered Boss mode. The panic at not knowing what was going on in her hotel had dissipated.

"Miranda, do you mind excusing us?" she said.

Once Miranda was gone, she glared at Leon. He was fully dressed now, in tailored pants and a collared shirt, looking more like a distinguished businessman than anything else.

"I know you've had a tough time," she began. "But Mr. Leon, can you please tell me what happened? I need to be ready for any backlash. I'm sure you understand."

"Just Leon," he replied.

He was wearing cufflinks now. Once he was done, he turned to face her, and once again, she was drawn to his eyes.

"I am terribly sorry that this happened at your establishment—which is an outstanding one, I must say. What happened here was a childish prank gone wrong, but still a prank nonetheless. I came here with friends and will be meeting them shortly after I leave. I promise that your hotel won't appear in the gossip rags."

Besi found herself nodding at everything he said. His words were calm and measured; he weighed everything before speaking as a shopper would select the best fruit at the market.

"There is really no reason to worry," he repeated. "My assistant will soon be here."

"All right," she said. "I'll be outside if you need anything."

It was after she had returned to her office that she realised that he hadn't really told her anything.

***

Free at last, Leon thought. Even though he was still bound in other ways. Like to this world, for one. He slipped into his shoes and stole another glance at the owner of the hotel as she walked away. He shook his head. Now was not the time to dwell on how beautiful his rescuer was.

When he thought of it, the last woman who had saved him had been bewitching, too. A human who had wandered so deep into the wooded forests that she had ended up in his world of daemons—varied spirits, wraiths, strange and curious creatures; Forest Home.

This had happened at least a hundred years ago if one was going by time as the humans today calculated it, but Leon recalled it as if it were yesterday. He could see her face peering down the hole he had been trapped in and left to die. Forest Home was a dangerous place, even for those that lived it in.

Several sharpened wooden stakes had pierced through his body, the pain rendering him witless, and she had saved him with his own magic. To repay his debt to her, he had looked the other way and let her roam Forest Home; a place that was forbidden to humans and had four guards to ensure this rule was maintained.

That one action would irrevocably change his life. Just his bad luck that the next time he had been dropped into a hole, she hadn't been there to save him. Nonetheless, she was still the reason he was free and thriving.

The door creaked open, and Rike, his assistant barged in. She looked so much like her ancestor, the adventurous huntress who had saved him and now left him in the care of her descendants.

"Who was it this time?" she demanded, crossing her arms over her chest. "I keep telling you not to trust people knowing your propensity for getting betrayed."

Rike was always protective of him, which he found funny at times because she wasn't the supernatural being in this situation.

"It was Becca and Razaq. They seem to have taken my phone, too."

"Damn it," she cursed. She eyed him from his head to his feet, her concern evident in her eyes. "Should I hex them? I will hex them."

"No need." He tapped her on her shoulder. "Let's go home for now."

***

In his study, Leon settled heavily on the oversized leather chair. It was strategically placed in front of the window that offered a stunning view of his garden, but this late at night, the view was blocked by thick velvet curtains. He removed his cufflinks and placed them on the ebony accent table before leaning even deeper into the chair.

"You know they just called me to ask if I was available," Leon said. "I had no suspicion ..."

"I say this with all my love," Rike replied as she picked up his cufflinks. "But you never have any idea."

He groaned. "They took pictures of me! In a very indecent state."

"I'll sort that out, don't worry." She walked over to the mini-bar on the other side of the room, next to the desk. "You're not going to end up on the Internet."

"Thank you, Rike." He accepted the glass of aged whiskey she handed to him and downed the drink in one gulp.

"While we're on the topic, I have an update on what we've been looking for," Rike said as she refilled his glass.

When Leon had found himself in this world, it had been Rike's grandmother who had saved him. But his relationship with the family stretched even further back— aeons ago, her ancestor had saved him in the Forest Home.

On this side, he happily entered a contract with the Folahan family where they managed his wealth and provided him a cover for his apparent immortality. Rike was different from her predecessors—she'd come in four years ago and surprised him with her multiple piercings, tattoos, and bleached Afro. He had initially assumed a young woman like her would not be interested in taking over the family business, but Rike was well-versed in the tradition of magic that had been passed down from her mothers. She was also more than happy to modernise the relationship her family had with Leon.

She was the reason his architecture hobby had become beloved by the crème de la crème of Nigerian society. She was the reason he'd made it to the headlines. He liked laying low and wanted to keep it that way, but Rike had other plans. She wanted him to leave with a bang, as she put it, because she was sure she would be the one to help him return to the Forest.

"Fuck it," she'd said. "You're going to be out of this world soon. Just go large then go home."

True to her word, she was good at making things happen. Now thanks to her, they had the first lead to getting him back home that he had come across in decades.

"I have established contact with the seller," she was saying as she swiped through her tablet. "And I'm this close to placing the order. The seller is saying it'll take a couple of weeks to reach Nigeria."

"We don't have weeks," he started, then grinned at the absurdity of that statement. Both of them knew that he had been trying to find the wand—the emblem of his power that had gone missing when he'd landed here—for a very long time. "Travel to wherever is nearest to the seller and take the next flight back."

"I've always wanted to go to the Bahamas," she said, a lopsided grin on her face.

He narrowed his eyes even though he was smiling.

"All right, okay," Rike launched. "I'll go to New York tomorrow ... I mean, later today ... and be back before you know it."

"Great." He nodded.

He would not think about how his wand had found its way across the ocean. To the person who was selling it online, it was an authentic African antique belonging to the Yoruba people of southwestern Nigeria. To Leon, it was a personal treasure not of this world, not only a one-of-a-kind gift made for him by the Forest, but intimately tied to his duty as a guard.

From the few daemons that had come to Earth after him, he'd learned that the Forest had gone into disarray since its Western Guard had disappeared. With such an imbalance, the already violent place became more precarious as the more evil forest creatures multiplied and wreaked havoc on the peace-loving ones.

It didn't matter that he was now buying back his own property or that it had been stolen from him initially, even before he could have figured out how to create a portal leading back home. Before, it wouldn't have occurred to him to check the websites Rike knew of. And this statue looked so much like his wand, the only way to know for sure would be to hold it in his hands. It was imperative that he return home.

"Let me call the travel agent," Rike announced, already on her way out the study.

"Before you go," he said just as she was about to open the door. "Kindly order for some flowers sent to Gazania."

The thought had swept through his mind, and he'd grabbed it. He had just met Besi Agbajor, but he'd felt a connection he wanted to pursue, and not because he had a thing for human women saving him from trouble.

Rike paused, brow raised. "The hotel? Who should the flowers be addressed to?"

"The manager," he replied, trying to keep a poker face. "What? I'm just extending my thanks for her cool-headed resolution of an embarrassing situation."

She did not say anything, but Leon could feel her gaze boring into him. Sometimes, he swore she used her magic to make it feel like the back of his neck was on fire.

He shifted in the chair and finally looked over his shoulder to where she stood by the door.

Finally, she spoke. "What's up? Are you trying to set yourself for another betrayal? You could die this time."

"Like I said," he repeated. "I'm expressing my thanks. She saved me."

"Sure," she said, rolling her eyes. "You never listen to me anyway."

Leon heard her murmuring about how she would still have to clean up after him before she could close the door behind her.

CHAPTER TWO

Besi opted to take a cab to Caesar's because she knew she would be too tipsy to drive back home. The bottomless mimosas promised on the flyer Chizua had shared were just what she needed. Three months into running Gazania, it was time to let her hair down, and she had literally done that. The braids she had been wearing had been taken out yesterday, and now, her straightened hair floated past her shoulders.

Chizua was the instructor at the private yoga classes Besi had attended a few times. They'd connected from the first class, and what a relief to finally be meeting outside. From the moment she walked into Caesar's, Chizua raised a hand and waved at her—she was seated at a table to the far right, near one of the floor-to-ceiling windows that made the restaurant look bright and spacious.

Besi noticed Chizua wasn't alone. Beside her sat a woman whose hazelnut skin clashed with the bright red wig she wore. The face looked familiar—she may have seen her at yoga class.

"Besi!" Chizua jumped to her feet to give her a tight hug. "So good to see you. This is Oyife. You remember her from class?"

"Hello." Besi stretched out a hand to Oyife, but the woman stood up instead.

"I'm a hugger. Is that okay?" Oyife asked, already stretching her arms.

"I hope you don't mind, Besi," Chizua said as they took their seats. "We're already on our first mimosas, and the wings are coming up soon."

"We got peppered and barbecue wings," Oyife chipped in.

Besi was only ten minutes late, but it looked like the party had started without her. Chizua waved to the waiters at the bar. Once she'd caught their attention, she turned to her.

"So you have to tell me about the flowers you received. I've been dying to know more."

Besi shook her head. "I already told you, they were from a guest at the hotel."

And that was the only information she would give. She wouldn't talk about how she had seen said guest in his underwear, or give details on how his briefs pressed against him and left little to the imagination. She gave a shuddering sigh at the memory of the fleeting but intense feeling of his body against hers.

Chizua had surprised her last week with a visit to Pan, the Afro-Asian fusion restaurant housed in Gazania under Besi's initiative. In the brief moment they had talked in Besi's office, Chizua had noticed the flowers. With red roses, chrysanthemums, and tuberose, they were hard to miss. Chizua had commented on them at least a dozen times in the ten minutes she'd spent in her office. She had even taken pictures in protest to what she called Besi's lacklustre demeanour.

"They looked absolutely gorgeous," Oyife said. "No one has ever sent me flowers. I mean, that guy must be very romantic."

"I hope you don't mind, I showed her pictures," Chizua quickly added. "But really, was that all? He came to your hotel, fell in love with you, and then sent you flowers?"

"He did not," Besi started, then paused when a waiter appeared with a tray of drinks. "There was no falling in love."

The champagne flute was halfway to her lips when Oyife yelled, stopping her.

"Let's take a selfie first!" Oyife said, raising her phone.

Chizua rolled her eyes and leaned towards Besi. "Oyife has about fifty thousand followers on Instagram. Everything must be documented."

"Yes o." Oyife chuckled.

After the pictures were taken, Besi hoped the conversation would veer in a different direction, but her new friends had other plans.

"He asked me on a date," she finally revealed. "But I turned it down. I contacted his personal assistant with my thanks, but that's it."

"Why?" Oyife asked, clicking her fingernails against the table. "Isn't he the popular guy that makes furniture?"

Besi made a mental note to limit the information she shared with Chizua in the future.

"He is. But which Nigerian man is called Leonidas?"

Chizua laughed. "Come on, Nigerians have all sorts of names, and you know it."

"And this particular Leonidas is fine!" Oyife said. "Wasn't he attached to that upcoming actress?"

Oyife was only repeating things Besi had discovered herself in one weak moment when she'd admitted she was thinking about Leon way too much and had Googled the name on the card attached to the flowers. So she knew Leon and the actress weren't attached—all he'd done was make all the furniture for her house.

Her new friends were singing the man's praises, but the truth was that after the flowers and her thank you with a side of rejection, she had not heard from him again. It had been a week, so it was safe enough to assume that enough time had passed and she would not be seeing him again.

Thankfully as their second round of wings came with more drinks, the conversation shifted to Oyife's new book club.

With each drink, Besi felt more at ease with Chizua and Oyife. So much that she gasped when she finally looked down at her watch and realised the time.

"Oh my," she groaned. "There's that art exhibition at the gallery in Wuse 2."

"True, the one with Zuliat Nuhu, right?" Chizua said. "Let's all go. I think we've had enough here. Are you okay with that, Oyife?"

***

As soon as they got to the gallery, Besi was on the lookout for Zuliat Nuhu. It was Zuliat's first exhibition. The young artist and photographer took photos recreating historical moments. Her work focused on women from different ethnic groups and showed them in elegant hairdos, wearing extravagant fabrics, and sitting before reconstructed scenes. Her photos genuinely looked like images from colonial archives except, in her work, the women held a silent dignity. Besi already knew the portraits she would be buying for each of her grandmothers.

Once she saw Zuliat, she cornered her shamelessly and immediately took on the role of the fangirl.

"These are so beautiful," she gushed. "My grandmothers would love this."

"Thank you," Zuliat replied, a shy smile on her face. "I've always imagined what life was like for our grandmothers and their mothers. It's a joy bringing what I imagined to life."

"I'd like to know more about your technique," Besi said. "Is that okay?"

Before Zuliat could reply, Oyife appeared beside them. Besi had to swallow a groan at the interruption.

"Guess who's here?" Oyife's eyes sparkled with barely contained excitement.

"Who?" Besi frowned as the young artist excused herself.

"Him," Oyife whispered, placing her hands on Besi's shoulders and leading her downstairs, spinning her 'til she saw Leon.

Seeing the man that had occupied so much of her thoughts recently sent butterflies aflutter in her belly.

He was dressed colourfully, in pants and a shirt tailored the traditional way. His head was bowed in conversation with someone she recognised as one of the gallery's staff. They both stood before a stunning work of art that she also instantly recognised as the work of Bruce Onobrakpeya. She had seen it in the gallery earlier that month and had been daunted by its price tag. Legends remained out of her league.

"He's looking at us!" Oyife said. "Shoot! He's coming this way."

With each step Leon took towards them, heat spread across her body. By the time he was close enough for her to smell his spicy scent that hinted of cloves and frankincense, Besi was finding it difficult to breathe.

"Good day," he said, nodding politely. He shook her hand and then reached for Oyife's, who grabbed with both hands.

Even as Oyife gushed over him, Leon's eyes stayed on her. And the more glances he snuck at her, the more times the image of his wide shoulders bare of any fabric crept into her mind.

"How did you like the flowers?" he asked as soon as he was done taking several selfies with Oyife. "I hope it was not too forward of me. I just wanted to express my gratitude."

"They make a beautiful addition to my office," she replied.

Over his shoulder, Oyife winked as she slipped away.

He smiled, and Besi noticed the shadow of a dimple on his right cheek. She needed to breathe, and it seemed like Leon was taking up all of the air in the gallery. She started walking, and he followed her, falling into step beside her.

"I'm yet to receive a response to my invitation," he said.

Ahead of them was the balcony. He held the glass door open for her.

The cool evening air caressed her face and helped her regain some composure.

"I'm sure you received my thanks," she said, shaking her head.

"Indeed, I saw the email." He leaned against the ornate balustrade. "I meant my invitation to dinner."

"I saw that you were speaking with Nick back there," she said, her gaze on the tiled rooftops of the buildings opposite the gallery.

That was safer than looking at him, his long legs, or his big hands.

"Oh, you're familiar with Nick?"

She nodded. "Are you getting that Onobrakpeya piece?"

"I am, as a matter of fact." He tilted his head to look at her. "You know of him?"

"Of course I do." She laughed. "I've been a fan since we learned about him back in secondary school. His works are hauntingly beautiful."

"You appreciate the arts," he remarked, then shifted closer to her.

"I like to think I do. I showed up to support the young upcoming artist."

"Zuliat's works are remarkable," Leon said. "It's actually eerie how accurate it is."

Her skin tingled at the hint of longing she heard in his voice. "You like history?"

"You could say I'm a student of history."

When she looked up at him, he was staring into the distance. Overcome by the urge to hold him, she lifted her hand to touch him.

"Besi!" Chizua called, making her way to join them. "Oyife told me you were here. Hello, and nice to meet you, Mr. Leonidas."

Besi chuckled quietly. It looked like Chizua could not miss the chance of meeting Leon herself.

She took this opportunity to escape, to stop herself from doing anything foolish. It wasn't exactly a quiet exit as she could feel two pairs of eyes following her every step. But the minute she was back among the crowd mingling in the gallery, she started reconsidering Leon's invitation. *Honesty to oneself is premium*, her grandmothers would say, and Besi admitted it to herself that she could not stop thinking about him. She'd been fighting this attraction, but would it be so bad to give in to it?

After placing payment for the portraits she had selected for her grandmothers and dropping her address for the delivery, she went in search of Leon. He stood in concert, surrounded by people enthralled by his every word. As soon as he noticed her, he excused himself.

"I'm leaving," she said and then mentally gave herself a kick. "I mean, I wanted to say goodbye."

"I am honoured you thought of me," he replied, a genuine smile on his lips.

"I'd like to take up your offer for dinner," she announced. "Here's my card. We can make plans during the week."

He stood still for a moment before snapping into action. He accepted her card with both hands, and his smile grew wider.

***

"This isn't too much, is it?" Besi said, smoothing her hands down the curves.

Propped on her dresser was her phone, on the other end of the video call Adaku, the best friend she had left in New York.

"Hmm." Ada adjusted her glasses in an exaggerated manner. "It's casual and sexy. Perfect for a first date."

"That's what I'm going for."

Besi leaned towards the mirror and applied a fresh coat of red lipstick. She wore a pair of leather pants that gripped every curve. They would be too hot to wear any other time, but the nights of rainy season were cool enough to pull off this look. The pants matched a green off-shoulder top while her hair—now back in its natural state—was drawn back into a puff.

"I can't believe you still have that hideous thing," Ada quipped as Besi smacked her lips at the mirror.

"What thing?" She looked down at her phone.

"That statue," Ada replied, her distaste evident on her face even through the grainy phone screen.

Besi looked over her shoulder at the parting gift her former colleagues had given her. They knew she loved art, and the statuette was something she appreciated—a squatting figure with bulbous eyes holding up its left hand; a prime example of African art that her colleagues said came from a second-hand antique shop in Brooklyn.

"Oh, you mean Ife? He helps me concentrate sometimes."

That was why she had moved it from its usual spot in her study to her nightstand when she couldn't concentrate on her meditation practice.

"You gave that thing a name!" Ada shrieked. "God forbid."

Besi rolled her eyes and gave her puff a light pat. "You're supposed to be helping me prepare for my date, in case you've forgotten."

"So remind me again, what's the plan for tonight?" Ada asked.

"Just drinks." She slipped on dangling long gold earrings in each ear. "I'll allow a drink or two and then I'll be back home. I want to see if there's more to him."

"Okay, babe, have fun!" Ada said. "I'll call you if I don't hear from you in two hours."

"Make that three. Thanks, friend. I love you!"

"Love you, too," Ada replied before ending the call.

Besi would probably have been better served telling Chizua to be her guardswoman for the night. However, the fact that the yoga instructor was already Team Leon dissuaded her. She needed a neutral party, Ada thus being the answer.

She arrived at Jerk Place, the Caribbean restaurant she'd recommended they meet at, early. She expected she'd have to wait for Leon, but he was already there. He stood up as soon as she entered through the doors.

A lightness settled about her when she saw him. She'd only just arrived for dinner, but felt buzzed, like she'd downed a few tequila shots.

"Good evening," he greeted. He stood for a few seconds, just taking in her presence. "You look exquisite."

She hugged him. Maybe it was the fact that no one had ever used the term 'exquisite' to describe her, or maybe it was how good he looked in teal dress shirt and slim-fit pants. It felt so good just standing there in his arms that she held on for just a second longer before pulling away.

Due to how small Jerk Place was, it was usually crowded. Tonight, though, it was empty save for Besi,

Leon, and the staff. They sat next to each other at the bar. She shifted in the high bar stool and brushed shoulders with him. Every breath in surrounded her with the scent of his spicy perfume.

"What drink do you desire?" Leon asked, leaning towards her to show her the menu.

"I'll just have a whiskey sour," she said, clearing her throat. A huge grin broke out on Leon's face, making her pause. "What, did I say something wrong?"

"That's what I was thinking of ordering, too," he said.

The drinks arrived swiftly, and she took a sip. Leon pointed to one of the carvings that lined the wall above the bar; he had been staring at it while the bartender made their drinks.

"Do you know how to tell which ones are genuine?" he asked.

"The wood is darker?" she guessed.

"True hand carvings are uneven," he explained. "The imperfection of the carver is revealed in the work."

"Where does your interest in art come from?" she asked.

"Well, you could say I grew up with artistic people." He shrugged, taking another sip from his drink.

"And where was that?" Despite her snooping online, that was one thing she'd never found out, any personal detail on Leon.

"Yaye," he said. "It's in Ilaje, in Ondo state."

"Were your family furniture makers?"

A wide grin broke on his face. "You looked me up."

"Well …" Her face tingled, but she resisted the urge to pat her cheeks. "Everyone does that these days. Are you going to tell me what happened that night at my hotel?"

"I suppose I should." He coughed.

By the time Besi's second drink was down to its dregs, she realised she did not want to go. She couldn't figure out why she had opened up to Leon in this way, pouring her heart out about the scandal at the hotel and how the aftermath had made her parents doubt her business skills.

Her watch told her almost two hours had passed, leaving her with one more hour before Ada checked in.

"Are you hungry?" Leon asked suddenly, as though reading her mind. "Because if you are, I have a proposal."

"I'm listening." She tilted her head.

"I would like to take you to three of my favourite places to eat. One each for a starter, mains, and dessert."

He had come with his driver, and they drove ahead while she trailed behind. After tapas and a shared plate of biryani, it was time for dessert. Besi didn't have much of a sweet tooth, but she was willing to stretch the night with Leon a bit longer.

That must have been why she had no complaints when the frozen yogurt spot Leon recommended had closed when they arrived and he suggested another place instead. They were driving across town, and when she remembered to glance at her phone, she found twelve missed called and a long string of messages from Ada. Besi had to slip into the bathroom to record a video message for Ada; knowing her best friend, just a text saying she was fine wouldn't be enough.

When they arrived at the crepe place, they found that though it was open, the kitchen was closed and not taking any more orders. They stood beside each other in front of the counter, neither wanting to leave.

"Boniface, is that not you?"

Besi glanced back at the bent, elderly man standing behind them. Her hand flew to the base of her neck. She shot a look at Leon who seemed just as confused as she was.

"How do you still look the same?" the man explained, gesturing towards Leon with his walking stick. "The last time I saw you was 1967, before the war."

"I am sorry, sir," Leon said, turning away. "You must have me confused with someone else."

"But I am not," the old man said. "Your help changed my life, and I've been wanting to thank you. I thought I'd never see you again."

Leon placed a hand on Besi's shoulder, steering her towards the entrance.

"What was that about?" she asked once they were outside.

The man had not followed them out, but she'd gotten a glimpse of his disappointed face through the glass doors, and it was already haunting her.

"I haven't the slightest," Leon said.

In the hubbub, his arm was now around her shoulder, and his grip tightened, holding her against him.

A knot was forming in her belly. She looked over her shoulder towards the direction they had just come from. The man was now saying something, mouthing words that she could not decipher at the distance.

Daemon.

Shuddering, she shifted closer into Leon's hold.

CHAPTER THREE

"This is fake," Leon pronounced. He cradled the statue between his forefinger and thumb—it looked much larger in the picture.

"I can't lie. I was shocked when I received the package," Rike replied. "But there's no way to know until we try."

In the early hours of the morning, she drew a circle on the dewy grass with off-white chalk. They stood in the heart of the garden behind the house. Surrounded by mango, moringa, neem, and the occasional palm tree, this half-circle was Leon's sanctuary. The space had scattered stone sculptures as well as ornamental shrubs and vines that shielded it from prying eyes. It would also serve as a portal if Rike proved successful.

"You've been in such a bad mood lately," she said, still stooped in the grass. "We need positive energy today."

Leon scoffed, knowing his bad mood had to do with running into an old acquaintance on his date with Besi. Everything was going so well until Julius Ayanda showed up. Julius had been Leon's neighbour when he lived in Ibadan in the 1960s.

As someone from the Forest stuck on Earth, he was skilled at covering up his tracks. When he disappeared and created a new identity for himself, he did not expect to see anyone from his past life.

However, it had to happen in front of Besi, who was so perceptive, she knew something was wrong and was now seemingly avoiding him. It did not help that he badly wanted to see her. Even today, he had woken up from a dream where he was saved from the trap, but instead of the huntress' face, he'd seen Besi gazing at him with longing in her eyes.

"I'm pissed we spent so much money on a counterfeit," he grumbled.

Rike paused to chuckle.

"Did you just say pissed, Grandpa?" She laughed again.

Done with her preparations, she rose to her feet and motioned for Leon to stand in the centre of a portal she had drawn on the earth. Should this work, he would be able to slip through it and return home. Around the circle she had drawn in the grass were a white bowl of water and a white plate of grilled chicken and sweet potatoes, offerings to the ones who guarded the spaces between worlds.

"Are you ready?" Around them, the world was waking up as the sun rose, spilling its brightness around them.

"It's not going to work," he replied.

"You could do with a little more enthusiasm," Rike offered.

Then, she just delved in, sprinkling the water from the bowl on the ground and calling on the forces of nature to bear witness. They had done this before, and he knew when it was his cue to summon the energy in him and direct it towards the statuette, channelling it and commanding it to open the portal at his feet.

As he concentrated, heat rushed through his veins, leaving fire in its wake. He could see the strained colours of his aura, carrot orange with strokes of midnight blue. His eyes widened at the growing flash of light that spread up from the ground. Eventually, he had to narrow his eyes at the brightness.

He quickly glanced up at Rike in surprise. Then, something gripped him, tightening his limbs to his side and sending waves of electric shock through his body. In a blink, darkness came. He fell to the grass, shudders racking through his body.

***

Rike had a theory ready by the time Leon came to.

"I think your energy levels are depleting," she explained.

"You mean to say I'm dying?" he quipped. He sat propped up with pillows on his king-sized bed, a blanket tucked around him. That couldn't happen. If he died, Forest Home would perpetually be in chaos; it would never know peace.

Rike stood amidst the array of pillows on the floor. She scooted closer.

"It would seem so," she said. "I want to believe this happened because we were so close … for the first time, but you fainted. You've never fainted. You don't even sleep."

Leon ran a hand over his face. He recalled he had also blacked out after the episode with the handcuffs at Gazania. Could that have been the reason he'd been unable to save himself?

He leaned back, and lifting his left arm, used it to cover his eyes. Back in Forest Home, death only came when someone else killed you. To think that his end had finally come after spending so long in this prison called Earth.

In the darkness behind his lids, Besi's face appeared, unbidden. He shook his head forcefully—he had seen her, too, when that force had clamped over him.

Time to get up. He shifted, but Rike lifted her hands up in warning.

"I don't think that's a good idea," she warned.

"You couldn't possibly mean my standing up?" he grumbled. "Come on. I'm not a weak human."

She stood back and let him discover for himself that his legs would just not cooperate and support him. Humbled, he slid back between the sheets and leaned against the stack of pillows once more.

"Rike, I need a favour."

She cleared her throat. "Anything."

"I need you to call Besi Agbajor at Gazania" he started.

"Really?" Her face fell. "At this time?"

"At this time," he insisted. "If I'm going to die, I might as well enjoy it. Do you know the last time I enjoyed a woman's company? Nineteen ninety—"

"Three." Rike rolled her eyes. "The year I was born, I know. What message do you want me to deliver?"

"I will write a note. And you deliver dessert to her."

"I came here to learn about other worlds." Rike shook her head. She brought out her mini notebook from her pocket and started jotting.

***

"Madam," Tope at the Reception said over the intercom. "There's someone here asking to see you."

"Who is?" Besi asked, impatiently tapping a pen against her chin. The call had been a welcome distraction because she could not concentrate on the work in front of her, Leon being foremost in her thoughts.

"Her name is Rike, from a Mr. Leonidas."

"Send her to my office." She remembered Rike from that fateful night that now seemed a distant memory.

Since the first and last date with Leon, she had chosen to keep her distance, which was made frustrating by the fact that she couldn't stop thinking about him. Something was not quite right, and she wasn't entirely sure she wanted to delve into anything with Leon if her intuition was tingling.

Yet, her arm still tingled where he'd held her that night, and when she closed her eyes, she was bombarded by images of him topless, of the brief tantalising feel of his body against her.

Besi shook her head. Of course, when she thought of it, she recalled there had been no alarm bells from the get-go. They'd only appeared after that old man had come in talking as if he knew Leon.

Logically, there could be a number of explanations like the stranger being senile, but her mind had created a story about a long-lost family with dark secrets that Leon was hiding somewhere. She had heard more than one horror story about men who created entire new identities for themselves just to woo women.

That was one part of her mind, though. The other part still wanted to see him. This tug of war was wearing her out, even as she knew it was always better to be safe.

"Come in," she announced once she heard the hard tap on her office door. She shifted in her chair and patted her hair.

Rike was just as she remembered, petite and full of energy as she burst into the office carrying a paper bag in her arms. Part of the sleeve tattoo on her left arm showed as her shirt sleeves were folded up. Besi saw mostly abstract designs—bands, lines, arrows, and crosses.

"Good day. My boss asked me to personally deliver this to you," Rike explained, skipping as she placed the bag on the desk before Besi.

"Good afternoon, Rike. What's in here?"

She peeped in and saw four small tubs of frozen yogurt.

"He wasn't sure what flavours you liked, so he asked me to get as many as I could," Rike was explaining. "There's plain, chocolate, green tea, and cherry."

"Oh." Besi looked at the bag once more. For a minute, she was speechless. "How come he couldn't bring this himself?"

"He's sick."

The words echoed in her head as cold dread washed over her. "Sick? What's wrong?"

"He had a minor accident and is bedridden. But he is slowly getting better."

"What hospital is he in?" Besi swallowed. Somehow, she had pushed her seat back from her desk. She needed to call on her inner calmness.

"He's not at a hospital," Rike replied. "He has been discharged now, is what I meant to say."

"Okay, that means he's getting better."

"He is," Rike replied, jutting her chin. "You should call him. I'm sure he'll appreciate that. Goodbye"

Now alone once more, Besi tarried. She put the yogurt away in her office fridge, grimacing at the way the fridge door didn't close until she slammed it. Leon had been sick all this while, but he had reached out through calls at first, and now this. Returning to her desk, she reached for her cell phone then put it back down again.

After picking up her phone for the third time, she dialled his number.

"Leon, how are you?" she said as soon as she heard his "hello". She held back a sigh of relief at the sound of his voice. "I heard you had an accident."

"I'm good," he said, his voice grating. "Better now I've heard from you."

Usually, she would have rolled her eyes at that kind of comment, but at that moment, she smiled. He sounded jovial, and she could hear the voices of other people in the background.

"Is this a good time?" she asked.

"Yes," he said. "A few of my acquaintances have come to pay a visit."

"That's nice of them. I would like to pay one, too."

"Actually," Leon started. "They are planning a banquet for me. It'll be at my home, and I'd like to personally invite you to attend."

"You're all healed?" she asked, then remembered Rike had said he'd been discharged from the hospital. "When is it? I'll be there."

"I'll have Rike forward the details to you."

"Speaking of Rike, she just left my office. Thanks for the dessert."

"It was my pleasure. I was dissatisfied with how our date ended ..."

There was a long, awkward pause.

"We can talk about that later," she rushed. "I'll see you soon."

***

As soon as he hung up, Leon knew he had made a mistake. The small smile that had touched his face at Besi's call fell when he looked at the people scattered around his room.

Eze sat on the low sofa at the other end of the room, reading a book. Ibrahim leaned against the horizontal dresser, glaring at his phone, probably in search of his next victim. Iyene, the Red Lady, stood serenely beside the curtains, looking out the window.

The daemons that called Forest Home theirs were of different races united under the force of the Forest—which was a living being in its own right. The four guards of the

Forest were split evenly between the pacific and the fierce daemons; Leon, as the Western Guard, was of the former.

This coterie of friends were mostly like him, although none of them held such an important position back home. Some of them were stranded on Earth, but they'd all chosen to live with humans. They were the stuff of the average person's nightmares; a religious person might call them demons if they were to see them in their real forms. But here in his room, they looked like models in a magazine spread.

They had surprised him with this visit, suspiciously coinciding with a time Rike was not at home. Leon suspected they knew something was up and had come to investigate.

Despite his usual trusting nature, he held back from announcing that he was nearing his end. He told them he was in bed because he was trying to be more human, which had made them all laugh. In his attempt to avoid suspicions, he'd hastily agreed to their suggestion of a party. He was trying to appear like he was simply resting, something his kind did from time to time. This was hard when three pairs of eyes—and about twelve underneath that glamour—followed his every move. Where was Rike when he needed her?

"Is everything okay, brother?" Iyene asked soon after Besi's call, her gaze still trained somewhere beyond the open window.

"Just a human friend." He tried to keep his face straight and not betray his interest in Besi. "She'll be coming to the banquet you have for ... planned for me."

"I hope she brings friends." Ibrahim grinned. He was one of the bloodthirsty ones with humans as his targets. "I keep saying they aren't as filling as they used to."

A sharp pain pierced Leon's chest. He cleared his throat. With his luck and the kind of creatures that forced their company on him, he had every reason to be worried.

"Now, now." That was the Red Lady. She looked over her shoulder at Ibrahim who avoided her gaze. "We have agreed not to cause scandals in Brother Leon's house."

The others snickered. Iyene made her way towards Leon and sat beside him on the bed. As one of the Red People, she was graceful and kind by nature. She was also beautiful, with dark, curly hair that reached her shoulders and her red-gold skin. In the Forest Home, the Red were trustworthy, but Leon could never be sure given his history.

"Your garden looks different," she said quietly.

He avoided her gaze. He could stand his ground in any other situation, but something about people in his personal circle made that difficult. It was his curse.

"Brothers," Iyene said. "You should get going. Leon and I have a personal discussion."

Eze and Ibrahim followed her command as if this were her home and not Leon's.

"Take care, Red Lady," Eze said. "We shall see you at the party this weekend."

"You'll probably need more rest later." Ibrahim leered at Leon.

When it was just the two of them, Iyene grabbed Leon's hand before he could draw back.

"Just giving you some of my energy." She held onto his hand so tightly, he couldn't budge. Her strength surprised him. He had heard tales of the Red even before his banishment but had never experienced it himself. "You need to take it easy with trying to go back there."

He gritted his teeth at the burn emanating from where she held him.

"There is home," he said. "And home is being destroyed. I need to be there."

"And we're on Earth," Iyene replied, intensifying the transfer, her exterior unbothered even when he started convulsing. "It's not so bad here. Maybe your new friend will help you realise that."

She spoke as if she wasn't the one who brought various daemons that came in with news of the ever-changing destructive nature of Forest Home.

Leon stiffened, alert even this deep into the misery Iyene was putting him through.

"I'm kidding." She let go of his hand and patted his shoulder. "I know you're needed back home."

Almost immediately as it had come, the pain dissipated. He didn't have to strain to see the orange and blues of his aura. His nose prickled with the strength of his familiar piquant scent.

"Accept my gratitude, Lady Red," he said, flexing his wrists and wriggling his toes.

"This kindness is mine to give." Iyene rose to her feet. "Those boys are too stupid to notice something is off. But I worry about what would happen if you were to fail again. I'll see you at the party."

CHAPTER FOUR

From outside the wrought iron gate, Leon's house looked unassuming. All Besi could see was lots of greenery until five minutes after the security guard waved them in and the taxi advanced towards the dwelling. The three-storey mansion loomed large from the driveway.

"Just what I expected from him!" Oyife squealed in Besi's ear as soon as they stood in the grand foyer.

She had been a ball of excitement from the moment Besi had picked her and Chizua up. Besi had imagined Leon surrounded by friends and decided she would be bringing Chizua along, too. However, it seemed Chizua did not go anywhere without Oyife.

The place was crowded. People roamed up and down the two staircases that curved up to the second floor. Others gravitated near the entrance and farther down between the staircases where they sat and chatted, some with drinks in their hands. Highlife music blared all around them, some already dancing to the rhythm.

"Let's get drinks first?" Chizua suggested, shouting over the music.

Both Besi and Oyife nodded. As they made their way deeper into the house, Besi found that she was craning her neck in search of Leon.

"I see you, Besi." Oyife winked at her. "Don't worry. As soon as I see him, I'll let you know."

She smiled her thanks. They were getting drinks from the bar when Rike appeared.

"Good evening, madam," she greeted Besi, nodding to the other two.

"Please, call me Besi. These are my friends, Chizua and Oyife."

Rike repeated her greeting and immediately looked back at her. "My boss is eager to see you."

"Oh." Her cheeks heated up. "And where is he?"

She looked at Chizua. They'd just gotten here, and she wasn't going to dump them.

"Go meet him," Chizua said, shrugging. "It's fine. We didn't come here to be third wheel."

"Yes, we have our own plans," Oyife agreed. She already had a drink in one hand and her phone in the other.

This was not how she'd envisioned the evening turning out, she thought as Rike led her up the stairs to the second floor.

"I hope you liked the frozen yogurt."

"Yes, I did." They were walking away from the party. As the music dimmed, she wondered if Leon was still bedridden. "He's not still sick, is he?"

"He isn't." Rike paused in front of a closed door, a frown on her face. "He's actually much better."

As soon as they stepped in, Leon jumped to his feet. He crossed the space and pulled Besi in his arms. She closed her eyes and leaned in, his now familiar fragrance wrapping her with warmth. It felt so good that she missed him as soon as he pulled back.

"Oh, goodness," he said. "I hope that's okay?"

"What was?" she asked.

"The sudden hug," he replied, his soft gaze on her stoking a fire in her tummy. "I missed you."

"It is okay." She looked up at him, and in that moment, it hit her how much she had missed him, too. She reached a hand up to his cheek. "How are you?"

"Much better." He took her hand in both of his. "What would you like to drink?"

"Whiskey on ice."

"Rike, if you would please."

She had forgotten they were not alone. Now, she could look away from Leon to see that they were in his home office.

He led her towards two armchairs poised at an angle facing an open window. The cool evening air brought with it the scent of petrichor; Besi sank into the leather chair and inhaled deeply. She only opened her eyes when Rike placed two glasses on the table between them, the clink alerting her to this. Leon was staring at her.

"So you invited me to a party only to hide me?" she asked.

"The banquet wasn't my idea," he said, feeling for his glass. "I'm happy you're here."

"Why do you keep saying banquet?" She laughed. "No one calls a house party a banquet."

He lowered his head. "I've been told I'm a bit old-school."

"That's cool." She nodded. "It's different." She took a sip of the whiskey. "Rike said you had an accident. What happened?"

"It was an unfortunate accident ..." he began.

When he didn't continue, she shifted to peer at him. He wasn't looking at her like before, his gaze now on the brown liquid swirling in the glass he held.

"Was it that bad? Wait, you don't have to answer that." Emboldened with a bit of liquid courage, she stood up and adjusted her dress. "May I?"

She stood in front of him.

He leaned back in his chair and looked up at her, a question in his eyes.

"Besi," he whispered huskily.

She straddled him, and almost instinctively, his hands went to her waist, pulling her closer.

"Seeing you made me realise—" she said as she cupped his face, "—that I missed you."

"I missed you, too," he replied.

Their lips met without hesitation, as though they had kissed a thousand times before.

Leon's were soft and full, and he nipped at her bottom lip gently. Their tongues danced slowly and lazily. His hands tracing a haphazard path up and down her back, increasing her pleasure.

Finally, she pulled away. Their foreheads pressed together, she grinned.

"I think we should go downstairs," she said. "I left my friends behind."

She could feel him stiffen beneath her.

"You brought friends?"

"Yes, I didn't think you'd mind," she said, stroking his cheek.

"I don't," he assured her. "But you're right. We should go downstairs."

***

Besi couldn't wait to leave the meeting and as usual had to make herself calm down with deep breathing exercises. It was five p.m., and she was at Gazania's head office in Lagos. She'd taken the first flight out of Abuja and had been in meeting after meeting the whole day. They had even eaten lunch while poring through the data on satisfaction targets of all four of their hotels. At the moment, the general manager of their Moroccan branch was rounding up her presentation on the next quarter's projections.

Soon, she thought, tapping her pen against her chin.

When the meeting was adjourned to the next day, she waited 'til everyone else had trooped out of the room. Her parents were here, and she wanted to at least make the effort of looking serious.

"Besida," her mother called as she came to sit beside her. Lolade Agbajor was slender and dark-skinned, her salt-and-pepper hair styled in twists and held up in an elegant updo.

Besi had gotten her mother's tall figure and cheekbones but was seriously lacking when it came to her grace and poise.

"How am I doing, Mrs. Agbajor?" she replied. There was a policy against calling her parents Mum or Dad in the office.

"You're doing well, dear." Lolade smiled at her. "There are areas for improvement, however, and I want you to look out for them."

"I will." She nodded. Even as a child, Lolade had always made her sit down and realise why she was being punished. Besi would prod them for a full review later.

"Have you heard from your brother recently?" Lolade asked.

"He's currently in Vietnam." Her parents didn't exactly approve of Mene's career choice, but her brother didn't care. He was known to disappear for weeks and reappear suddenly, all in his bid to be a travel blogger. "I'll tell him you asked after him."

"I wonder when he'll stop wasting money and start earning it." Lolade shook her head. "We're really grateful to have you here, Besida."

Besi couldn't contain her grin.

"But I'm sure you're eager to see your grandmothers now," Lolade said. "Let me not hold you back."

When she'd been growing up, everyone had found it odd that Besi's paternal and maternal grandmothers lived together. In the bungalow set apart from the main house were Grandma Adisa and Grandma Alero. With age came the knowledge of what it meant to be a widow, and her grandmothers were both widows with only children. They'd found ways to bond despite their different ethnic backgrounds, and it made more sense for them to live together in the city than the villages they both claimed to be sick and tired of.

The traffic delayed her on the way home, but as soon as they turned into Lugard Avenue, Besi started fidgeting. Once she was past the gates, she bypassed the main house for the bungalow. Efe, the woman who took care of grandmothers, opened the door.

"Besi!" Efe screamed, and squeezed her with her ample arms.

"Aunty Efe, good evening." Slipping a plastic bag into Efe's hand, she whispered, "For you."

"Did I hear Efe called Besida's name?" Grandma Adisa shouted from within the house.

She found her grandmothers in the sitting room. She knelt down first in greeting before hugging them both.

"What will you eat?" Grandma Alero asked.

"Efe, is that soup ready?" Grandma Adisa shouted. "Will you take tea while the soup is prepared?"

"I'll eat with you," Besi said, smiling. "In fact, I will be sleeping here."

She was in the hot kitchen assisting Efe in plating dinner when her phone rang. Looking down, she saw Oyife and chose to ignore the call. She was with family, after all, but they kept coming. After the seventh call, a message came in: '*Please call me back, it's urgent!!!*'

"Is that a man?" Grandma Alero said, pointing to Besi's phone with her lips.

"A friend of a friend. But speaking about men, you promised me a folktale."

"Oh, no." Grandma Adisa smirked.

"Please," she pleaded. "Grandma Adisa, you promised."

"Let us eat first," Grandma Alero said.

After dinner, she was clearing the plates when her phone buzzed again. This time, she answered Oyife's call.

"Hey, Oyife, what's up?" She tried not to sound upset. "I was eating dinner with my family."

"Besi ... hey," Oyife said.

The sombre tone of her voice was so unlike her that she was immediately concerned.

"What's wrong?" she asked, stepping out to the quiet of the night from the kitchen.

"See, I know it will sound crazy, but I'm not crazy," Oyife whimpered. "Something wasn't right with Leonidas, with his friends ... at the party. Something isn't right. My pastor has prayed for me, but I just wanted to warn you."

"Warn me?" she said, grimacing. "I don't understand, Oyife."

"I didn't understand, too. I started having weird dreams after the party. It affected my health, but my doctor said I was fine. My sister dragged me to her church, and they said I had de-demons."

"Okay ..."

After that steamy kiss with Leon, she had spent most of the night dancing with him and then Chizua. She recalled

Chizua explaining that Oyife had left with a tall and dashing man. None of that shed any light on why Oyife was calling her right then.

"You think I've lost it, right?" Oyife jeered. "Something happened to me in that house, and it had to do with the people there. The pastor confirmed it."

It was never Besi's thing to disparage anyone else's experience, so she chose the least obstructive path.

"I hope your health is better, Oyife."

"It is, I told you ..." Oyife groaned. "Wait, you don't believe me, do you? I'm just trying to warn you."

She kissed her teeth and hung up suddenly. Besi looked down at her phone, confused.

"Besida," Efe called from the kitchen. "I think they are ready to tell you that story now."

Inhaling deeply to clear the confusion left from Oyife's call, she headed back indoors. She found both her grandmothers in the veranda.

"Is it story time?" she asked, a nervous smile on her face.

"Well," Grandma Adisa said. "Which one do we tell?"

"How about the one with the three brothers who were fishermen?" Grandma Alero suggested.

Grandma Adisa kissed her teeth. "We've told her that before. Do you want to hear it again?"

Besi nodded. She settled on the rug and looked up at Grandma Adisa expectantly.

Grandma Adisa proceeded to tell her a story that started with one brother breaking his hand, then the other brother fell down, and one by one chaos reigned as more accidents continued to befall both human and animal until it reached the King's palace. It was up to a mysterious woman descended from Heaven to prevent catastrophe.

"Now that your mother's mother has finished saying her chaotic tale, let me say mine," Grandma Alero said.

***

In the downstairs studio, Leon carved into a chunk of wood. With his energies amplified, he was back working on his commission. All this felt like a waste of time knowing that the Forest was being destroyed every single moment he stayed here. Nonetheless, his hands were tied without his wand.

Rike walked into the space, her humming interrupting his concentration.

"The Red Lady is here," she announced.

"Did she say what brings her?" Leon set his tool on the worktable.

"She did. I felt an odd presence in the house last Friday, and I've been doing some investigation."

"And you're only telling me this now?" he cried out.

"You were with Besi," she explained. "I didn't want you to worry."

He was at a loss for words. Regardless of Rike's intentions, he was worried now.

"But I do want you to hear what the Red Lady has to say." Rike tilted her head towards the door. "She's in your study."

Iyene sat poised on the same oversized armchair Besi had occupied that night, a teacup in her hand. Leon took his seat on the other chair and leaned forward.

"Greetings, Sister Iyene."

"Greetings," Iyene replied and blew gently over her tea. "Your assistant must have told you why I'm here."

He nodded.

"Then I won't beat around the bush. I've heard rumours."

"What rumours?" he demanded.

"That Forest has given up on daemons," Iyene replied. "That Forest is dying, which would mean the blood-thirsty daemons have gotten their way. Who knows where they will go next?"

"No!" He leapt up from his chair and started pacing.

He recalled when Forest had chosen him to be the Western Guard. While he couldn't remember Forest assuming any shape or form, he would never forget the pulsing bring light that felt like home, joy, and all things good. To think it was his naïveté and carelessness that led to the destruction of Forest Home.

"Still, you're closer to returning that you've ever been, it seems. Your last attempt brought something over to this side."

He froze.

"One of us," Iyene continued. "It's someone you'll remember; the Southern Guard."

The world grew still around Leon as the hair on his nape painfully rose.

"What else do you sense?" he asked, his voice shrill.

"Not much else except that you should be careful," Iyene went on. "You've been silent on what exactly led to your arrival here, and I gather you have enemies there. But I think this is bigger than you. If Forest is defeated, they may be looking to expand."

She paused to sip at her tea, utterly calm despite the gravity of her words.

"And that is why I am working on protection spells," Rike chipped in. "You'll need amulets on you at all times."

"I can protect myself, Rike." He waved her off. "What we need is to find my wand, double down on that."

"You should accept her help," Iyene warned. "And I will do my part in reuniting you with your wand."

CHAPTER FIVE

As Besi stepped off the plane at Nnamdi Azikiwe Airport in Abuja, Leon was on her mind. A smile graced her face as decided she would ask him out on an impromptu date.

She waited 'til she was seated in the taxi heading to town before calling him. They had been doing that a lot recently, speaking on the phone and not running out of things to say.

"Beloved, I'm afraid I can't," he said in reply to her lunch invitation. "I will be speaking at an event at Transcorp."

"What's happening there?" she asked.

"A conference for artisans," he replied. "You're welcome to attend if you wouldn't get bored."

"Will there be crafts for sale?"

"There usually are."

"I'll be there."

After hanging up, she saw that her taxi had already passed the City Gate. She would go home, change, and head to the Transcorp hotel. Her mind only briefly scanned over the hotel that she hadn't been in for about a week. After the strain of working under the close supervision of her parents and the fact that she was now in charge of putting together a feasibility plan for a new Gazania in Dakar, she deserved just one day.

In the hotel's Congress Hall, she slipped into the darkened auditorium. She had made it just in time to catch Leon on stage. The projection on the screen behind him announced in bold letters *'Blending traditional woodwork with modern technology.'*

Seeing him prance across that stage in the traditional-styled trousers and tunic proved enough to send heat through her body. Her heart swelled with a mix of pride, desire, and something else she was not ready to name. As she was ushered to an empty chair, Leon held the audience's attention with the story of how he'd started planting trees for every one that was cut down for his woodwork.

The room loved him, and wild applause rang out once he was done. Before he could make it down the stage, a crowd had him surrounded. Besi stood just outside the circle feeling a sense of déjà vu when he looked at her and winked. She tilted her head towards the door where crafts from different artisans were for sale before heading out.

He found her bargaining over a set of plates from a pottery seller.

"Welcome back," he said from behind her, his breath on her bare neck raising goose bumps across her skin.

"Thanks." She grinned at him. "You were awesome on that stage."

"I'm pleased you found my talk useful. I think I can have supper now. Are you still interested?"

"Supper?" She couldn't help but giggle. It was evening time already and a tad late for the lunch she had proposed. "I am interested in supper. Where should we go?"

Leon's driver dropped them at the restaurant beside Jabi Lake. They sat on the upper floor that looked out onto the still waters and the highway bridge in the distance.

Besi leaned against his shoulder as they waited for their orders to come in.

"You know what?" she asked, encouraged by the glass of wine in her hand. "You never talk about your past."

She felt him stiffen against her. She glanced up, and right before her eyes, a wall went up. She noted the way his eyes dimmed, the way he seemed to shift ever so slightly away from her. The slow smile that had been on her face all day faded away.

"What are you hiding?" she probed.

"Nothing," he said, even as he was moving away from her. "It's just … I've been hurt. Very badly."

She touched his hand. "We all have, Leon."

"Indeed, we have," he mused out loud. "I should probably explain what brought me to Gazania and left me handcuffed in the bathroom."

She perked up. That had been almost a month ago, and this was the first time Leon had opened up about it. She listened to him narrate his challenges with friends and the usually awkward, sometimes dangerous, situations they led to.

"So understand that I don't mean you any harm, Besi," he concluded.

"I see," she said. "Your friends actually had you kidnapped?"

"I have many more stories like that," he replied.

"That must have been traumatic." She sighed. "Thank you for sharing that with me."

***

Leon's mansion was incredibly lonely without guests. Besi's heels clicked on the tiled floor as she followed him to the parlour upstairs. After dinner, drinks at his place was her idea. She was just eager to spend more time with Leon after he'd opened up earlier. The distraught look on his face she he'd told her about his past hurt still caused a slight numbing in her heart.

"Port or white wine?" he asked, squatting in front of a mini-fridge.

"Is there nothing else?"

He shrugged. "The only other alcoholic beverage here is beer."

"I'll have the port then."

She stifled a laugh at the phrase Leon had used and admired the acrylic painting of Lagos' iconic yellow buses.

"I thought it perfectly captured the chaos and vibrancy of the city," Leon said of the painting as he poured out their drinks.

When he appeared beside her with a glass of pink port, she settled on the L-shaped sofa and patted the space next to her. With him beside her, they toasted and drank in silence. It could have been awkward, but she welcomed this, at ease and felt comfortable enough to bury her head in the crook of his shoulder. She breathed in his scent.

"Leon," she called his name as she cupped his cheek and turned his face towards her for a kiss.

Their lips met in an electrifying embrace. She shuddered, pulling him close, opening her mouth so that her tongue licked his lips. Their tongues danced, gliding across each other. Leon kissed her deeply, causing her to gasp for air. Grabbing at his shirt, she pulled him above her while shifting 'til her back met one of the cushions on the sofa.

"Besida, I've wanted you so badly."

The way he said her name sent a shudder through her body.

"Take me," she urged, putting his hand on her breast.

Groaning, he placed an intense kiss on her lips. He then moved to deposit small kisses along her jawline and down her throat while squeezing her breast gently through the sheer top she wore.

She threw her head back when his fingers pinched her hardened nipples through her clothing. She clung on to Leon desperately, wanting more.

When he pulled away, her eyelids fluttered open with alarm. He stood, his arm outstretched towards her. Hands entwined, he led her to his bedroom. He didn't bother turning on the lights before he started undressing her. When she was naked, he buried his face in her stomach and breathed in deeply. Leon traced his tongue over the contours of her midriff, dipping it into her belly button slowly.

His hands holding her waist kept her from spilling over. Besi trembled, gasping for air. She felt so hot all over, and he hadn't even touched her where she ached most for him yet.

"Tell me how you want it," he whispered as he pushed her on the bed.

She moaned out her instructions. Pulling his head to her chest, she arched her back as he dragged his tongue over her nipple while cupping the other breast. His fingers played with one nipple while he sampled the other with long licks and light bites.

She held on to his shoulders, her breath coming out in puffs. Her hips felt like they were molten lava. She craved that thrill and wanted him to make her body pulsate.

"You are entirely captivating." He breathed her praises in her ear while his hand traced a path down between her thighs where her wetness grew.

Burying his face in her neck, he rubbed slow, torturous circles on her clitoris. A wave of emotions swept over her.

"Kiss me there," she whimpered, clinging to him, her fingers digging into his back.

Besi's mind went completely blank when Leon's lips followed the path his fingers had taken. He tasted her gently at first before devouring her. Pleasure dripped out of her pussy, pooling beneath her butt. It felt so good, she grabbed his head, holding him in place as her hips ground against his face.

Even as she moaned her release, he continued his pleasuring, slipping a finger into her. He lifted his head up. She felt him looking at her but could barely make his shadowy figure moving above her through her half-lidded eyes. Stretching down, she grabbed his dick and shuddered at the size and feel of it.

"Condoms?" She could barely formulate the question.

"I'm afraid I don't." He shook his head. "But we don't have to. I just want to make you feel good."

At that, her eyes popped open, and they met Leon's intense gaze. Nodding, she said, "Keep doing this then."

He cradled her in his arms as his fingers brought her to another climax.

***

Besi was abuzz, and she suspected it was due to Leon's effect. She was taking yet another day off work, leaving Miranda in charge of things. Though now afternoon, she was still in her yoga pants from her morning exercise. She lay in bed chatting with Ada and dishing out details on Leon when a call came through.

"Mene!" she yelled. "You're in Nigeria!"

"In Abuja as we speak," her brother replied. "What's your address? I came to the hotel, and you're not there. Missing work during a week day? How unlike my sister."

Somehow, skipping one day to spend it with Leon had turned into two, and she didn't feel too bad about it.

"Come on." She laughed. "I'll text you my address. Most cab drivers know the area."

She was hugging her brother fifteen minutes later. It had been months since he'd gone off on his Southeast Asian adventure. While she defrosted food made by her cook every weekend, he filled her in on his latest adventures.

"So while I was backpacking, you met someone." Mene grinned. "What's his name? I want to meet him."

"Why, Mene?" Besi took the jollof rice out of the microwave and put in the steamed vegetables next.

"He has you, Uptight Besida, skipping work, for one. I'm supposed to be the irresponsible child of the Agbajor clan."

"Come on," she said. "No one has called me that in over a decade."

"Yeah, yeah. Let's have dinner while I'm here."

She rolled her eyes, but a huge grin spread on her face when she grabbed her phone and texted Leon, inviting him over to her place for dinner. He agreed immediately.

***

Leon had his driver drop him off in Besi's estate. The preparation to return to Forest Home was going nowhere, even with the Red Lady's help. She had recruited a seer to detect his wand, but all her messages had been cryptic—it was somewhere close but far; the figurine rested in an unlikely place.

In the meantime, all he could do was prepare. Dnres, the Southern Guard, had yet to reveal himself. Leon tapped his pants pocket, feeling the weight of the amulet Rike had prepared for Besi. The plan was to find somewhere in her house to install it and to keep it hidden from view.

He wasn't sure how she would feel if he gave her the amulet upfront, but he also didn't want to be the cause of any harm befalling her. When all this was over, he would retrieve the amulet, and she would never know.

He rubbed the back of his neck as he knocked on her front door, the skin there suddenly prickly. It was opened by a man who looked so much like Besi, one could take them for twins.

"Hey!" He shook hands with Leon. "You must be Leon. I'm Mene. Nice to meet you."

"Nice to meet you, too." He smiled.

"Come on in." Mene ushered him down the short hallway into the sitting room. "We're just getting things ready."

"I'm really feeling that necklace." Mene gestured towards the beaded amulet Rike had made for him as Leon took a seat. "It looks ancient."

"It is an ancient design made with modern materials," he tried to explain. As soon as the words had left his lips, he realised they must not make much sense.

He heard something clatter in the kitchen before Besi's head appeared at the doorway.

"Hey there," she beamed at him, then turned to Mene. "You, come help."

Alone now, Leon rubbed his neck again. He thought he was nervous, but this felt different. Heat spread from the back of his neck upwards to his head, driving him dizzy. This reminded him of his and Rike's failed attempt at opening a portal. He rubbed his sweaty palms and stood up—he needed to ensure Besi remained safe. He removed the amulet from his pocket and slipped it somewhere between the cushion and the back of the sofa. His head now swam; he needed to splash some water on his face.

He made his way to the kitchen on unsteady feet to find Besi and Mene setting up the dining table.

"Sorry to interrupt. Where is the convenience?" he asked.

"Convenience?" Mene teased.

"Down the hallway," Besi said. "The door to your right. Are you okay?"

"I'm fine," he replied. "I just feel slightly faint."

His vision distorted as he walked down the hallway. He opened the door to the right, but there was no bathroom in here. Instead, it looked like a study. He reached to pull the door shut, but his vision trained on a figurine. The statuette sat on a bookshelf, on the third row, short but slim, in the figure of a kneeling woman, the length of his hand, and it had fit perfectly during their adventures in the Forest Home.

This was what made him react this way—his wand was trying to communicate with him. As soon as he held it, a surge of energy drifted through him.

"You led me here," he stated.

Once reunited with his wand, he knew. His wand was behind his pull to Besi—the reason he saw her together with him in the Forest when he dreamed.

"There you are." Besi appeared behind him. "We're done setting up, and—"

"Why is this here?" he asked, his eyes never leaving his wand. He needed to confirm that it hadn't been here all along.

She frowned. "That is a gift from my former workplace, in New York. I told you ... Why—"

"It shouldn't be here." He had spent years searching for this statuette just to find it here sitting in the house of the woman he thought he was falling in love with. He didn't mean to, but his voice rose. "Tell me why it's here."

Besi's frown deepened. "I just told you."

"Do you have any notion how important this is?" he shouted. The Forest may have been lost already while he tarried about, wasting time. He narrowed his gaze at Besi as though seeing her for the first time. There was no multi-coloured aura or distinct scent, but her kind were crafty. Leon couldn't believe this was happening again. "What are you?"

At this point, Mene came in and immediately stood between them. "What's going on here?"

"I don't know." Besi shook her head. "There seems to be a misunderstanding regarding my gift."

"Dude, I know you like art, but this isn't necessary."

"Isn't necessary?" Leon's shoulders fell. "You wouldn't understand what's necessary. The entire world as you know it is at stake."

"I think you should leave." Mene stood authoritatively, regarding Leon as though he were insane.

Leon nodded and made his way towards the door.

"My sister's artwork," Mene objected. "Leave that behind."

His hand tightened against his wand. "Not a chance in hell."

"You will." Mene reached for the wand, and Leon's grip on it tightened.

It happened so fast. A bright orange spark jumped from his hand and hit Mene. Besi screamed and rushed towards her brother writhing on the floor, grasping his arm.

Leon stared at the scene before him wild-eyed. He dropped his wand on the floor and slipped out into the night.

CHAPTER SIX

"What just happened?" Mene scratched his arm.

Besi shrugged. "I'm not sure … He loves art."

"Somehow, I don't think that has anything to do with what just took place," Mene said, hugging her tightly. "You all right?"

Besi leaned against her brother. There was a first time for everything, and she had never seen Leon like this before. He'd looked angry, but beneath that anger had been despair, an intense sadness she could still feel.

"What do we do with all that food now?" Mene said uncertainly.

Suddenly, she remembered Oyife's mysterious call. Her phone still in the kitchen, she retraced her steps there and called Chizua. Within thirty minutes, Chizua was at her doorstep with Oyife. They all sat down around the dining table in the kitchen, but the meal—jollof rice, grilled chicken, and a leafy salad—was ignored as the spotlight beamed on Leon.

"Something isn't right," Oyife said. "And I mean spiritually."

Chizua rubbed her friend's arm. "Oyife has never been the religious sort, but whatever happened at Leon's house spooked her out."

"I'm telling you," Oyife insisted. "You know famous people are involved in all sorts of cults."

Besi shot a glance at Mene who sat opposite her, arms crossed, quietly taking it all in.

"Oyife," she began then swallowed. "Did … did Leon try to attack you?"

"No, he didn't attack me." Oyife shook her head vehemently.

Of course, she knew this for sure because he had spent most of the night of the party with her. She'd had to practically drag him out of that study.

"You mentioned dreams. Was he in them?" she asked gently.

"No ..." Oyife crossed her arms over her chest. "It wasn't him. It was one of his friends."

"Birds of the same feather flock together," Chizua said as she helped herself to some of the rice.

"It's not just that," Oyife continued. "The pastor that healed me, she said they are all demons."

Silence descended over the dining table and stretched for a few uneasy moments.

"I know I must sound crazy, right?" Oyife said, a sad smile on her face. "But I was sick, and I didn't feel better until I was taken to that church."

"You read a lot about energies and intention, right, Besi?" Chizua slid in to offer some help. "You should get it if you look at it from that angle."

She had never felt anything but positivity with Leon, if she didn't count today and that weird episode with the elderly man on their first date.

"I think what everyone agrees with here—" Mene finally said, "—is that Leon is dangerous."

"You can't say that," Besi replied. "I'm sure there is a perfectly reasonable explanation."

Her friends and brother looked concerned for her, and that made her even more riled up.

"Oyife, I'm truly sorry you experienced what you did, but Leon isn't behind this," she said, surprising herself by the force of her defence.

"Besi ..." Mene began.

"Leon isn't behind this," she repeated defensively. For some reason, her friends thinking badly of Leon rubbed her the wrong way. "And I'm going to prove it."

***

This intense feeling was definitely shame. Leon lay in bed with the curtains and blinds drawn, leaving him in darkness. He had no excuse for his outburst at Besi's. What was supposed to be a joyful time had darkened when he'd seen his wand. As soon as he'd lain eyes on it, memories had come back.

The betrayal, the pain of being thrust down that hole, what felt like centuries of darkness until he'd opened his eyes and found himself on a farmland. He'd thought he was back home 'til wandering into the nearest village had erased that notion from his mind. He'd been surrounded by humans, and it had taken him a while to know what the year was and where he had landed: 1937, British Nigeria.

When he'd fallen into this universe, his wand had been with him, and he had always known it had come here, too. This was confirmed when his path crossed with the Red Lady, and through her, he learned that the Forest had been devolving into lawlessness. At a point, he had imagined that the Forest would do fine without him as a guard if his wand stayed behind. But it had come here with him, and he hadn't seen it in 1937—he had been searching for it for so long. Everything he had been carrying for the past eighty-two years had hit him when he'd seen his wand.

Perhaps the most startling thing was the realisation that his wand had been calling him all this while. The inexplicable pull that had drawn him to Besi from the time he'd crossed paths with her at the hotel was the work of his wand. That meant she was not in control of her feelings, either. As hard as he tried to tamper down his disappointment, he kept failing.

He shut his eyes, stretched a hand to massage his temple. Now that tranquillity had returned to him, he knew he had no basis on which to blame Besi. She was not immortal, had not been alive long enough to have stolen his figurine and deliberately hidden it from him. If she had been a daemon all along, between him and Rike and the entire house full of his kind, someone would have noticed that.

He really liked Besi, and his outburst had proven that he had no business being with her. Someone like him deserved to be alone for eternity in service to maintaining Forest Home's balance. That was the original curse, wasn't it? And now that he could go home any time he wanted, how would he face Besi to ask for the figurine?

He threw his covers over his head when he heard a knock on the door. It could only be Rike, and he hoped his lack of a reply would dissuade her as it had these past few days.

To his chagrin, she burst into the room.

"You're behind on your client orders," she said as she switched on the lights. She hastily threw back the heavy curtains and then finally pulled the covers from him.

"I require rest," he groaned.

"I have let you mope for eight days now."

They had reached this agreement the first time she had seen an episode of his after friends he had drawn particularly close to for over a decade had ended up betraying him. That had been the last time he'd allowed himself to hope that people around him wouldn't betray him eventually. Rike's modus operandi was to give him just eight days to feel whatever he was feeling.

"You still haven't told me exactly what happened," she repeated. "Either you talk to me now, or I call Madam Red."

"You seem awfully fond of Iyene recently."

Leon made a hasty attempt to change the subject. He didn't want to see Iyene, not at this point. The Red Lady would remind him of his duties to the Forest, and the already intense pressure on him to return home would increase tenfold.

"You know, Boss?" Rike was setting up a meal on the small round table beside the window. "She's actually friendly, plus she's helped you like five times now."

"She's only that way because her kind can't help it," he said, still in the bed. "It's in their nature. Everything from the Forest operates within established boundaries."

"Okay, so shall I call her while you eat?"

"I have no interest in eating or in speaking with anyone at the moment. I am meditating ..."

"Fine, I'll call her." Rike brought out her phone from her dress pocket.

"I found my wand in Besi's home," he announced.

The hand holding the phone stilled beside Rike's ear. She made her way towards the bed, but he sprung up and out from it, avoiding her.

"How? She can't be a daemon."

"Exactly what I thought. But not at the moment I saw my wand. I realised the truth, and I lost it."

"She broke up with you?"

He made his way to the table and sat down heavily on the armchair. "We might as well have. We weren't going anywhere. I was always going to get back home. The Forest needs me."

Rike's brows drew together. "But you clearly like her ... Is this what you've been trying to convince yourself all this while?"

"Do you think you can break into her house?" he asked as he brought a spoonful of the spicy fish soup to his lips and sighed. He missed food, even though he wasn't exactly hungry.

"Seriously, Boss." Rike fished into her other pocket and brought out his phone. He'd dumped it with her when he'd returned home that night. "She has been trying to reach you. No matter what you did that night, she's willing to hear you out."

"And what am I to tell her? Oh, darling, I'm just a daemon who was kicked out of his universe and landed on Earth eighty-two years ago?"

"You could try that." She shrugged. "Wrap this up first before I push you."

Leon focused on his meal.

#

Even though she threw herself into the Gazania expansion project, Besi knew she was just bidding time 'til she sought Leon out. After countless meetings with Jama, the Dakar-based consultant her parents had brought on board, she was almost ready to send the feasibility report with the rest of the team.

With work done and Mene on his way to Angola, she set out. She suspected he had extended his stay just to ensure she was safe, but deep down, she knew Leon wasn't dangerous.

The last time she'd been at Leon's house, someone else had been driving. She put in the address to his house on her GPS as she still had the message from the party invite. Directions had never been her strong point, especially in a new city, but even she was surprised when she found herself at a dead end. She looked at her phone once more for the address and then glanced around her. Between the trees and tall gated houses, this could be anywhere in Abuja.

She reversed and drove slowly, looking for someone to ask for directions. It was just her luck that the area was deserted, and to make things worse, night was fast falling.

She exhaled in relief when she saw a lone man walking ahead of her. Carefully, she parked and hailed him.

"Good evening. Please, I'm looking for—"

As soon as he looked at her, she froze. It was like she was staring at a grotesque masquerade where his face should be, the holes where his eyes should be appearing cloudy like a storm brewed within. She reached to wind up her window, to shift her car into drive, but she couldn't move. Her limbs locked stiffly as the strange man approached her car.

"This is what he holds precious?"

He leaned against her car. The smell of burning sulphur choked her throat, making her whimper. He laughed in her face and opened the door easily even though she always locked herself in.

Besi willed herself to move. A coarse hand touched the side of her face, and she saw red. When she blinked, she saw a forest filled with monsters tearing themselves apart. They saw her and charged at her. She tried to run but couldn't make her legs move. She couldn't even open her mouth to scream.

"Do you see what he really is?"

The voice came from inside her head.

She desperately wanted to close her eyes, but even that was impossible as creatures from her worst nightmares descended upon her. She felt a prick on her arm, and the force that held her head upright let go just enough so that she could look down and see the life being drained out of her. They were biting into her skin, sucking her blood.

She screamed into the void.

***

Leon sat on a low bench in the verdant sanctuary of his garden. His bare back pressed against the roughness of a mango tree with low branches that brushed leaves against his face every time the wind rustled.

Lost in the stillness of the garden, he did not hear Rike's approach until she cleared her throat. Opening his eyes, he saw that she stood right in front of him. Her outstretched hands held a flat stone carved with deep impressions.

"Sorry to interrupt your meditation," she said. "But does this make any sense to you? One of the security guards found it in front of the gate."

Leon's eyes widened as he studied the stone. He reached for it, and upon contact, it disintegrated. Both of them jumped back, gawking at the spectacle that had just taken place before their eyes. A familiar sulphuric smell hit him, and with it came a cloud of dark moss green.

"Something found me the last time we tried to create a portal." He swallowed. "It is indeed the Southern Guard."

"Who?" Rike muttered. "What?"

"The one that sent me here. Dnres." He stood up. "He has Besi. We have to—"

"Wait." Rike stopped his movement. "Are you sure? You could tell all that from a rock?"

"Yes," he said, rushing towards the gate. "I'll find him."

"Wait, Boss." She ran after him. "Let me take you there."

"This is personal, Rike. I need to handle this alone."

"Then take this at least."

He waited impatiently while she tied a new amulet to his left hand, this one a lone white feather tied to a string. It struck him that this should have been how driven he was to return to Forest Home. He should have left by now, but he'd tarried, meditating and exercising in preparation for the battle ahead.

Now, however, the battle had come here, and he was rushing to save Besi in a way he hadn't for the Forest. Yet, he didn't hesitate. He only waited long enough for Rike to secure the amulet, then he sharpened his senses, focusing on the signature of Dnres. Then, he did something he hadn't done in a long time—he vanished into thin air.

He re-materialised in the park.

Dnres crouched before him, Besi nowhere to be seen. Under the cover of the night, his old friend wore a human body, but Leon could see past it to the multiple horns and eyes that made the Southern Guard.

"You shouldn't be here," he said.

"Neither should you," Dnres grunted. "You should be dead, yet I saw your light. We threw you down that hole, and here you've been living large!"

Leon stepped forward, and Dnres immediately retreated.

"Don't move," he warned.

Dnres pointed to the left, and Leon looked to see Besi on the grass, struggling against the nightmares Dnres had tossed her in.

"Why?" He charged towards Dnres and only stopped when he heard Besi scream.

He looked at her again and saw that her life force had dimmed. At that, he stopped moving.

"You always had a weakness for human women," Dnres said. "Allowing them to come to our side, to destroy things."

"What do you want?" he spat.

"I see you're no longer the peace-maker you were in the Forest," Dnres instructed. "Take off those amulets and fight me one on one."

Leon eyed the amulets around his neck and his wrist. It struck him that Rike's protection must have been why Dnres couldn't approach him directly. He had put Besi in danger.

"You will let her go first," he said, tugging at the necklace. "Your grievance is with me."

Dnres shrugged and flicked his fingers. Besi stilled, but he kept his hand in the air, ready to continue his torture if Leon did not comply.

Leon removed the amulets and tossed them into the bushes. He didn't have time to prepare before Dnres charged at him. The Southern Guard went straight for his chest, the source of his life-force. Claws pierced through his skin as Dnres searched for the small bead that would extinguish him.

Using all his strength, he kicked Dnres off him. He then went on the attack, throwing punches packed with both his physical and psychic strength, pounding Dnres with the force of all the years he had spent lost on Earth. He was going to crush Dnres, extinguish his light, and put an end to this madness.

Leon's energy overpowered his friend's, but with each punch, he realised he couldn't do it. Perhaps because he'd never been a fighter, Dnres took every hit but was not going down. He turned the tables once more when he grabbed Leon's throat. His sharp fingers pressed into Leon's chest and moved slowly through the muscle and mass, searching. He was inching closer and closer—Leon pushed at him, but the daemon was rooted firmly to the spot.

A soft song reached his ears in an ancient tongue. Bright lights erupted all around him, and for a second, he thought his existence was over, 'til he saw Rike looking down on him.

"What happened?" He blinked and clutched his chest, found he was still whole.

"I followed you here," Rike said. "I couldn't let you face this alone."

"Dnres?"

"He's gone. He doesn't agree with my amulets."

Leon shuddered. "He's not gone."

Dnres had made this seem personal, but if the Red Lady was right, his appearance on Earth signalled that the chaos happening in Forest Home was spilling over.

CHAPTER SEVEN

Something cold and bitter snaked its way down Besi's throat. She saw the forest again, and fear clutched at her. But this time, it looked light and airy. In the clearing was a woman dressed like she belonged in a historical movie with multiple wrappers and an elaborate hairstyle. Her skin was a bright red as though she had been dipped in blood, but she had a smile on her face. Everything about her aura felt loving.

The first thing Besi saw when she opened her eyes was the most stunning woman she would probably ever see. The woman's curly hair framed her heart-shaped face, with feline eyes accentuated with eyeliner, her clear skin reddish with golden tones.

She must have spent minutes staring at the woman, lost in her calm and loving aura before the horrible memories started drifting back to her in bits and pieces. The woman moved closer to her and placed her hands over Besi's clutched arms. The smell of honeysuckle surrounded her as a cool tranquillity enveloped her.

"You're at Leon's house," the woman said softly. "Do you remember coming here?"

She shook her head through the flashbacks that jolted her.

"You're safe now." The woman stroked her cheek. "Let me get you some tea."

"Who are you?" she asked, clearing her throat.

"They call me Iyene." She smiled. Iyene had not moved, but there was now a steaming cup of tea in her hands, which she offered to Besi.

"I think I saw you ... while I was asleep." She struggled to find the words. "It was in a forest ..."

Iyene said words she couldn't comprehend; they sounded like a totally different language.

"That's my home," Iyene explained. "Our home."

"Is that somewhere in Nigeria?" Her throat still felt parched, so she gulped the tea.

"Well, it's ..."

Iyene paused and glanced at the door. A heartbeat later, it pushed open, and Rike and Leon trooped in.

Besi's heart soared at the sight of Leon. He beamed at her, and it triggered a recollection of him shrouded in brilliant colours and charging towards the monster that had attacked her.

"Well," Iyene announced. "I believe this is my cue to leave."

On her way out, she paused beside Leon. They looked at each other, not saying a word, but it seemed like they were having an entire conversation. Besi felt a new energy sift through the room—gratitude. All too quickly, it was just her and Leon.

"I'm sure you have many questions," he said, pacing across the large room. He was avoiding her, cautious with his movements and trying not to come too close to bed.

"Just tell me everything," she said, drinking the last of the tea. She was feeling like herself again, balanced and in charge.

"Where do I start?" He leaned against the windowsill, crossed his arms over his chest, and stared at her.

"Start with today. What happened?"

"Today, you were attacked by Dnres," he started. "Their kind is fierce and feed on life forces and attack through hypnosis and sometimes dreams. But the Forest saw it wise to make him one of its guards."

"Okay ..." She wrapped the coverlet tighter around her shoulders.

"They are daemons with an 'a', the closest way to describe them ... us ..." Once he'd started, Leon found that he couldn't stop talking. "Me. Iyene who helped heal you. I am not from here. I'm actually from ... there. I have been trapped here for decades, sent by the daemon that attacked you. That figurine artwork you say is a gift. It's my wand. Losing it is—"

"Wait, no." She vigorously shook her head. "You're human."

"I'm not." He couldn't meet her gaze. "I've been living here since the 1930s."

"No," she objected. Of all the things she had imagined about Leon, this was the most outlandish. "You're kidding. There is a rational explanation."

"It's why the man at that restaurant recognised me. We shared a bungalow in the 60s," he explained. "You've seen it yourself."

"When?"

"At your home, when I held the statuette."

She had seen the electricity that had jumped from Leon's hands and hurt Mene. They'd both seen it, but it had gone unmentioned as there had been no reasonable explanation.

Leon wouldn't look at her as she got up from the bed.

"So you have magic?" she asked.

"You can call it magic," he affirmed. "I am ... I used to be the Western Guard, and that wand helped me with my duties. I lost the statuette when I landed here, but I didn't lose everything."

"How am I to believe this?" She was saying the words, but that calmness from earlier hadn't let go of her.

Just what was in the tea? The past few hours had slapped her in the face with magic and more magic, but to learn that Leon, the man she was falling for, wasn't even human? She should be screaming and running out of the house. Instead, she wanted to find her purse—the statuette was in there. She needed to see.

"Use your magic to find my car, then."

"Rike already did. It's in the garage."

"All right." She lifted her jaw. "Take me there."

Her purse was where she had left it on the floor, at the back. She palmed the statuette and pushed it at Leon.

"Show me," she demanded.

"What do you want to see?" he asked uncertainly.

"Everything."

He took the statuette from her and eyed it. She blinked and drew back when she saw those sparks again.

"I won't hurt you, Besi," he promised. "But I'll show you."

A dazzling orange filled the dark garage. She smelled cloves and frankincense as the walls closed in on her. Out of nowhere, she was plunged into darkness.

Slowly, it faded away 'til she saw a bruised and battered Leon shivering in the depths of a hole. She saw the forest Iyene had showed her, a place of luminous brightness and the feeling of home.

Images from Leon's life passed before her eyes like a vignette. She saw him lost and trying to find his way home again and again. Each time he failed, he was weakened. She saw the betrayal he had told her of, the way people that drew close to him always turned on him, over and over. She saw Iyene giving him her life force and witnessed the fight between him and Dnres.

By the time he had shown her everything about his long life, Besi was on her knees, gasping for air. Her eyes teared up as she rose to shaky feet.

"Besi." He reached for her.

She pulled away. "I-I need to go home."

***

Rike pulled the curtains back, flooding the darkened room with sunlight.

"Eight days have passed?" Leon asked from the bed.

"Precisely. I've got sweet potato chips, sautéed vegetables, and peppered fish. Your meal is ready."

He dragged himself from the bed and to the round table by the window. He dug into the meal and felt better but only slightly considering he had lost Besi forever.

"I trust preparations for my return are set?" he asked.

"Yes." Rike looked at him concerned. "So this is it?'

"You always insisted that you would be the one to send me home." He shrugged.

"So I have a confession. I haven't finished with the preparations."

He glanced up at her, his brows furrowed. "A few minutes ago, you—"

"I lied." She played with a thread at the hem of the short dress she wore. "I don't want you to go yet."

"Rike." He laughed dryly. "Whatever is the matter?"

Her phone chimed, and she looked at it. "Yes! Okay, just give me a moment. One second!"

She was out the door before he could react. He wondered why she was acting so strangely and turned his attention back to his food. Now reunited with his wand, his energies were amplified. He knew that Dnres was no longer on Earth, but that didn't mean he would not return.

He shuddered at the thought of Dnres harming Besi again. Once he returned to the Forest Home, he would ensure balance was restored, then he would hunt the Southern Guard down and banish him for good. And then, he would guard the forest like he'd always done.

His shoulders slumped. All of a sudden, going back didn't seem as enchanting as it once did. For so many years, he had wanted to return to the Forest Home, and now, he was questioning himself.

A low knock sounded at the door.

"Come in, Rike. And be prepared to explain yourself."

"It's not Rike. It's me."

Leon jumped to his feet at the sound of Besi's voice. He blinked to ensure he wasn't dreaming.

Besi was indeed in his bedroom, wearing a sheer pink maxi dress, her hair braided in a ponytail.

"Hello." She smiled at him. "You look horrible."

He rubbed his stubbled chin. "Excuse me."

He channelled his energy, and in a flash, it was gone.

"Okay!" She jumped. "I was not expecting that."

"I'm sorry," he rushed.

"No worries." She sighed. "I have a lot to learn."

"Besi, why?" He shifted from one foot to the other. "Why are you here?"

"Rike cornered me." She laughed. "She told me you were leaving forever, and I meditated on it. This is the wildest thing ever, but here I am."

She moved towards him, and he opened his arms. He was holding Besi, something he'd thought he would never feel again. She tilted her head up for a kiss, and he leaned in.

"I really like you, Mr. Otherworldly."

"I really like you, too, Ms. Human." He held her face and deepened the kiss.

***

Besi had not made a mistake coming here. Waking up in Leon's arms, she didn't want to let go. He kissed her slowly, and she knew he didn't want to let her go, either. However, he had to, and she understood.

It was for their safety. The world as she knew it could be overrun with daemons like the one that had attacked her if Leon did not go back, as the Red Lady had warned. She appreciated this, but it didn't make accepting it easier. In the early hours of the morning, she worked with Rike and Leon in the garden.

Rike marked the earth with the white chalk where the portal would appear. Besi helped her, placing clear glasses of water and cooked food for the four navigational points. Leon sat in meditation, acclimatising himself with his wand. Although Rike and Besi moved slowly, it seemed as though everything was set too quickly. Leon stepped into the markings, and he looked at them.

"Be safe," she said, her voice croaked.

"I will." He smiled at her. "I will return to you, Besi."

The carrot orange of his aura radiated from him, its warmth stretching towards her.

One moment, he stood there, and the next, he had vanished.

Besi choked on a sob, then another one. Tears streamed down her face. Rike held her hand and squeezed it tightly.

EPILOGUE

At the launch of Gazania in Dakar, Besi shone. She smiled for the cameras and tried to express her excitement in halting French, but her mind was still on Leon. It had been four months since he'd crossed back to Forest Home, and his promise still remained unfulfilled.

Everything around her reminded her of him, and not just the memory of his kisses. Rike had delivered selected furniture handmade from Leon's collection to Dakar. Even with this success and with her solid network of family and friends, Besi felt alone. It was difficult to have found something that she couldn't talk about with anyone. But then again, who would believe her? On days like this, she imagined how difficult it had been for Leon to reveal his true nature to her.

Soon after he had left, she had made Rike take her to Iyene out of desperation. She'd needed to know if Leon was okay. Under the Red Lady's supervision, she had seen the Forest Home glowing in welcome.

It had embraced Leon after his long exile, balance having been restored. News of his return had swept through the forest as he had paid visit after visit to the troublemakers who were inciting trouble as well as anyone who had harmed him or attempted to. While he didn't extinguish their light—it was always difficult for him to do that—he'd made them swear before the Forest itself to their own extinction if they tried to harm him or others. The unruly ones had left him no choice but to engage in battle.

The vision had told her he was hard at work. She just had to be patient—he would come back to her.

***

On the beach, she sat down on a spread towel. Under the shade of a large umbrella, she flipped through a photo book. The air stilled, something shifting in the atmosphere. Ever since Leon, she had found herself more sensitive to energies, and this one felt familiar. It smelt like cloves and frankincense.

The book fell from her hands as she stood up and looked around. She tore her sunglasses from her face when she saw Leon emerging from the ocean as though he'd just gone for a quick dunk. She rubbed at her eyes. He was still there, walking purposefully towards her.

She ran into his arms; he was real. This wasn't a dream. "This isn't a dream."

It was Leon's voice, and she had been talking out loud. "How?" she asked.

"I got some help," he explained. "And I have some gifts, too."

"What does that mean?"

"It means I am retired. There's no more magic," he said. "I'm not immortal anymore. I live and I will die, but I will return to the Forest Home, and you're welcome to come with me, too ... if you decide."

Besi laughed out loud. She kissed him.

"Thanks for leaving that option open for me. Is it still dangerous?"

"It's a lot more peaceful than it was when I left. The new Western Guard is less prone to accidents than I am."

He held her close, breathed in her aura, and knew he had made the right decision. This is what love felt like, and it was a gift he was never going to let go. Besi was his anchor, his proof that he could trust, and with her, he was ready to start living life free.

THE END

ABOUT THE AUTHOR

Bambo Deen is a romantic grew up not seeing herself in M&B books she loved reading as child. She always wanted to write about lovers crossing paths on a bus to Abuja or about hot Africans making love under the canopy of the forbidden forest. She writes fantastical and paranormal love stories. Keep up with her on https://www.facebook.com/bambodeen/

Finding Love in Betrayal

FISKE NYIRONGO

BLURB

A love story full of hope and seeing beyond differences.
Mbawemi is an heir to the throne in a kingdom of witches, wolves and hybrids. Hybrids are considered the lowest form of creature in the kingdom. In enters Sangwani, a hybrid king who is anything but what Sangwani thinks of hybrids. Can their love build bridges?

CHAPTER ONE

Mbawemi's dreams took her to worlds unknown every time, a trick she'd learn at age four and forbidden by her parents. She knew how to stay hidden from the dangerous creatures in her world, her most prized attribute to date being her skill in camouflage; one passed on from her paternal side.

Tonight was different—she was exposed, the forest she found herself in being too dark. Her feet bled as the hard floor made cuts into her bare soles. She heard the thing pursuing her through the trees grow closer, its growl menacing and the air around her smelling rancid.

Her body gave out when she came to a tree she recognized from her previous run across this part of the forest.

"You are trapped here. Just let me in," the creature said.

She heard it growl much closer now, the rancid smell permeating all around her.

"I should have known you would have a pretty voice. At least the creator gave you something beautiful to work with because you are so ugly," she said.

It emerged from behind one of the trees.

"Why do you always go where you are not welcome? Have your bastard parents not taught you that none of them or their offspring are welcome outside of their cosy little palace?" it asked.

Mbawemi had never seen a hybrid creature in its real form up close, only from the museum in the palace and the video games she was forbidden from playing.

"I can go wherever I want. You are not the boss of me," she said.

The creature laughed as he drew closer to her. He walked on two hind legs, his face as foul as his scent. He stood a few feet away from her face now.

"We don't usually feast on your bastard flesh, but I will make an exception for you," he said as he bared his teeth and wrapped a claw around Mbawemi's throat.

She closed her eyes, willing herself to remember the spell that would work in this forest. Then she recalled this was the only place where her powers would not work, no matter who she was.

She heard the horns sound in the distance and wanted to be dead in the second that followed. The palace knew she wasn't in her bed like the perfect daughter she was known to be and the future queen of the kingdom. Her parents would be less than pleased, and their punishments would be much worse than what this creature had in mind for her.

"Well, you can kill me. I'm dead meat anyway now." She laughed.

The creature paused, and she concentrated on its eyes. It had the most dazzling eyes she had ever seen in her life. The purple irises with the outsides glowing in a blueish flame were a waste on such an ugly thing.

"Your people are here. I guess I'll have to find another feast tonight. You should learn something from your witches. They know not to seek things that might end them," the creature said.

Before Mbawemi could reply, she saw the mist, pink and white, rise from the distance, and she smiled at it.

"I'm thinking you shouldn't stay for—" She looked around her, but the creature was gone. Just like the mist that had appeared out of nowhere, the hybrid had disappeared.

"You better get back to the palace, young lady. Before your parents devise more serious punishments for you," a figure said as it formed from the mist.

"Grandma Towa!" Mbawemi said as the shape fully formed into the woman she hadn't seen in weeks. "You came," she added as she saw another form beside her grandmother.

Towa's identical twin sister, Tawanda, was dressed similarly to her. Their pink-dyed white hair and outfits all looked just as dazzling as the first time they'd changed their look.

"You didn't think we would miss your birthday, did you?" Tawanda asked as she took Mbawemi into her arms. "Now, before your parents send out hunters throughout the kingdom, let's get you back into your bed."

The two older witches morphed back into the mist, carrying Mbawemi away in it.

***

The creature that had been with her only minutes ago watched the scene from above in the trees. He was just a boy himself. He had gone after her when he'd heard the heartbeat of something that didn't belong in his world.

He'd heard something else pursuing her and had known exactly what that was—a part of him, too. It had stopped its hunt only when it had seen him emerge from the shadows, an unspoken law held over its head: He picked the first hunt. He was, after all, king of the forest.

***

"I don't think she realizes what she is and why she doesn't have to go outside the perimeters we agreed on years ago with them."

The king rarely raised his voice, but Mbawemi heard him clearly through her bedroom in the West wing. His throne room was two floors down and on the Eastern wing of the palace.

"C'mon, child. She's a curious one. I remember raising someone like her moons ago," Grandma Towa said.

Mbawemi laughed at that. She'd gotten the gene for adventure from her father, and Towa reminded him often of that fact.

"She'll grow out of it. Just give her time, my love," her mother's voice said.

She knew not to get comfortable by the softness in her mother's tone. While her father got the most angry whenever she went missing, it was her mother who belted out the punishments—the most atrocious kind of misery she wouldn't wish on her worst enemy, not even on the creature she'd encountered in the woods.

"We don't have time to wait for her to grow up. There are too many threats to us out there. She needs to understand that," her father said.

"He was in the forest with us. We felt him. He didn't try to harm us. Maybe he is different from his lineage."

Her eyes grew heavy when she heard this. She let the sleep take her to new lands now.

***

"You have to conclude an alliance with one of the families making a tribute this year. That's the only way we strengthen our blood lines and kingdom, Your Highness," Niza said.

Niza was her chief advisor. She'd promoted the woman from her position as governess to that of the future queen's advisor, a decision that had not gone well within the kingdom's council, but she couldn't bring herself to care.

Mbawemi was taking her second bath of the day. She wanted to know more about the kingdom that would be hers one day; she wanted to be a good queen. She went to see the affairs of the realm and had not shied away from the touches of the ordinary people and the hard work of the day.

"And what about me choosing a mate more suited to myself, Niza? Isn't that my right as future queen? Or does all this freedom mean that I now become a slave to some ancient rules?"

"Well, you could, you know, have someone else. If you have someone else in mind, that is. To fulfil your other needs from time to time." Niza said the words without humour.

Mbawemi was briefly embarrassed by the suggestion.

"Never mind. I will fulfil my duties. I just wish I could have what Father and Mother have, you know. Something much more real."

"Your father and mother met the first time on their wedding night," Niza pointed out. "And they are the most in love marriage I have witnessed in this castle."

Mbawemi smiled.

"You'll be fine, Your Highness. Is there anything else I can help you with?"

"No, thank you, Niza. That will be all. I'll be down in a second," she said as she got more comfortable in the water. She knew that was a lie.

The palace was lively today. Towa and Tawanda had their best witches selected already to bring in their talents and skills that would be used in the pick for Mbawemi's future husband and consort.

"Your Highness. We don't have everything set for the final event. You will be more comfortable in the Great Room," one of the servants said to Mbawemi.

She brushed him off as she went to sit near the stage where the whole show would take place in a few hours.

"Go, Tawanda! That looks amazing, I should choose you to be my consort instead," she joked.

Towa and Tawanda had the helpers of the candidates in a queue, showing them how to navigate the traps and creatures throughout the stage only there as an illusion. The sisters were in their usual pink Chitenge dresses, their hair in the bun style Mbawemi only wished she could perfect one day, their dark skin covered in white dots around their faces and chests.

This brought her back down to earth. All the female members of her family would be spotting the white marks on their bodies until her new marriage was consummated, with a new heir on the way. It made her sad that this was what her life would be in a few short weeks—having sex for the purpose of securing an heir without any love. It could end in two ways: either a loveless union, or like her parents who fell in love after their joining.

"Child, I've been making these happen for two hundred years. We can teach you one or two things," Towa said as they come to stand near her.

"It's all coming together. I just hope it is not as bad as I think it will be," Mbawemi said.

"You are dressed up already. Look at you. That gown is something," Tawanda said as she took in Mbawemi's appearance.

She wore a brown, floor-length ball gown with accents of gold peppered in that made it shimmer with the tiniest movement in her body. The gold also held a secret that only Mbawemi and her seamstress knew. She'd embedded a spell into the fabric of the gown—only the one person who could read it would become her consort. When she'd read the rules of what she could do to contribute to make the tribute harder, she had come up with the idea alone and only told her seamstress days before she'd been done with the gown.

"It will be over soon. You'll see what I mean one day," Niza said as she came to stand with them.

They remained quiet as the room previously alive with activity became absolutely still as people now went to get ready for the main event.

CHAPTER TWO

Sangwani had a hard time getting used to being ruler of the forest. He didn't know how to rule over people who defied him at every turn. It had been six years since his father had died. Six years since he'd had to be on the throne proving to be more of a headache than anything.

"We don't attack them on their land. We have an agreement in place with them; we have had it for the past century," he said as he circled around the creature that looked like him.

"You are still a boy! You don't understand that they will come for us some day. We have to get ready. We kill as much of them as we can now before it's too late."

Sangwani saw the defiance in the creature's eyes, the same one he had encountered since he'd gotten the throne.

It was futile to argue with the older creature, though. He chose to let the matter and him go.

"You can leave. Stay away from the boundaries."
***

The sight still made his heart ache. The spirit of his father, the great Mako, visited him from another realm whenever he found himself on the edge of saying fuck it all. He always came, but the spirit never counselled him with what he needed.

"What now? I am not in the mood for you, old man."

"She will come through to you like the ground you stand on. You will fight it at first, but she has your heart already. She's going to be the promised queen, freeing our people and uniting us across all the realms," the shadow said.

"Well, I have no use for your words of wisdom, like always."

"You have to let her in, Sangwani. She'll be here soon."

Sangwani turned—the shadow had more emotion than he'd heard in his father's voice even when he was alive.

"What does all this mean, Father? Don't go. Please don't go." He almost sobbed.

The shadow flickered before it puttered into the air. Sangwani had another reason to add to the shitty day he was having. He had someone who would make some things better for him, but even going to the cabin that was his favourite place in all the forest didn't make him quicken his steps.

"Your Highness, it's great to see you this side of the forest. What are you doing here visiting us lowly creatures?"

Chapansa regarded him with the same suspicious look as the day she had been brought into his house by his father. Two years younger than him, she was the young sister he had always wanted, and to date, he always regarded her as he would a blood sibling.

"And you have the audacity to walk here without your guards after you cut down the boundaries without asking me!"

The mutual affection from her end was gone and buried.

"Good to see you, too, Cha. How is our mother doing? Is she going to live with you forever now?" Sangwani asked.

"He should have left the throne to me. I would be more of a leader than you could ever be. You are too soft, Sangwani," Chapansa said.

"It's a good thing he's not your blood father, then." Chapansa looked down to the ground beneath them when he said those words. "I'm sorry. That was uncalled for."

"You always know how to hurt people when they are down, don't you?"

Mwaka was every bit as bitter as the day she'd lost her king and the greatest warlock/wolf she had ever known.

"Hello, Mother. It's good to see you, too."

"Don't you ever say that to my daughter. She is my blood, your father's blood. We made a covenant for her to be a part of our household. She's your father's child as much as you, more than you will ever be."

"Thanks, Mother," Sangwani said as he started to walk away. "Thank you for this glorious family reunion."

"Sangwani, wait," Chapansa shouted. "I have something for you."

She was a skilled hunter and fighter, or like they were called by the witch population, half-breeds. She had the skill to track down all information from the supernatural communities of witches, warlocks, werewolves, and other shape-shifters.

"I found this on our border with the wolves. They have something going on. I found witch signs with them," Chapansa said.

She led a map that lit up when she ran a hand over it, and Sangwani was taken into her mind from when she had seen the forest border.

"What does all of this mean? Wolves and witches have never been known to meet each other willingly unless it's to get rid of the anomalies like us," he said.

"I don't really care because whatever they have planned to do with that bastard royal family will be the least of what they deserve," Chapansa said.

"I'll keep an eye on it. Just to be sure they are not planning on exterminating us." Sangwani snorted.

"Thanks."

He now just wanted nothing more than to go far away from his world, and he did exactly that as he transformed his body into the shape-shifting part that would keep him safe in the witch/warlock world. Maybe he would see the girl who had plagued his dreams for years now.

CHAPTER THREE

The ceremony had started outside, but Mbawemi couldn't be bothered to exit her bedroom to check on the progress of her suitors. She heard the excited giggles of her cousins as they filed out of her room, but she just sat on her bed, sulking.

"I know that look. I had the same one when I was on the other side. Your grandfather was the one in his room hearing a group of young women fight to call themselves his queen consort. I sulked through the whole process, too. He was a prince, but I didn't like him."

"And you expect me to somehow pick someone who's not royalty?" Mbawemi joked.

"You don't have to do anything but just sit there. We have another trick up our sleeves this year with your dress," Towa said. "I saw it already, child. The right one will, too."

"I don't know what to expect," Mbawemi admitted.

"They are not as bad as we thought they would be. Just come outside for a bit. You can come back in until we are down to the last two," Tawanda said.

She walked out flanked by Towa and Tawanda.
***

Sangwani watched Mbawemi from his spot in the crowd, her eyes every bit as beautiful as the day he'd saved her in the forest moons ago. The grown-up version of her didn't hold a candle to the one he had concocted in his dreams. She was now almost as tall as him. She took his breath away in the brown gown she wore that had accents of gold that called out to him.

It was like a siren's song emitting every time she moved. He admired the outfits of the old women by her side. He hated the royal family with everything in him, but he couldn't deny they were the best-dressed creatures he had ever seen.

He didn't know how he'd ended up coming to this part of the witches' world. His shape-shifter's body had a mind of its own, and it had led him to the palace walls where he'd fitted in with the hundreds coming into the palace. He didn't know what he was doing here or much less what was going on.

"Does anyone have any claim on this warlock?"

A scream emitted from beyond the stage where shirtless young warlocks all navigated obstacles that were nothing but rabbit traps to everyone else. He groaned when he realised what was taking place.

"So old-fashioned and primitive," he said to himself.

The warlocks around him regarded him curiously as they all stood at least two feet away from him, like they somehow knew he wasn't one of them.

He was trained for anything out of the ordinary. He had failed his father years ago, but he knew when he smelled something unusual. He didn't alert them, for fear of being found out himself.

The first wolf appeared out of the stage above them. With its murderous look, it took into its mouth the warlock announcer who had just before being lusting over the bodies of the half-naked warlocks.

"Mbawemi! Guards, take her away."

He heard the voice he had been dreaming about over and over. The voice of the man who had launched the attack against his father all those years ago.

He approached the king and queen and saw he was too late to give him the same fate he had given to his father. A wolf already crouched between him and his target.

He became aware for the first time that some of the witches were helping the wolves. He saw a middle-aged witch walk towards the princess with a murderous look in her eyes. The princess was frozen in place.

"Now!"

He heard one of the older witch twins as they disappeared into a cloud of mist, holding on to the princess he had come to know as Mbawemi.

***

"Mum and Dad!" Mbawemi said as she was dragged through the forest and brought to an underground cabin.

"There's nothing we could do for them. It's not only the wolves who are part of this. They put a boundary when they attacked."

"An assassination? By who?" she asked.

"Witches and warlocks. We warned your father. He was becoming too relaxed about the reports of meetings taking place between the wolves and warlocks on the northern border."

Mbawemi was too numb to cry, the grief she was supposed to feel quickly replaced by the need for revenge.

"I have an idea who is behind this," she said.

"Niza?" Towa nodded.

"She was pushing me to be strict on issues Father was relaxing over. Like the attack on the half-breeds that took place years ago. She said he had the forest under his control, but he left the son of the king he killed to rule."

"And she wasn't around when the attack happened," Tawanda said.

"They will comb through every nook and cranny in the kingdom. They would never think to search for us here," Towa said.

"Where are we?" Mbawemi asked.

"In the middle of the forest," Towa replied.

"What? Where we are the number one hunted creature? Grandma, I don't—"

"I thought I was dreaming when I found out that we had full-blooded royal witches in our presence."

The door to the cabin burst open after a cunning voice spoke.

"We don't want any trouble here. This is part of the royal family's property," Tawanda said as she and Towa came to stand in a defensive pose in front of Mbawemi.

"I know what this is," the creature said as it morphed into a beautiful human woman, one that held familiarity to all the three royal women. "I hear you are not part of royalty anymore. A new queen was crowned. So I can kill you right now and not get any recourse from the new queen. I might be doing them a favour, anyway."

She stalked closer to the twin old witches and the younger witch who stood behind them.

"But I won't. Your bastard father is dead, I hear. He was the one that ordered the ambush against my father. And now, he is dead, too. We are even." She smiled.

Mbawemi lost her fear in that moment. Hearing the stranger gloating over her recent loss was too much. Towa and Tawanda had anticipated her move as she charged towards the woman. They held her back as she launched one spell after the other onto her.

"You can't even fight, and you think you can take me on?"

Sangwani had tracked Mbawemi and the others to this part of the forest. But he hadn't expected to find his sister attacking them.

"What's going on, Chapansa?"

The booming voice resounded through the small underground place, and all their eyes were drawn to the door—one pair in irritation and the others in wonder.

"Your Highness, I was just giving the visitors the ground rules for coming onto this neutral land."

Chapansa looked into Sangwani's eyes with irritation. She called him 'your highness', but he heard the clear disrespect in her tone.

"You are not supposed to come onto this land uninvited. They could kill you," he said to his sister. She rolled her eyes and excused herself from the group.

"You shouldn't have run so fast from saving your family. They now think you are running scared."

"You and your family are very undiplomatic, it seems," Mbawemi said as she slipped out of the tight grip Towa and Tawanda had her in. "You can't possibly know what it's like to lose some one you love." She scoffed.

"Now look who's being undiplomatic?" Sangwani said.

He was intrigued by the pull he felt towards her and disregarded the feeling in the next minute.

"Come on, Grandmas. We are going to get back what belongs to us," Mbawemi said.

"You are not thinking clearly. Look, my father was killed, too," Sangwani said.

"Never compare our fathers. Your father was a bad, mad king. Ask your subjects."

"Beyond your perception of him, he was my father. I could give you a lesson about who your parents truly were, but I'm too diplomatic, unlike you," he said. "It won't do you any good to go after the ones you claim are behind the attack now. You have to first think, plan."

He saw the defiance in her eyes.

"You call my father a mad king. One thing I learnt from that madness is that it came from a place of not thinking through rage. Trust me on this one. I know what blind rage can do to a person. You are welcome to stay."

He followed Chapansa out of the cabin.

"It pains me to say this, baby, but he is right," Tawanda said to her.

"We will be dead come sunrise if we go to them now," Towa added.

Mbawemi felt the first signs of grief and fatigue, and she nodded to Towa and Tawanda, and they let out collective sighs.

As Sangwani left them, he heard the clear sounds of mourning, and he remembered his own grief years ago. Theirs had been different; there had been no crying involved—they had each retreated to their corners of the forest.

"You don't bully yourself in when you want to get something in return from others, Cha. This isn't something we can do without allies in place," he said.

"We have two old witches who look like they are more into fashion than they have ever been in perfecting their skills, and a younger witch who is just as fashionable but looks like she has never gotten a nail chipped in her entire life," Chapansa said. "And you expect those to help us to win the popular vote for us to get the kingdoms to be all ours?"

"You have no idea who those two old women are. They have a direct lineage to the first witch. They have more power in a chipped fingernail than you could ever muster over centuries."

"I hope you don't regret it," she said as she disappeared back into the thicket she had come out of.

Mbawemi circled back into the house when she heard their conversation end.

"No, please don't leave now. You are really a very good eavesdropper. Chapansa didn't even notice you there," Sangwani said.

"You are either a masochist, or you really must need us for something for not killing us as soon as you saw us," she said as she rounded to come near him.

"Your hand is bleeding, and your dress is torn in the midriff. Get that fixed before you start to question me, Your Highness," he replied. "None have her, but many want her?"

Mbawemi ignored the loud beating of her heart as she looked into the eyes she had dreamt about for years now.

"What?"

"Your dress. It had those words in its fabric right in your midriff. 'None have her but many want her'. She's yours as soon as you say these words. From the book of marriage and love by your kind."

"How did you ... what did you do?"

"I know about my ancestors, too. More than you can imagine," he said. "I will see you around, Princess."

Towa and Tawanda found her hours later standing in the same spot as her brain wondered what all this meant for her.

"You are cold, baby. What are you doing outside? I thought you went to sleep?" Towa asked.

"He was there at the palace. He gave me the answer to my dress, what it had in its embroidery."

"Oh," Towa said.

"What does that mean? That he could read it? Half-breeds don't know how to read," Mbawemi said.

"I have a feeling he is a different half-breed. He can blend in with us. He got behind the palace walls when we have measures put in place to stop their kind from ever setting foot in there."

"What your Grandma means is, don't trust him. He seems to be after something," Tawanda said.

Mbawemi was embarrassed that the thought thrilled her. She was more aware now that she wouldn't mind to give him something. And she just knew it was clearly written on her face.

"I don't trust him. That's no problem for me," she said.

It was the truth. She didn't trust her body's reaction to him.

"Good. We need to get some sleep," Towa said.

They knew they wouldn't get much sleep. Not until they'd avenged their family.

CHAPTER FOUR

He watched her. Every day that followed, he had her in his sights. The three of them kept within the boundary of their habitat. He saw the longing in her eyes as the days passed. He wanted to make it better for her; somehow, he had become more attached to her even when he saw how inaccessible anything between them was.

One day, he followed her out to the waterfall above their underground home. She disrobed, and he didn't avert his eyes. They traced across her dark skin. She was a tall woman, he realised once again, all limbs, and only her breasts and other female prominent parts stood out apart from her tall stature.

"You are now watching the enemy take a bath? Don't be so pathetic, son. You can have ten who look like her easily if you are into such."

Mwaka still had the same disappointed look and contempt she had for him. But this time, he noticed she also had amusement in her eyes.

"Mother? What are you doing here?"

"The same thing you are doing," she replied. "Maybe not exactly the same. I heard that we had guests in the forest. I wanted to see for myself what all the fuss was about. Your guards told me you come here to check on them."

"It's not what you think."

"That you are making friends with the family of the man that killed your father?"

"You and I both now know her father didn't come up with the idea to kill Father," he said.

"He didn't stop it, either. He sided with everyone. Not that I was surprised."

"You know he became unstable. He wasn't going to let his reign go by without attacking the wolves and the witches, Mother."

"You sound like you are now an activist for both sides, child. Remember who you are before you defend them. You are nothing but an abomination to them, to her, too. Do you think she would ever willingly go to bed with you?" She sneered.

"I'm keeping my people safe. I don't need your approval to do so."

"Fine. You are going to regret this, Sangwani. Mark my words."

In their tense stand-off, they didn't notice that Mbawemi had noticed their loud conversation.

"Are you stalking me now?" She held onto her bath robe tightly as she looked at the mother-son duo so consumed in their talk, they hadn't heard her approach them.

"We were checking on you, to make sure no one is disturbing your time in the forest. Weren't we, Mother?" Sangwani said.

"Oh, yes. You resemble your father, young lady. I once would have given anything to be his queen back in the day, but your mother got to him first. Well, that was then, but I found my own prince, just as handsome but more daring than your father."

"We will be leaving soon," Mbawemi said stubbornly.

"And where are you going to go, Your Highness?" Mwaka asked. "When they have bounty hunters among every species now hunting you?"

"We have some allies we have contacted ... You know what, never mind. Please excuse me. My grandmothers will be worried if I don't get to the cabin before sunset," Mbawemi said.

"I can now see why you are drawn to her. She is hundred percent her father's child. She also isn't a fool. So keep her close but not too close. We will need her."

"We have had the same plan in motion all this time, and we have never gotten past our dislike for each other to discuss it. We need to talk, Mother. Our survival depends on it."

"I agree. We'll come to you."

She was gone before he could say another word to her.
***

"Where have you been? You know it isn't safe for us to split up anymore," Towa said as Mbawemi looked out of the door to make sure no one had followed her back to the cabin.

"I was taking a bath. Is that not allowed anymore, or am I to ask for permission from you now?"

"Have you gone mad? You don't talk to your grandmother like that, young lady! This isn't a democracy we are in. We follow the rules we all agreed on," Tawanda said.

"I'm sorry, Grandma. I shouldn't have snapped at you."

"What's wrong? You looked upset when you came in," Towa asked.

She was too tired to argue.

"I found the hybrid king and his mother watching me while I was taking a bath. Well, it was him who was watching me at first, I gathered from their conversation."

"Did they do anything to you?" Tawanda asked as she came closer to her.

"No. No, nothing like that, but it's so irritating that we are being watched every single second like we are criminals."

"It won't always be this way, Mbawemi. We will be in our rightful place soon. I promise you."

"About that. Do we have any information about the Chuma Coven?"

She didn't miss the glance Towa and Tawanda shared.

"Your mother's coven send you their best wishes, but they won't join you in reclaiming the throne," Towa quietly said.

"I was expecting that. It doesn't make it any less painful to hear," she replied. "I will retire for bed now. I will see you in the morning. Good night. Thank you for staying with me."

They remained standing minutes after Mbawemi went to her room.

***

"Good morning, Your Highness."

"You can stop calling me that. I'm too busy to worry about some half-breed king's insults. Don't you have a kingdom to rule? Or is this a do-as-you-please place like the stories I've heard about you people?"

"And you think me calling you 'your highness' is an insult?" Sangwani asked.

His booming laugh sent birds scurrying in all directions.

"You are really a full-blooded witch. Your kind knows how to get under our skins." He smirked.

Mbawemi saw the way he looked at her body. She shuddered when his thoughts became clear.

"I don't know what you are talking about," she said as she hurried off into the woods beside the cabin.

"You know what I'm talking about, but I also know how repulsed most of you are by our existence. What our witch ancestor did for love is foreign to most of you," he said sadly. "Looking at how you still choose your mates was very primitive and barbaric to watch."

"We are all barbaric to some creature out there."

"You are trying to get rid of me. It isn't working. What are you doing in the forest nowadays? I have been too busy with kingdom duties to follow you around these days," he added, emphasizing the last words.

"Kingdom this, kingdom that. You sound like a little—"

"She's been coming to see me," Chapansa said, interrupting Mbawemi as she emerged from the trees above them and landed in the space between them gracefully.

"Your sister is teaching me how to fight," Mbawemi said.

"You belong to the most powerful coven in the land—"

"Look where that got most of us for believing that. The majority of us are dead, the rest in hiding or flat out cowards. I need to learn how to fight," Mbawemi said.

"Can I talk to you alone, Chapansa?" Sangwani asked

"Start on those moves we ended with. I'll be right back," she told Mbawemi.

"What do you think you are doing?"

"Teaching a girl how to fight? Is there anything wrong with that?" Chapansa asked.

"I know you. Now would you like to repeat the true answer for me?"

He didn't mean to, but he transformed into his wolf—a sure way to get a half-breed to obey protocol was for the leader to transform into his wolf. His alpha wolf was to be obeyed.

"You always have fought dirty when it suits you. Fine, I need her to lead us to where the wolves and witches are. I have a feeling we are next on their hit list. The dead king was very liberal, maybe too liberal when it came to us. They will fix that now that they took the throne by force."

"So you want her to be bait?" Sangwani asked.

"You are using all the bad words. I said I want her to lead us to them. I'm teaching her to defend herself, for that matter. She won't be bait."

"Great, sis, very benevolent of you. Bravo. Then why doesn't she know what your plans are? Why didn't you come to me with this first?"

"She'll know soon enough. It's not like she thinks I'm doing this out of the goodness of my heart. Secondly, you would have shut me down before I even got all the words out."

"Not my problem that you get wrong ideas every time that blow up in your face." He turned. "I'll sit in on this training, if you don't mind," he said to Mbawemi who was already on her second fighting stance.

"What? Why?" she asked.

"Its fine, Your Highness. He can give us some useful commentary and help," Chapansa said.

CHAPTER FIVE

It took them days for Mbawemi to know how to use the basic fighting stances. They continued with the same routine, with no idea what was happening in the outside world. A spell had been cast on the kingdom of the half-breed population. Time stood still for them—things stopped growing; they remained in the same old winter for months before questions started being asked, before they started to complain about the presence of the dead warlock king's child in their midst.

"I told you to get rid of them weeks ago. You never listen to my words of advice," Sangwani's uncle and advisor said.

"I respect you, Chirambo, but this is not the place nor the time for you to start on your lectures. We decided that having all of them would be an added advantage for us if we have to go into this battle."

"Permission to speak?" a woman said.

He recognised her as one of Chapansa's friends and the first person who had made sexual advances on him unashamedly. She had been his comfort the first few months after his father's death, until she'd told him she wasn't interested in anything more with him.

"Granted," he replied.

She walked up to where he sat with his advisors. Sangwani felt the stirring in his pants at the sight in the corner of his eye—Mbawemi watched their meeting somewhere around them.

"The presence of the witches among us is costly for us, but it also is an added advantage. The princess has told me how training the younger witch is proving to be successful even without her using her powers. I think they should stay," she said.

"You can't all be seriously considering to shelter one of the most deadly creatures whose ancestors have hunted and killed us for years," Chirambo pleaded.

As Chief Advisor to the dead king, Sangwani's father, he had thought his advisement to the mad, blood-thirsty king stressful, but he was just as stressed dealing with the son. Sangwani was equally as stubborn as his father, but he had a more diplomatic approach to matters.

"I have the final say. Princess Mbawemi and her grandmothers will live under our protection for as long as they need. And that is final," Sangwani said.

The group dispersed as soon as he uttered the words, some grumbling among themselves while others walked away solemnly. None of them trusted the witches. He supposed it was a mutual mistrust. Mbawemi didn't trust him; she clamped up every time he went to watch her train with his sister. She was more free, he'd noticed, when he stayed in the shadows.

"You are really good at hiding. Who taught you how to do that?"

"I'm not that good if you felt me there. You heard me before you saw me," she replied as she stepped down from the branch she had sat on to eavesdrop.

He didn't tell her he could feel her breathe even in her cabin from his bed.

"I'm just good at hearing sounds." He smiled.

The devilish smile she had come to know and resent made her stomach tighten to an almost uncomfortable knot. *He's never going to be yours*, she thought.

"I didn't expect to see you do things the way we do them, too. You also have advisors?" she asked.

She didn't notice the hint of irritation that crossed his eyes. She always assumed they were so different from each other.

"You thought we were savages who probably eat human babies for our dinner and never plan and discuss how every such decision would affect us?" he said. "My mother is or was a witch depends on how you term a powerless witch. That makes me what, three quarters of witch? That makes me almost as civilised as you, right?"

"Wow, no, I didn't mean that. I was just surprised, that's all. And you are not savages. You are more kind to me than my own family has been to me."

"Are you crying?"

"No, I'm not crying, stupid. I'm just drying my allergies," she lied.

"How far do you think they'll stretch this winter?" he asked. "As you heard, the locals are growing more anxious that we have been stuck in the same cycle for months."

"I have no idea. What I can tell you is that whoever is at the other end of the spell either recruited every witch they could find or he or she is one powerful witch."

"Can all three of you get around the spell, punch holes in time to make it less effective?" he asked.

"We haven't tried all together. My grandmothers and I are saving up our energy for when it's time to leave."

Sangwani nodded in understanding.

"I want to teach you some of the olden ways the witches had," he said.

He saw the flicker of surprise in Mbawemi's eyes as she registered his words.

"You mean the bloody ways? You know about that?" she asked.

"I'm half-witch, Mbawemi. You and your ancestors seem to forget that."

"Do the olden ways include blood rituals?" she asked.

"Yes, but we can improvise—"

"With what? It demands a human or creature sacrifice to get access to any of those spells, and even after, you have to make blood sacrifices often."

"We have a wolf we caught lurking on our Western boundary with the wolf population," he said.

"No."

"You don't even feel any bloodlust for your parents' murder? She was one of them who entered the palace. I remember her," Sangwani said.

"We know who are responsible for calling for the killings, and believe me, my bloodlust won't be quenched until those people are treated the same way they treated my family," she said. "I don't blame the small players in this. They were following orders and under manipulation from someone much more cunning than them. I know this more than ever now."

He heard the double meaning in her words clearly.

"It's not the same. Your father was the king. He could have pulled out of the war when he saw that he was being used," Sangwani said.

"He regretted everything," she said.

She drew closer to him, but he took a step back.

"Did he tell you that? Or are you speaking for a man who would have made amends on his own if he wanted before he suffered the same fate he gave out to others?"

"You are getting upset. I should leave," Mbawemi said as she backed away from him.

"I'm not upset, more irritated. By this."

Mbawemi braced herself for the attack she thought was coming, but all she felt was the softest lips brush along her own. Sangwani's grip on her arms should have hurt her, but all the sensation in her body had gone to the nerve endings in her lips.

She was frozen against him as his mouth moved with purpose. His tongue traced along her lips before she did what her body asked of her—she opened her mouth and kissed him back. The only sound around them was the soft collision of their lips against the other's and their heavy breathing.

When Mbawemi's hands started to unfasten the drawstrings on his trousers, something stopped Sangwani's pleasure-filled mind.

"Hey, hey. We don't have to," he whispered.

"Oh my God. I'm sorry, I shouldn't have done that. Grandma will kill me. I'm sorry."

"Why are you apologizing? It's not like you attacked me. I kissed you."

If Mbawemi's dark skin had been lighter, it would have shown how embarrassed she was by this.

"I should go," she said as she saw him look at her lips and the rise and fall of her breasts through the cotton white shirt she had on.

"You should," he agreed.

"Sangwani?" she called out to him as her footsteps led her away from him.

He turned to look at her, and for a second, she was tempted to turn back around.

"I'm sorry we took your dad away from you," she said.

Sangwani let his guard down, and he hoped he wasn't wrong.

"He needed to go somehow. I don't blame the ones who thought so. I just wish they gave him a chance to reform. He wasn't an all-around bad person. He just didn't know how to be good," he said.

Mbawemi nodded. "He would have been proud of you."
***

The words *he would have been proud of you* played in Sangwani's mind until the following day. It found him on Mwaka's door step, seeking some answers he knew would provide him some clarity.

"What did Chapansa do now?" the older woman asked as soon as she saw him.

"Can't I come to see my mother for morning greetings?"

"Shut the door on your way in. Those hooligans are now allowing their children to leave carcasses on my doorstep and even right inside if the door is open," she complained.

"You decided to come and live here so—" He stopped when he saw the look in his mother's eyes. "And I didn't come here to give you a lecture," he added.

"Good thinking, boy. Now say what you have to say and leave me alone," Mwaka said.

"Do you remember how Dad almost sent me to that boarding school that accepts all creatures, even us hybrids?"

"Tabernacle: Home of the Weird and Slightly Crazy."

"You do! What happened? I never asked what happened."

"Well, as such places go, they dragged their feet over accepting a hybrid. It closed down before we could get you in the door," Mwaka replied. "You came down here to ask me about your failed academic career?"

"No, I want to know what changed the man who wanted me to learn among different creatures. The man I knew as a boy changed, and I want to know why."

"He just found out the truth about the wolves and witches. He put so much effort into learning about each side, more than his father and grandfather did. Then when Chapansa's biological parents were killed by the wolves, he thought he would make the witches see that they needed protection and maybe acceptance, too."

"Why didn't he talk about it? All of this."

"He was ashamed of how he had opened himself to both sides with much vulnerability, like a stepchild looking for favour. He promised himself that he would never be weak again," Mwaka said pointedly now.

"He took it out on us, that disappointment. It wasn't supposed to be like that. He became weak because everyone hated him, even his advisors."

"You father lived his life. He wasn't in his best state of mind towards the end, but he was a good man. He just needed a second chance to change. You can learn some things from him."

There was ice in his mother's voice now. He didn't know if he had offended her, but he realised that for the first time, they'd talked about his father without a shouting match ensuing.

"I hope things can change one day, for all of us," Sangwani said as he rose to his feet to plant a kiss on his mother's forehead.

"She's all over you. I do hope you know that whatever it is you have going on with the girl is temporary. She will never willingly choose you."

"My heart is unbreakable, Mother. Remember."

His stomach twisted uncomfortably at his mother's words, but he kept a smile on his face.

CHAPTER SIX

Mbawemi was grateful that when she got home, Towa and Tawanda had been outside the house. She changed out of the blouse and skirt which now had his scent all over them and sprayed the perfume she had squeezed out of the roses out front before she redressed. She smelled like herself again when she went outside to check on her grandmothers.

"I told you!" she heard Tawanda exclaim just as the impenetrable wall the witches had placed around the forest shuddered before a gap appeared in it. It stayed open for a few seconds and closed up again.

"You did it, Grandma! I thought we were waiting for sunrise to get started again?" she asked.

Towa and Tawanda exchanged a look before Towa spoke.

"Your mother's family is being held hostage. They are asking for you to come out of hiding for them to be let go," Towa said.

"What?" Mbawemi asked. "I ... I thought they were safe? They didn't even retaliate when Mum was killed. They have kept their distance from me and were unwilling to help me. They are on their side. Don't they see this?"

Her mind was now running through all the scenarios of why they had taken her mother's family.

"That's not entirely true. Your mother's brother came to us days after they said they couldn't help us. He agreed to provide information for us from the council," Towa said.

"Uncle Joseph? He is one of the high-ranking members of the council."

"Not anymore. He hasn't been for a while now. He was pushed out when they realised that his loyalty would always be to your parents," Tawanda said.

"Someone found out he was sending us information. They must know where we are exactly by now. This was built by your grandfather's father, a way to escape in case something like this would happen. It isn't safe anymore. We have to act now. To get out before what they have planned finds us," Towa said.

"Then we better get started. Which spells are we using this time?" Mbawemi asked as she rolled up the sleeves of her cardigan.

"We got something from the olden books. We need everything we can use. It's not easy, Mbawemi ..." Tawanda said.

"I'm ready," she replied.

"Okay. You smell different. New perfume?" Towa said as they formed a circle.

"Something like that," she replied.

The moment was forgotten as their chants began. It echoed through their bones, the power that escaped through their pores. It circled around the clearing in the forest where they stood.

***

Sangwani watched as the mist wrapped around the invisible wall. He was in a trance as the three witches' chants grew louder. He heard the first crack along the unseen surface, then another and another until the cracks formed a pattern that resembled a person's outline. The invisible shards melted away, and as soon as they did, the wall grew itself back.

"We can do this until each person we need is out of the wall," he heard Mbawemi say.

He shifted back into the shadows with a smile.

"They are ready," he said out loud to the other shadow standing beside him.

"Good. You are ready for this, too. I can't come, not until I can defend myself again. She will need you. And I don't mean what you think. I can smell her on you."

"You didn't mention me falling in love with her. Besides, I got you out of the palace before you could be shredded to pieces. It qualifies me for being a mate for Mbawemi."

The shadow scoffed before a hiss of pain came out from it.

"Don't hurt her," it said as it now disappeared back into the cocoon it had been placed in.

"I would never think of it," Sangwani replied. "Unless she asks me to," he added underneath his breath.

***

Mbawemi had had sleepless nights from her overactive imagination for most of her life, but it didn't compare to the lack of sleep that came from a body throbbing with need and which couldn't be satisfied by her own touch. He lips screamed for attention, and her body drummed with yearning which had her almost out of the cabin in search of the hybrid that had started all of this.

The morning light made her groan as she'd now had an entire night of no sleep. She had a minute to think before she decided that using a potion to hide her tired face and more tired body would do. She looked the same as she would if she had gotten eight hours of sleep. She left the cabin in search of Chapansa.

"You are awfully early today for someone who didn't get any sleep at all last night," Sangwani said.

He leaned against a tree, in his casual wear of drawstring trousers and a T-shirt that tightly covered his upper body, showing off his defined muscles.

"How did you ...? Never mind. Where's Chapansa?"

She stepped back when she saw clearly that he was looking at her like he had yesterday.

"She's busy with the troops. I will be teaching you today," he said.

"Oh. I'm sure you have much more important things to do. Besides, I have learnt all I can from her. You don't have to teach me more."

"Then take me on." He smiled.

"What?"

"I said, fight me if you think you are that good of a fighter now."

"I should help my grandmothers. This isn't a good idea," she replied.

"You should really not get used to running away from me," he said as he blocked her path. "I want you. I know you want me, too. You would have already struck me in my balls if I even mildly irritated you."

"I shouldn't do this," she said underneath her breath, but her hands reached for him.

She ran them slowly up his arms, felt him shiver beneath them, and landed her touch on his face. She kissed him first this time, explored his body with her hands while her lips and tongue explored his lips and mouth. They shared one kiss after the next for what seemed like hours and only came up when they had to breathe.

"You should leave if you don't want this to go any further," Sangwani said, his voice full of need.

Mbawemi went back to kissing him. She didn't stop when she heard something snap and break; she didn't tear her lips away from him as he sank into her with a groan that vibrated throughout her body. Instead, she rode the ecstasy her body chased with him.

It didn't end until the sun was now shining through the trees, announcing the early afternoon. Two bodies lay in the middle of a cocoon made out of dried bamboo and surrounded by plush blankets.

Mbawemi had fallen into a much-needed sleep against Sangwani who had remained surprisingly awake as he watched his witch lover sleep. His mind was running through everything he had since learnt about the family he had sworn he would destroy one day. One of them had snuck into his heart the very first time he'd seen her at fifteen years old.

She had been amused, not scared, when she'd seen his wolf form, but the one who had hunted her had not been amused when he'd gotten ahead of his hunt. It was protocol for the king's son to get first hunt even during a hunt in progress. She wasn't an animal—he'd outlawed the hunt of other creatures in the forest when he became king. He knew what the others feared in them, the impulses that could not be controlled when a hybrid tasted the blood of another creature.

Mbawemi stirred against him before she went back into her deep sleep.

***

"Dad? Is that you?"

Mbawemi knew she was dreaming when she saw the deep purple silks above her and the lilac fields that stretched beyond her without an end.

"I have been waiting for you, baby. We have all been waiting for you."

She saw behind him her grandfather, Towa's husband who had the same grin she missed often.

"I don't understand. What is this place?" she asked.

"It's where we go when we have unfinished business on the other side. You have to help them, Mbawemi," she heard them all say in one voice. "They need you. You are the key to everyone's problem."

"How can I help them? I couldn't even protect you and Mum. Where's Mum? Mum?"

***

He heard the first whimper escape from her mouth just as the sun went down in the sky.

"Mbawemi? Wake up, you are dreaming. Wake up," he said as he gently shook her awake.

"Oh my God. Mum."

She went willingly into his arms as he cradled her in his lap. She hid her face against his neck as she silently wept.

They stayed in that position for a while until she stirred, breaking the moment.

"I'm sorry. I'm sure you wake up to more stable women after sex. I should leave," she said as she bunched up the bottom of her dress to get into her shoes.

"You were calling out for your mother a minute ago. C'mon, lie back down with me. You look drained. Have you been having the dreams often?" he asked.

Mbawemi went back into his arms without a second thought. His hands returned to stroking every inch of her skin. It comforted her but also made her question how right it felt to be in his arms.

"No. I think Towa and Tawanda cast a healing balm spell around our cabin. We haven't had time to grieve for long."

She had not thought of that. She only knew that as days had gone on, the raw ache in her heart had eased more.

"What did you see? You were talking. I thought it was something good," he said.

"It was at first. I saw my father and his father and some other family members. I noticed when I talked to them that my mother wasn't there."

"Oh. Why do you think that is?"

"We never had an easy relationship, my mother and I. It was always her raising the future queen, and I really never quite made it past the daughter-mother relationship. My dream confirmed what my subconscious knows. We didn't get to have a real connection, and I hate them more for taking that away from me," she said.

"What did it look like?" Sangwani curiously asked.

"Lots of purple," she replied.

He didn't want to tell her, not yet. She had been invited into the Land of the Valley, a bridge between the dead and undead. Her mother wasn't there, and she would soon find out.

"We didn't even get a chance to practice," Mbawemi said. Her dream was forgotten as she remembered the last few hours.

"Oh, maybe not. I trust Chapansa. She gave you as good as she knows," he said as he laid her down on the ground again.

"We are being bad."

"Shut up.'

Mbawemi answered with a laugh which was cut off by his lips that latched onto hers now. All thought was forgotten.

***

"I'm in deep shit. Oh my God, Sangwani, wake up," Mbawemi said.

He didn't awaken until she landed a fist to one of his shoulders.

"You made me late. It's dark out," she continued.

"Hey, calm down. You are not in danger here." He tried to placate her.

"Towa and Tawanda will know immediately when I enter that cabin. You are all over me!" she said, her voice full of frustration.

"You weren't complaining," he joked, but stopped when he saw the deadly look on her face. "I'll walk you. Let's go."

The cabin was silent and dark except for the lone light that streamed out of one window. Mbawemi knew she would be walking into an ambush, but she couldn't be bothered to feel bad. She was an adult now, she decided. She would tell them the truth and would move on from it.

"Where have you been?" Tawanda stood in the doorway of the cabin as she looked at Mbawemi.

"I was practicing—"

"This late?" she asked.

"Oh. Thank you for walking her home. You can leave now. You have done enough," Towa said, turning to Sangwani.

Mbawemi felt naked as Towa and Tawanda looked at her suspiciously.

"I hope you know better what the penalty is for getting a witch pregnant," Towa said.

Mbawemi wanted the earth to swallow her whole in the seconds that followed.

"I didn't ... I didn't. She doesn't want me like that. I have integrity, too. She can control that part of her," he replied.

Mbawemi had never seen Sangwani nervous in the time she had known him. Now, he couldn't meet anyone's eyes.

"Good. It won't happen again. I suggest that you stay away from my granddaughter," Towa now said.

"Grandma!"

"She will make that decision on her own. I didn't force her into anything."

The shy and nervous Sangwani was now replaced by the cocky hybrid king, and Mbawemi warned him silently.

"We have a meeting in three days. We ask for your presence," he said. "Good night, Your Highnesses."

"He sure is pretty to look at, at least this version of him," Tawanda said.

The tension around them diffused by the obvious trail Tawanda's eyes followed.

"We should get you a leash or something. Our ancestors would die if they knew what you have done," Towa said.

"Give her a break, Towa. She's allowed to have feelings. It's not like she wants to marry him and have children with him," Tawanda said.

"That's how it started with the witch and the wolf. It is rarely simple when you get yourself entangled with someone so different. Our ancestors knew why they forbid it."

"The hybrids haven't been a problem in years now, Grandma. We have been here for months, and none has so much as attacked us or caused us any disturbance," Mbawemi said. "Maybe we should really reflect and see how all this can work out for our good. We have lost witches and warlocks because of this law, and it is time we changed it."

"Are you in love with the boy?"

"No. I am not talking about me and Sangwani. Sangwani's mother, she's a witch, too. I felt it last time I was with her."

"You know that when one's powers are stripped, we don't call them a witch anymore? She chose the other side; she can't be allowed to come back."

"We need everyone we can get, Towa. Listen to the child. We have been betrayed by people we grew up with already. Kids we helped to raise now hunt us. We need her."

They found Sangwani near the waterfall, a place he had been drawn to since he'd seen Mbawemi bathing last time.

"Hi. Can we speak to your mother?"

"My mother? Why?" he asked.

"We'll tell you as soon as we talk to her," Towa said.

"She can be of help to us," Mbawemi said.

He nodded in understanding.

"You want to give her back her powers. Well, while that's a good gesture on your part, I don't think she will appreciate it happening now when you want to use her to fight with you. She isn't particularly fond of witches."

"I can speak for myself," Mwaka said as she came out from behind a tree. "I found an old friend lurking outside my door. I thought I should return her to her rightful owner."

A pale hand emerged first from the same tree, and out came a woman who wobbled on a cane as she walked.

"Samwa? Mum?" The collective voices of Towa, Tawanda, and Mbawemi resounded as the woman walked towards them.

She wobbled more on the stick before she fell down. They all ran to help her up, but she rebuffed their efforts.

"You can never change, can you, Samwa?" Mwaka said as Mbawemi slid to the ground with her mother.

"We saw you ... the wolves, they surrounded you." Mbawemi saw where her mother's gaze was focused. "You? You saved her?"

"She keeps forgetting that part most days," he said.

"I need some water," Samwa said as she gasped out breaths.

"Her ribs are still on the mend. Help me get her inside," he said as he lifted the frail-looking woman.

"Why?" Mbawemi asked when Samwa was settled in one of the tiny rooms in the cabin. "Why did you save her? Why did you keep it a secret from us?"

"She was worse off than you see her when I managed to get the last wolf off her. I didn't want to give you false hope when you have lost so much already. I know what it feels like."

"So you kept it from me to spare my fragile feelings?"

"I didn't say that."

"She's really her mother's daughter," Mwaka said.

"Mother, stay out of it," Sangwani said.

"You can leave. We don't need you anymore here," Mbawemi said. "I meant you, not your mother."

"I will come back some other time, child. You should try to calm down until then. I can't help you if you don't respect what the king, my son, has done for you and your family," she said.

Mbawemi wasn't one to believe in coincidences when it came to her world, so as she looked at her mother's frame as she slept, she looked at the bright side in all of this. She'd had a parent literally come back from death. It had to count for something.

"Don't you wish it was your father who'd survived this and not me? It would have been better for you."

Samwa's voice sounded stronger than it had been earlier, and Mbawemi thanked the lucky herbs she'd made her drink before she lay down.

"You need to sleep some more, Mum. It's the prolonged pain. He should have told us. We would have made you better by now."

"Your father was amused by your antics. It was always funny to him how you could go missing in a second," Samwa said. "It scared me, how carefree you were. I didn't know whether to punish you more after each disobedience or to loosen my hold around you. I was raising a future queen, and I wanted you to act like one from birth."

"I didn't mean to make things hard for you," Mbawemi whispered.

"It wasn't hard, baby. I just didn't see that even in my strict rules, you managed to have fun and spread joy all around the palace."

"Remember that time I put the lizard in Niza's tea potion?" Mbawemi laughed.

"The bitch deserved it," Samwa said.

Mbawemi gasped.

"Mum!" she said.

"What? I know it was she who orchestrated this whole thing. I saw her standing on the balcony facing the courtyard with a silly grin on her face."

"She won't get away with it. We'll make sure of it."

CHAPTER SEVEN

Two weeks later, they all stood as a united front as the invisible wall shuddered and melted away into nothing. The wolves who guarded the boundaries were easily disposed of. It didn't take long for them to cut through the first layer of the wolves and the next. Fighting hybrids were no match for the wolves, and they knew this when they suddenly all retreated to let them pass through.

"We don't have time for them. We will come back," Sangwani said when he heard the growl that Samwa let out when she recognised some of the wolves.

"Mum, listen to him. They will get their punishment. We need to get to the palace," Mbawemi shouted through the deafening howls of the wolves as they carried away their dead.

Chapansa led the charge ahead of them, and they were at the palace walls by sunrise.

"We have known this would happen. Niza and the warlocks have put a spell around the palace that would require years to work around. We don't have that long. You protect the witches as they work. Nothing should move you from your spot," Sangwani said as his army surrounded the walls with more situated around Mbawemi, Samwa, Towa, Tawanda, and his mother.

They cast spells for days. The wall showed no signs of coming down until Samwa called on her brother's spirit who was being held hostage inside the palace walls.

"Joseph? Can you hear me?"

A mirage appeared as she chanted, her breath mixing with it and creating a white trail.

"I felt you, I knew you were still alive. Forgive me, sister—"

"We don't have time for that, Joseph. We need your help. Where did Niza put you?" she asked.

"The Eastern wall dungeons," he replied. "We have always mapped our surroundings from childhood. How can I help?"

"We are on the Eastern wall. Do you remember the Chikulu spell? We need you to be our compass, connect to our power source. Can you do it?" Samwa asked.

"I'm on it. I have to find a wall," he said.

The others, who had not heard the communications the siblings had shared, waited for her instructions.

"That spell was outlawed," Towa said.

"It kills everything in its path," Tawanda added.

"We know what we are doing. Mbawemi, you remember this spell, don't you?" Samwa asked.

"Like the back of my hand," she replied.

"Let's get the throne back in our family," Samwa said. "Now."

They chanted the old spell—it was fresh in some minds while in others, it took some time to get the words right.

Sangwani exchanged looks with Chapansa, a silent 'what the hell' passing between them when flames rose from the five witches' bodies.

"Sangwani? We need you," he heard Samwa call out to him.

"Is it done?" he asked.

"No, we need your power," Samwa said.

"I don't have—" He stopped when he saw the flames rising from his own hands.

"Half-witch father and a full-blooded witch mother. You have enough of us in you," she said.

"Now!" Mbawemi shouted as the first part of the wall fell.

The hybrid army charged into the palace walls, and she heard the first sounds of the struggle.

"Niza has to be found. She won't be stopped until she's found," Samwa said.

"You won't find her here. She's gone," Joseph said. He staggered out of the courtyard, his hand on his stomach as blood dripped onto the marble ground.

"Joseph?" Towa was the first to reach him as he fell to the ground.

"She's going to the wolves," he said. "They have an agreement that she will be under their protection until she's strong enough to come back to take the kingdom again. The rest have gone back to their covens."

"That's all, Joseph. Take him to one on the rooms in the Western wing," Samwa ordered one of the soldiers.

"They won't be too happy to shield a fugitive, especially when they find out what we have done to all who planned the assassination. Prepare the chamber," Mbawemi said to one of the guards who stood between her and Sangwani.

Killing had always repulsed her when she heard how her ancestors dealt with treasonous witches and warlocks in their midst. Yet, she didn't flinch as body after body went down the gallows.

She watched it all. She didn't have mercy on the people who had almost killed her, the people who were responsible for the death of her father. She knew Sangwani held the same resolve as these were the same witches who had convinced her father to go to war with the hybrid population and had killed their king in battle.

"They'll send her back by sunrise," Mbawemi said.

"One thing I hate about wolves is how they change sides so quickly," Sangwani said. "Not that it isn't good for you this time, but they need to be taught how to stick to a side."

"They go with what will benefit them in the end, and I'm sure Niza gave them something they couldn't refuse. It's time we teach them a lesson by giving them something they cannot refuse."

"Keep your enemies closer," Towa agreed.

"We need to involve them in ruling the kingdom, like we have other creatures," Samwa agreed.

***

It didn't take sunrise for Niza to be returned. The wolves had already done the job for them. She arrived in two parts, one tastefully put on a spike, a peace offering from the other side.

"We need a much more solid representation of how far we have come. A union that will show everyone that we can all coexist and without mistrust or being ostracised," Mbawemi said in a toast at dinner the following day.

She signalled for Sangwani to stand.

"We would like to invite you all and the kingdom to our wedding in two months," she continued.

"What?" he hissed underneath his breath.

"Just smile and wave. Don't pretend you are not a tiny bit happy," she replied.

The congratulations ran through the dining hall until they were left alone.

"Where are you going?"

"To bed. Is that okay with you?" she asked.

"I prefer to be the one to propose marriage to my girlfriend other than the other way round," he said.

She was struck by how different he looked in her world—the man she had seen as uncultured and brutish had fit in easily with her people.

"You look great," she said.

"You are trying to change the topic," he replied.

"This is my world. I say who I will marry. Or don't you want that? You have another woman in mind?" she asked. She was half serious.

"I've been pining after you since I was fifteen years old. You want me to remind you of our first meeting, Your Highness?"

Mbawemi averted her gaze when a look that made her shiver came into Sangwani's eyes.

"I've been in love with you for most of my life. I just want you."

One day, they would laugh at the way Mbawemi's mouth closed and opened without words each time she tried to speak. Instead, her feet drew her closer to him.

He watched her through heavy lidded eyes as she stalked towards him. She straddled his lap, releasing a groan from his mouth.

"Just promise me one thing?"

"What?" she asked as she nibbled along his jaw.

"I don't wear a crown," he answered.

"Deal. Now shut up before I get you a muzzle."

He laughed at her joke, and this time, she joined in, their laughs echoing throughout the palace, followed by their sounds of lovemaking. They had found a kindred soul in each other, and their losses were healing slowly by each other's side.

Love had won.

THE END

ABOUT THE AUTHOR

Fiske Nyirongo is a Zambian writer based in Lusaka, Zambia.

She was shortlisted for the 2019 Kalemba short story writing prize and her work appears in online spaces such as The Kalahari Review, The Go The Way Your Blood Beats anthology (Brittle Paper), The Writers Space Africa Valentine's issue, and Unbound online magazine. Her first children's title appears in Cricket Magazine's (Chicago publisher) Holiday themed issue in December 2019 and she co-created a Book with an illustrator and designer for the South African Book Dash model. She has upcoming work in an anthology produced by Blackbird Books (South Africa) and HOLAA Africa.

She is currently studying Public Health.

Connect with Fiske: https://twitter.com/ChimikaCha

Fiske Nyirongo

Dream Seductor

KARO OFOROFUO

BLURB

Ajiri runs away from the river kingdom to avoid an arranged marriage and settles in the human world. But her relationship and sex life is lacking until she finds herself torn between two men. Will she give in to the suggestive stares from the handsome human, or cling to the blue man who haunts her dreams and unleashes erotic desires that make her yearn for more?

CHAPTER ONE

The lights were out. Ajiri stood beside her bed and occasionally allowed her eyes to dart to her body lying peacefully on it. Nights had been like this for her since she'd assumed human form about a year ago.

On so many occasions, she had been conscious of leaving her body to rest while her spirit self worked on major tasks she couldn't complete before her body got tired and chose to retire for the night. But it wasn't only work. Some nights, she went downstairs to watch TV while her body slept.

One rule, however, was to not leave the house while her body lay asleep. Unprotected. Leaving it unprotected would give those who wanted her dead the opportunity they needed to do her harm.

The months that had followed her advent into the human world had been filled with things she'd never really thought to care about before. An example? The two supposedly dead men standing in the opposite direction of her bed, eyeing her sleeping body intently.

Not the first time she was encountering their likes. And they wanted nothing else but to kill her. On whose orders? She didn't know, nor did she understand what business she had with ghosts or entities, who mostly came to attack her in her dreams.

"I just want to know why you're after me. Who is sending you?" she asked the men.

"Our orders were straight to the point. Kill you. We were not told to explain anything to anybody." One of them sneered at her.

Ajiri wasn't fazed. The previous night, she had fought off three of their kinds. And although it hadn't been an easy battle, she was sure she could ward them off.

"The dead have no business with the living, you know," she said.

"And a mermaid has no place on land," the other ghost said. "Even if you succeed in warding us both, more and more of our kind will come."

"We are dead already. We can't be killed again," the taller one spoke. "We will only let you live, sweetheart, if you accept our offer."

"To be a mistress for your mad leader? No. I'm not interested in any man. Let alone a dead one."

"Then you leave us no choice."

"My father used to say something about grasshoppers not having the time to say goodbye when there's fire," a voice said from the window.

Ajiri turned to see the blue-skinned stranger who had wreaked havoc in her body every night and dominated her thoughts throughout her days. Blue fireballs burned on both his palms.

"Which of you would love to go first?" he asked.

He didn't wait for a response before throwing the balls at the entities. One of them dropped and writhed in pain. The other dodged and took off in the opposite direction, running through the wall of the room.

"Take care of this one, sweetheart." The blue man winked at her before running through the wall in hot pursuit of the second man.

Ajiri returned her attention to the one on the floor. He seemed to have somehow put out the fire, although he'd been terribly burnt.

"You said something about dead men not being able to die a second death, yes?" She mocked him.

"I will still carry out my orders." He coughed. His body smoked.

Ajiri stretched out her hands, and the same kind of fireball the blue man had thrown at the entities earlier formed on her palm, but bigger.

"No. Please," the ghost begged.

"Do you promise to go and never return?"

"Yes, yes! Please."

"Now leave. And tell the rest of your kind, they picked the wrong woman."

"Thank you!" He was struggling to his feet when a bigger fireball landed on his back. "Ahhhrrr! Arrr!"

He fell. The fire burned brighter and consumed him totally as he screamed for help. Not even a trace of his once black clothes could be found.

Ajiri looked up to see the blue man in the doorway. "You didn't have to kill him."

"It was for your safety. Imagine if he had the chance to go back and report that you now have a partner." He winked.

"You're not my partner. I don't know who you are."

"So you're going to pretend we haven't been having great nights together?" He moved closer.

"Stay away from me. You're the one who comes to seduce me every night."

"And you love every bit of it. Don't you? So much so, you can't help but think about me throughout your day."

Ajiri swallowed and turned away. He was right. Ever since he'd started to visit her dreams and seduce her every night, she hadn't been able to think straight.

"Please go. Leave me alone. I can take care of myself." She eyed her body sleeping peacefully on the bed, before walking to the window.

She couldn't deny she enjoyed his touch and longed for his thrust. But she couldn't give in to that. Not when she wasn't sure who he was.

"If I told you who I am, would you believe?" he asked as if reading her thoughts. "If I told you I know your real name, would you believe me?"

Before she could form a response in her head, she felt his lips on her bare shoulder. His arms moved to wrap themselves around her waist and held her firmly against his hard frame.

"Let me make love to you, please."

One hand moved to cup the soft moulds of her breasts as his lips moved to her neck. His actions sent shivers down her spine.

Ajiri wanted to protest. She wanted to tell him to stop. But she couldn't. She had been sexually involved with different men from the human race. They'd all claimed to be a stud and a romantic. But none of them had come even close to making her feel the way this stranger made her feel.

How could she chase him away when, deep down, she knew she wanted this?

"Come with me," he said, and led her to the bed, to the exact spot her body slept on.

"No," she protested.

"You'll be semi-conscious. And I wouldn't hurt you. I promise."

He led her to lie in her body, and in her semi-sleep state, he kissed her passionately and whispered all the things he'd love to do to her. He let his hand slide between her legs and caress her softness.

Ajiri's breathing switched to a different rhythm. Her hormones ran wild, the V between her legs dripping wet. One masculine hand ran along the length of her thighs, caressing, and then moved to her hip. He bent low and planted a kiss on her abdomen. Then, he took his lips downwards until his tongue caressed the swollen part of her sexuality.

A moan escaped her lips. Her hips arched upward, begging for more.

One hand reached for her breast again and caressed gently. Then, he moved up from the V of her thighs to focus on her nipples while his other hand caressed her body.

Ajiri was on Cloud Nine as the man raised his head up and went for her lips, kissing her passionately. But she didn't respond to any of his kisses even though she knew she wanted to.

"Please," he begged. "Let me claim you, my love."

"But I don't know who you are. And I can't give my consent to a man I don't know."

"I'm the man you ran away from."

His blue eyes shone in the dark. She looked at her dark hands against his blue skin and she was sure—had always been sure, anyway—that he was from her world. And if that was so, then he couldn't penetrate her. He could seduce her as he was already doing. But he couldn't have access to her core heaven as long as she didn't give him permission.

He ran one hand over her afro and pecked her forehead. "Would you prefer I taunt you with desire every night before you accept me?"

He took her lips again, and she felt her legs shake when his hardness rubbed against the wetness of her core.

This was torture. She wanted him. She wanted to say yes. She wanted him to ride her hard. The passion was driving her nuts. But she couldn't let him. Not until she was sure who he was.

He was back on her nipples now, nibbling away and caressing. He pulled himself down after a while, spread her legs apart, and buried his head again between them.

She gasped as the sweet sensation between her legs increased. Moans escaped her lips. Her hips arched forward again. But he didn't stop.

Instead, he looked up occasionally and said, "Let me take you, my love. Let us ride together to the higher heavens in ecstasy."

Beeeeeeeep! Beeeeeeeep! Beeeeeeeep!

She heard the ringing. It was morning. Both of them froze and glanced at the alarm clock. When she looked back at him, she didn't miss the disappointment in his eyes. And when he pulled away from her, the length and hardness of his phallus created images in her head.

He wanted her. That was for sure. But he was gentle in his ways, teasing her while waiting for her permission. In the human world, rape would have happened already. She couldn't be thankful enough for the protection her people had put in place against such. But then, she was not sure for how long she wanted to be protected from his man.

"I won't stop seducing you, my queen." He snapped his fingers, and his clothes appeared on his body. "I only hope you let me be the one to truly claim you, instead of some lousy human or entity who does not know the first thing about making love to our kind."

Ajiri's heart skipped at his last word. *Our kind*. She was right. He was from her world.

"You seem to know everything there is to it," she said and swallowed.

"I do. Have a beautiful day today, my love. And happy Halloween."

"This is Nigeria. They don't celebrate Halloween here."

"Some do. Put on something from our world today." He blew her kisses and disappeared.

CHAPTER TWO

Ajiri, already dressed for work in a pink jumpsuit that hugged her hourglass figure, white stilettos to match, and braids packed up into a ponytail, headed out of her mini duplex. No, she hadn't put on anything from her world as the blue man had suggested. The majority of Nigerians didn't concern themselves with such celebration. Just no need for it.

The black briefcase in her left hand contained some office file. Still so much to be done. Working her butt off to grow her fashion business to the top wasn't child's play. At least, certainly not in a country like Nigeria.

And now that she had reached the top, she worked double hard to remain there. Which meant always more work to be done.

She locked the door of the mini duplex and headed towards the car.

Her personal driver, Rabin, got the engine started while the security man, Emeka, opened the gate. Ajiri stepped into the back seat of the car. And as usual, she couldn't help but notice Rabin staring at her through the rear-view mirror.

She considered him a rude sort that hardly even said 'good morning' to his employer.

"What is it this time?" She rolled her eyes.

"I'm just wondering if you're okay?" His baritone rang full of concern, and his eyes lingered on her in a way that made her skip a heartbeat.

Not this now. The effects of intimacy with the blue stranger from her dream hadn't died down yet. Besides, she could still perceive his scent on her, and her panties would definitely get wet due to the images that ran through her head.

Having Rabin stare at her that way only meant more trouble. Only this time, with her driver.

"I'm fine, Rabin. What could possibly happen to me?" She tore her eyes away from him as it was best to put aside any form of attraction or distraction that morning.

"Nothing. I was just checking." He moved the car outside the gate and drove off.

Ajiri sighed and leaned back against the seat. She understood why Rabin was asking if she was okay. But her curse was hers to bear alone. No one she told ever believed what she was going through. Most people only told her she was looking for cheap publicity with the crazy experiences she claimed to have had.

And so, she had been silent but had moved to find other means to stay sane and safe from the attacks.

It didn't help that she felt alone in this world. Only in her dreams did she have a partner. At least, that's what the blue man said. If only her parents were with her. But then, that couldn't happen—not when they definitely would be mad at her for running away from home. Not when they needed her to marry Prince Ago and she refused.

She had no issues with the older prince. She just wasn't in love with him; his person, his features, and anything else that defined him. His younger brother, Yunad, was the one she had eyes for.

Since her growing up days, her mother, father, and even her personal attendant had said the Kingdoms of the North and South would be joined together by marriage. And since she was the only child of her father, she'd certainly be marrying one of the Princes.

Ajiri didn't reject the idea, not after she'd met Yunad at the tender age of eight. Or was it nine? They'd had a small adventure together, and for a few months after, he'd sent her secret letters that were both funny and lovely to a nine-year-old. That kind of sealed her love and trust for him.

She'd mentioned his name in almost every conversation that had to do with getting married or falling in love. She'd fantasized a lot about him and the things they'd do together. So it was really a disappointment when years later, now an adult, her father announced she'd be marrying Prince Ago instead of Prince Yunad.

She was heartbroken. And even though she had always been obedient to her father's wishes and commands, her heart rested with another—the brother of the man they wanted her to marry.

When she asked about Yunad, no one told her anything. She wrote and sent secret letters to him down south. But a response never came. She concluded that he wanted nothing to do with her, or had decided to obey his father's wishes of having her marry his elder brother.

Not like they'd both talked about marriage at such a young age when they first met. She had only assumed he'd want her. Well, she'd been wrong.

As long as Ajiri was concerned, running away from home had been one of the best decisions she'd ever made. But with no help from home, she had relied on her good luck charm and hard work to survive in the world of the humans.

She heard them talk about Mami water every now and then. Some of them believed Mermaids and Mermen were real. But others didn't believe.

However, those living close to the River Nile, as well as the locals in some of the nearby villages, claimed to have had one encounter or the other with mermaids and mermen.

She remembered vividly when she'd gone to visit the region the previous year. One man had recounted how he had gone for a long stroll with a friend at night. They'd sat at a beer parlour and gotten very drunk. While returning home, their legs had carried them in a different direction. They'd ended up some distance away from the river bank.

Unable to walk farther, they'd both fallen flat on their backs, too tired to move.

According to the man's story, they'd seen a woman emerge in the middle of the river, and she'd started towards shore with speed. Her body had been illuminated with a brilliant blue light. And when she'd gotten on the shore, she'd looked around, as if to survey the area to be sure she was alone.

He'd said his friend, out of fear, began to cry a very useless cry. It had caught the attention of the woman, and she'd walked up to them. He'd said contrary to fiction books and speculations, this woman had had no fishtail. She'd had legs.

She had asked them who they were and why they were at the river bank. But they'd been too drunk to say anything, let alone say something reasonable. Instead, they'd cried.

The friend had tried to get up and run away. He'd spoken in their native dialect as he did so. But the woman had walked up to him and struck him down. She'd gone over him, had placed her hand around his neck, and almost in an instant, had strangled him to death.

It was then words had formed on his lips. He'd pleaded for his life and promised not to tell anyone of what had happened.

Satisfied by his words, she'd scooped some water from the river with her bare hands and had forced him to drink. The man said the water she'd scoped sparked with blue light. He'd drunk, and his entire system became clean of the alcohol. His eyes had been clearer and his senses sharper.

He'd known he was not with an ordinary woman, and he'd been stunned by her beauty, even though she'd had scales on her forehead and arms.

She'd asked him to lead her to his home. He'd obeyed. There, she'd taken a few of his wife's clothes and put them on. She'd also asked a lot of questions—about food, getting a home, the best city to live in and so on. Since he couldn't provide all her answers, he'd given her his mobile phone and told her to ask Google.

But she'd been confused.

"How does this thing work?" she'd asked, but before he could talk, she'd moved forward and placed on hand on his head. During that short period, all he could think about was the phone, its functions and how to use it properly, both online and offline.

She'd taken her hand off and said, "Thank you. Now I know how it works."

She'd uttered some words, and her body had stopped glowing. She had transformed into a black, gorgeous woman, her hair a full afro. She'd promised to make him rich in exchange for the service he and his wife had rendered, and then, she'd left.

The man had gone on to say she'd kept her promise because, since that night, he had always met good luck in business. But then, he had lost a dear friend. And this friend always visited his dreams, demanding that he told the truth of what had happened that night, else he'd die, too.

His friend had been buried with no one really knowing the cause of his death. And even though his wife and kids had been taken care of, he'd still demanded the truth be told. The people may not be able to give him justice, but at least, they'd know why he'd died.

And so, he was sharing the story. Every day that went by, he shared the tale with the locals. Some of the men talked about visiting the river at night so as to meet a beautiful mermaid who would make them rich. They didn't care if it proved risky.

Ajiri had sighed and moved away from the crowd of people listening to him. If she had retained her old appearance, he'd have known right away she was the one— the mermaid who'd killed his friend and made him rich.

What he didn't know about that night was that she'd been running away from home. She'd been escaping from living the life her father had planned for her.

Since her time on land and among humans, she had hidden her powers and stayed away from anything that could point to her as a mermaid, including swimming pools and beaches. Her skin had a way of reacting to water, and she understood that if she were discovered, she wouldn't be able to remain on the land. Humans wouldn't be the only ones fighting her. Entities and native doctors would, too.

While most humans didn't realize the power they had, some did. And they'd fight her tooth and nail, even though she had been able to understand their kind of power and had even tapped into it.

But then, wasn't she already being attacked by entities? Their attacks accounted for more than anything she had ever encountered. If not for the human power she'd tapped into to increase her strength, she'd have long been dead.

Now, she had not only warded them off, but she had also killed a lot of them, and they could no longer touch her. They could only make attempts.

Her heart occasionally went out to those innocent humans who had no idea what was happening around them. Arrows, curses, and diseases aimed at her bounced off, thanks to her new protection. Unfortunately, they landed on anyone close to her.

Some of her workers had been hit in the past. The pain they'd felt had been instant, and they'd died a few days or weeks later.

Speculations were all over the place that she used her workers for ritual purposes and that's why she got richer anytime one of them died.

She'd dismissed the rumours until five of her workers had resigned on the same day. Then another five had followed the week after. The few of them who'd stayed back were obviously very prayerful—the big man up there protected them.

She had seen, countless times, arrows meant for her directed at those ones. But they all bounced off.

She encouraged the workers to keep up with their prayer life and even made them pray in the office every morning before the start of work.

No, she never joined them. She couldn't. But she was glad to make them keep their protection up.

With assistance from the few workers in her office, she had gone on to work her butt off to grow her company. A snap of her fingers could have given her all her present achievements and lots more. But she wanted to live the human life. She wanted to experience their suffering, their struggles, their happiness and achievements. It was the only way she'd truly understand them and relate with them better.

Talking about relating with them better, she stole a glance at her driver. Rabin was different. Right from the moment he'd approached her for a job, she had felt at ease with him. He seemed to understand her better than most other people did. Even Funke, her personal secretary, did not 'get' her as much as Rabin did.

Besides, whenever she experienced a ghost attack, he'd ask if she was okay, like he had done that morning. She'd once suspected he may be seeing the things she saw.

One day, she'd tested him. There'd been no attack, but she'd pretended to be going through one. Rabin had watched her closely and afterwards asked if she was okay.

That had been her proof that he did not see beyond the ordinary. He was just concerned about her well-being; he did everything to make her comfortable. Although, sometimes, he let his male ego control him.

Funnily enough, she found him attractive during such times. She couldn't understand why she never yelled at him instead.

Only three months ago, her last driver had died in an accident. She had sent him on an errand. But he'd never returned. News of his death had reached her when the police had run the plate number and discovered she was the owner of the car.

She'd quietly visited the scene and run a replay of the etheric record of activities on that spot. And she'd seen it. A ghost had been the cause of the accident. They had targeted him as a way of getting to her.

She'd been reluctant to have another driver after that. She couldn't have someone else killed because of her. But when Rabin had shown up, she'd warmed up to him instantly.

As attractive as he was, though, he avoided any form of body contact with her. She didn't know why. But his strict attitude, very manly figure, and his handsome features got her crazy at times. There were moments when she found herself longing for him, and she'd wonder what was wrong with her.

No way was she going to date or marry a human. If she didn't kill him, the entities would, and in an instant, too.

Beep! Beep!

Her phone, snapping her out of her thoughts. She came out of it in time to catch Rabin's eyes on her through the rear-view mirror.

"Are you okay?" he asked, keeping a straight face.

She sighed. "Yes. I'm fine."

She reached for her phone beside her and opened the message. It was from Funke. It read; 'Good morning, ma. Those fabrics you ordered have been delivered. The style artiste is here with the designs. All we need now is for you to go through and decide the styles you what for the next fashion show. Irene Osoba is here too.'

Ajiri sighed. So much for battling entities the entire night and being seduced by a blue man. She'd woken up early but had spent her morning thinking about all that had happened. The fabrics supplier and her company's fashion stylist could wait for her, but definitely not Irene Osoba, one of the proudest, most popular celebrities in Lagos. And she wouldn't sit thirty minutes to wait for anyone, let alone an hour.

Ajiri wanted to discuss having her as *Ajiri's Fashion* Brand Ambassador, especially as she had well over fifteen million followers on Instagram and Facebook. She'd also be the first to try on the new designs to be made for the company's next fashion show.

She looked at the time. Ten to eleven a.m. already. She looked up at Rabin, and again, she caught him staring through the rear-view mirror.

She frowned. "If you keep staring at me, how are you going to get us to the office on time?"

"I'm just making sure you're o—"

"I'm fine, Rabin!" she snapped. "Kindly keep your eyes on the road to avoid having an accident and still get me to the office in time. People are waiting for me."

"Okay."

He tore his eyes off her and focused on the road again. He increased the speed of the car, and not even her plea to be careful made him stop, at least until he got to the office premises and brought the car to a halt in the parking lot.

He stepped out of the car to open her door and help carry some of the items into her office.

CHAPTER THREE

"Hello, Irene. I'm so, so sorry for keeping you waiting," Ajiri apologized as she stepped into her private Reception to find the celebrity gisting away with a male friend of hers.

"If not that I love your brand, I would have long been gone." She grinned, got to her feet, and locked herself in a brief embrace with Ajiri.

"I don't doubt you one bit," Ajiri said and laughed. She looked at the male friend as he got to his feet. "And you're?

"Adebayo," he said, extending a hand for a shake.

"Adebayo is my fiancé." Irene grinned and locked one hand around his arm.

A silent way of saying 'this is my man. Back off!'

"Nice to meet you, Adebayo. And welcome to Ajiri's Fashion House."

"Thank you. I'm happy to be here at last." He grinned. "I've seen some of your designs online, and I've heard so much about this place. Irene doesn't stop talking about it."

"Why should I? Check out her style. She's the goddess of fashion!"

Ajiri made a face that said, 'she's right', and they laughed.

"Please come to my office. We have a lot to discuss, and I know you have other things to do. You celebrities are so busy!"

"But that's how we make our money!" Irene defended.

"I'd like to have a long chat with you two, but I have a meeting of mine to attend. I produce fabrics, too," Adebayo said, allowing a grin.

"Oh, wow! That's great." Ajiri was pleased.

"I'm hopeful we can do business sometime?" he asked.

"Definitely. If you have what I want." She smiled at him.

"I'll surprise you." He sounded confident.

"And he will. He is a man of surprises," Irene supported with a smile that did not reach her eyes.

Ajiri guessed again, it was her way of saying '*back off my man.*' She smiled at the couple and promised she'd check out Adebayo's fabrics. They exchanged business cards, and he left.

Ajiri, ignoring Irene's mood swing, led the way into her office. She gestured at one of the couches in the mini sitting area just in front of her office desk and asked Irene to take a seat.

She took the opposite couch and looked at the celebrity in the eye.

"I know what's going on in that head of yours, Irene. I know we're still getting to know each other, but if there's one thing you need to know about me, it is that I don't steal people's boyfriend or fiancé."

Irene's brows shot up. "Did I say you're stealing my man?"

"Your expression says so. You've been frowning since your fiancé talked about his fabrics production and proposed working together."

"Has it occurred to you that something else caused my mood swing?" She threw her head to the side, brows still up.

"Okay. If you say so." Ajiri smiled, even though she knew Irene was lying. "We should get to business." She walked to the table, reached for the intercom, and dialled a number. "Funke, please ask the supplier and stylist to come in."

The next hour and thirty minutes saw them picking designs, reworking some of them, and choosing fabrics, and then taking Irene's measurements.

At the end of their work and after a brief refreshment, Ajiri saw Irene off to her red Porsche at the parking lot. There, she turned briefly to her host.

"About Adebayo, he is actually a chronic womanizer." She grinned, "I just think he might come after you. You're a raving black beauty, you know, and he loves his women dark."

Ajiri smiled. "So how did a fair skin beauty catch his eye?"

"I just shook my booty in front of him. That's all." She gave a burst of hearty laughter.

Ajiri couldn't help but join her. "I'm not good at shaking my booty. So don't worry, I'll keep him off."

"Thank you." Irene hugged her, got into her car while promising to be back the following week for the photoshoot, and then drove out of the compound.

Ajiri kept a smile on her lips as she made her way back into the building. So much for men and their ways. In her own world, things were done quite differently. One Merman could have just one wife but as many concubines as he wished. There was nothing of jealousy or betrayal.

However, good or bad, the wife and husband were bound to stay together forever. They were never allowed to divorce as couples in the human realm did.

She had noticed a spark in Adebayo's eyes earlier when he'd first seen her. He'd looked like he had seen the most beautiful treasure ever. But Ajiri had long known she had such an effect on men, and Irene wasn't the first lady in a foul mood because her man seemed interested in black beauty.

Ajiri had warded off most of the men. She didn't want to make trouble or have trouble with her business partners. However, there had been a few men she'd given room to.

Some of them had been married to beautiful wives and had gorgeous kids. The others had been single. But one thing common among them was the wonder in their eyes during sex. They screamed in pleasure. Sometimes, she thought they'd die of it.

These men kept coming back. They wanted sex with her. Their wife, girlfriend, and even ex-girlfriends didn't give them a sexual experience even close to what she gave. But after a few weeks of having sex with these men, one terrible thing after the other seemed to happen.

Some died. Some caught a fatal illness that stopped them from being useful to themselves or their family ever again. It took a long while for her to realize that her genes are different. The pleasure she gave these men proved mind-blowing. But during orgasm, her juice transferred something deadly into them, and in turn, she was rewarded with a vital part of their life force.

It usually took a few weeks for the symptoms to show. Sickness and death were instant for the weak ones.

Only after the seventh man died did she understand she couldn't continue having a sexual relationship with men of the human race. She'd just have a trail of corpses behind her. It was one of the reasons she didn't want to see Rabin as anything other than her driver.

Sure, he was attractive. She doubted Irene had seen him when he'd taken her stuff upstairs to her office. But she was sure that if the fair-skinned celebrity had, she wouldn't have talked about Adebayo again, or cared if her fiancé had eyes for another woman.

Rabin, she had imagined, in his naked form would be better than a Greek God. She had fantasized about him a lot. But that was all that could ever be. He was human. Having an intimate relationship with him meant his death. And she couldn't live with another death on her conscience.

The man in her dreams was another issue to worry about. Sometimes, she dreaded going to bed at night because of him. Other times, she wanted him. His lovemaking skills were certainly above anything else she had experienced. But still, she'd prefer not to let him have her until she knew who exactly he was.

As for Adebayo, he'd have to be content with his celebrity fiancée or end up dead, like her previous boyfriends.

Ajiri stylishly looked around for Rabin. His disappearance could only mean he had gone to his regular food joint for breakfast, or was it brunch? She looked at the time—a few minutes to one o'clock.

Even she hadn't eaten anything since morning. She made a mental note to ask Funke to get her something to eat.

She was about to step into the one-story building when she felt a vicious presence. She sighed. Not again. She just couldn't be battling entities in her office environment. But since she was alone outside the premises, she turned around to face him—a young boy in a black hoodie shirt and black pants. He'd covered his head with the hoodie, making it difficult to see his face. A red fire burned on his open palms.

"*What do you want?*" she asked in her head.

It was the only way to communicate without drawing attention to herself. If not, people would call her mad or possessed.

"You don't remember me?" he asked.

"I don't. I meet a lot of people every day. Actually, your kind of people."

He took the hood off with one hand. Ajiri paused.

"*Think about the devil,*" she said. The man before her was not that young, but one of the men she'd had sex with who'd died a few weeks later.

"Yes. Think about the devil. I'm here to pay back."

"I didn't kill you."

"No. But you failed to mention sex with you, Mami water, can kill," he gritted. "Do you know what my death did to my family? My wife and kids suffered so much, because of you!"

"You should have realized you had a wife and beautiful kids before coming to me," Ajiri fired back. "Your attacks can't kill me. You should know that by now, else I'd have been dead long ago, so save it. What I can do is find your family and take care of them."

"Too late. Someone is already doing that. My wife is doing much better, and my kids are having the best education ever. Someone else did what you should have done a long time ago, and that someone wants you dead, since you keep turning down his offer."

"So he sent you?"

"Who better to send than a man full of hate and revenge for the target?" He started to laugh, wickedly. "These fireballs are not ordinary. Don't be deceived. It killed a merman I used it on just last week. And I'm using it on you this week. Arrrrg!"

He threw the first ball.

Holding the blue necklace around her neck, Ajiri whispered some incantations as she froze her body and jumped out of it. Her blue glowing figure with scales on her hands, shoulders, and forehead bounced the fireball away. A flowery plum of shiny blue, pink, and gold protected her heart.

"Tell the person who sent you, Mermen and Mermaids have levels of hierarchy. I know my roots. I know my bloodline. You don't mess with me." Her eyes shone with something that looked more like sympathy than hatred. The flowery plum expanded from her heart to cover her entire body.

"Impossible!" the man whispered. "Only humans have that plum in their hearts. Evil creatures like you cannot have it! Arg!"

He threw the second fireball at her. But the plum absorbed it and expanded further.

"I have spent one whole year in the human world. You don't think I found a way to have it for myself?"

"You stole it from someone!" he accused.

"I earned it. I worked for it. It is unfortunate that a lot of humans don't even know they have it. But I assure you they will awaken to it. You and I know the human race is unpredictable."

"I don't care about humans. My only business here is your death." He charged at her.

Ajiri charged back. They were almost colliding head-on when an explosion blasted them apart.

She flew back into her own body just in time to see Rabin shaking her vigorously and calling her name.

"What?" she almost screamed at him.

He looked very concerned. She tore her eyes away from him and looked back in the direction her dead lover stood in a few minutes ago. He was nowhere to be found. She wondered where that explosion had come from and who'd sent it.

"I walked into the premises and met you staring in that direction. You were not moving. Your eyes didn't blink when I waved my hands in your face. You were transfixed on that spot like a rock. Do you still want to tell me you're okay?" Rabin asked, his expression serious.

"I'm fine," Ajiri insisted. "I just thought I saw something."

"Something that would make you seem as though you're lifeless?"

"Stop it. I'm fine. Nothing happened."

She looked back in the same direction before turning around to head inside.

"One doesn't stand transfixed for a solid fifteen minutes, ma'am," he called out, making her stop in her tracks.

She turned back and obviously had something to say. But the passionate look in his eyes took the words out of her mouth. Was he in love with her? Was that why he cared so much? Did he know he'd die if she so much as allowed him to penetrate her? Because, after all, sex was where any relationship led to.

"I only wish you'll trust me more," he said, turned around, and walked toward the parking lot, probably to relax in the car while listening to music, his hobby.

Ajiri shrugged and walked inside the building.

CHAPTER FOUR

The rest of the day went by peacefully and was highly productive. The stylists were able to start work on the new designs. And thanks to her marketing team, both online and offline, the business raked in massive sales for the day. Items were packaged and ready to be dispatched the following morning to their buyers.

Adebayo kept his promise. He called at about four p.m. to invite Ajiri to The African Fashion and Fabrics Seminar hosted by his company, in partnership with Guarantee Trust Bank.

Ajiri, curious about the opportunities that might open up to her, asked a lot of questions. The answers she got proved satisfying, and she promised him she'd be there.

Adebayo had clearly been excited over the phone. He hadn't hidden the fact that he was glad he'd meet her at the venue, Eko Hotel and Suites.

"And please, it's a Halloween-themed event. If you can put on a costume, better."

"All right." She had rolled her eyes.

After the call, she'd sat back on her chair and started to search her phone contact list. She just wasn't interested in scandals, and she could already sense Adebayo was up to one. Irene's name came up on her screen, and she hit the dial button.

Ting-ting. Ting-ting.

Irene picked at the second ring.

"Hello, dearie."

"Hello, Irene. Hope you're grooving your day?"

"Of course I am. What else I'm I known for? I'll have the pictures all over Instagram soon." She giggled.

Ajiri could tell she was in high spirits.

"Don't get too drunk, though. Will you be attending The African Fashion and Fabrics Seminar?

"Nope! I wasn't even aware there was a seminar like that." She sounded really confused.

"Maybe your fiancé forgot to mention it to you. His company is hosting the event in partnership with Guarantee Trust Bank. It's a seminar I believe every fashion enthusiast should attend, as it is aimed at helping us go global. And since you're the new face and main runway model for our upcoming fashion show, I was hoping we could be there together to draw from whatever ideas and experience other guests would share," she finished.

"Awww ... All I can say, sweetheart, is thanks for letting me in. Of course, I would love to be there. Just let me know the time and venue, please."

"Its Eko Hotel and Suites. Eight to eleven p.m. on the dot. It's a Halloween-themed event. So please get a costume."

"All right. Thanks so much, Ajiri. I'll make sure to be there."

The line dropped, and Ajiri rested back on her chair.

So much for an invitation. Adebayo would really get the shock of his life. If he was already planning a romantic evening with her, then she definitely had two different shockers for him.

Four-thirty p.m. saw Funke helping her close for the day and prepare for the seminar. Funke should be with her there. But since the woman had a family to care for, it wouldn't be possible.

She helped Ajiri move her things to the car. Rabin stepped out of it and helped put the documents and fabrics onto the passenger seat.

The ride home took nothing less than fifty minutes, thanks to traffic.

Once at home, Emeka opened the gate, and Rabin drove in. He helped carry the documents and fabrics into the house and was heading out after bringing in the last item when Ajiri stopped him.

"Do you have anything planned for tonight?" she asked.

He turned around to face her. "No. Is there something you want me to help with?"

"Yes. I need to be at Eko Hotel and Suites tonight. I already booked two rooms for the night; one for you and one for me. There is a fashion seminar taking place there and I have to be present."

"Okay. I can drive you down there."

"Actually, I'll prefer if you act as my boyfriend or bodyguard."

From his expression, she could tell he hadn't expected her to think those words, let alone say them. She watched him prevent his lips from curving into a smile. Perhaps he thought it would pass across the wrong impression and she would change her mind.

"Is there someone you think may want to harm you?"

"He can't harm me. But I just need you as a cover that can, without words, tell him to get moving."

"It sounds like something I can do."

"Great! So we start preparing right away. I need to sort out some items so we can be on our way to the hotel. We can shower and get dressed there. The seminar starts at eight o'clock."

"Okay. Just let me know what I need to do."

"Nothing much. Just hang around. There are some documents I need to get from my study. And some I need to print out. Then I'll need to pick something for us from my storeroom."

"Okay, ma'am."

She walked into the mini duplex while Rabin walked back to the car, shut the door, and started towards the boys' quarters.

Ajiri went straight to work on her laptop and printed some documents. She also looked through some others before picking the ones she needed.

Thirty minutes later, she was in her fashion room where all new supplies of clothes and shoes for sales were kept. Her hands reached for a blue, floor-length fish gown. She had a crown to go with it. Being from the water, she only thought it better to wear something that would bring water and its fishes to mind.

Besides, she had always loved blue for special occasions. It was the colour of her home, and she missed home. A lot. Some days, she wondered what it would have been like had her father not insisted on marrying her off to Prince Ago. Perhaps she'd have been happy. She'd still have been with her family.

All the same, she was happy for her experience in the human world. She had met wonderful people and had wonderful moments. But she didn't like the grind. Everyone worked their arses off for wealth and fame, thereby ignoring more important issues, like the spirits that attacked them daily, causing one problem after the other in their lives.

Well, they didn't know it, and it wasn't like they could see beyond the physical.

She reached into the back hanger and picked out a black Italian tuxedo. Ajiri convinced herself she wanted Rabin in that suit because the man, who would act as her bodyguard, had to be well dressed. She only hoped seeing him in that outfit wouldn't turn her senses inside out.

He is supposed to be just my driver. But every day, he is getting under my skin.

Not just in the way he always asked if she was okay, but in the way he stared at her from time to time.

Somehow, she found his attraction to her scary. She couldn't help but wonder what would happen to him if they went all the way. All the men in her past relationships had been passionate. They'd showered her with love, care, and gifts. It had been beautiful to experience such. But they couldn't survive the paranormal. They couldn't survive lovemaking.

As much as Rabin was starting to get under her skin, Ajiri knew she couldn't let certain things happen, or else, he would die.

The only person she could have sex with, and maybe a relationship, was the man who had dominated her dreams. One thought of him made her wet. And he seemed to be following her all over the place during the day—if not, how else could he know she thought about him a lot?

She raised her head briefly to look at the time. Six o'clock neared, and they still needed to get to the hotel in time to freshen up, so as to make an early appearance for the event.

She was already heading for the door when she heard a disturbing sound. Not just any noise, but that of two people arguing, one yelling at the other, saying "she must not die". But the other party seemed to be insisting on the death of whoever this 'she' was.

Ajiri couldn't help but feel both men were referring to her. One of the male voices sounded familiar. The currents of energy from the disturbance told her these were no mere people arguing. She'd had enough entity attacks to know that. And she could bet on her life that it was the blue man from her dreams defending her from another ghost.

She left her fashion storeroom, dropped the clothes in the sitting room, and began tracing the noise. They were fighting now. It didn't take her long to realize it al came from outside the duplex.

She took the kitchen door and made her way outside. One of them was begging now, pleading for his life. The voice she assumed belonged to the man from her dreams was telling the other he'd show no mercy.

As she headed towards the boys' quarters, the noise got even louder—coming from Rabin's room.

She knocked. No response. She banged on the door until she heard him ask, 'Who is it?'

"Ajiri."

It took another ten minutes before she heard a bolt pulled back. The door gradually opened to reveal a bare-chested Rabin with only a towel around his waist. He was dripping wet as he probably hadn't had the time to dry his body.

"Is there something you want me to do?" he asked when she kept staring.

"Oh ... no," she said and mentally knocked her head.

She pushed past him into the room. Everything looked normal. The noise had stopped, too. She tried to find traces of what had happened, but could find none. No entity, no blue man.

She turned to Rabin. "Did you hear anything?"

"No." He looked perplexed.

"And you're sure?" She looked around, bewildered.

"Yes. The only noise I heard was from Emeka."

"You're lying!" She moved to stand in front of him. "Emeka is at the gate, doing his job. And this particular noise was so loud, two people fighting. You can't say you didn't hear it!"

Her frustration must be obvious by now. Suddenly, he was looking at her like he wanted to wipe this frustration off her face.

"I don't know what you're talking about, ma'am. You may just have been hearing things. So if you'll kindly excuse me, I need to put together a small bag for our stay over at the hotel." Rabin opened his door wide and gestured for her to leave.

"You're rude, Rabin. Very rude. Don't forget this is my property and I can kick you out anytime I like."

"I remember it's your property. And I remember you can be a pain in my neck sometimes. I don't know what it is you always see or hear. Maybe you need help."

"Are you saying I'm crazy?"

"I'm just saying you need help."

"I'm not going to fire you because you're the only driv—" She paused.

How could she let him know he was the only driver who'd not been attacked by those crazy dead people? She eyed him. He eyed her back. His rude stare melted her insides. She should yell at him instead of acting like a teenager.

"On second thought ..." He closed the door, reached for her hand, and pulled her up against himself.

His lips descended on hers, and he kissed her passionately. Funnily enough, she kissed him back, licking, suckling, as their lips battled for dominance.

His hand slid to her backside. He cupped and squeezed it against his erection. A moan escaped both their lips, and the passion they shared deepened as he led her towards the bed.

It took all of Ajiri's strength of will to pull back and push him away from her. They both were out of breath, but his expression told her—what just happened wasn't a mere fling. For him, it amounted to more. Was he in love with her? Was that why he seemed to always be looking at her? He had avoided any form of body contact all the while. Why now?

"I'm sorry," he said. "I didn't mean to overstep my boundaries."

Now, she wasn't so sure if she'd been right to let what had happened happen. How could he apologise for the powerful intimacy they'd just shared? How could he affect her so much in such a short period of working with her?

"Please get dressed and take me to the hotel."

She marched out of the room and back to the duplex. The images of Rabin couldn't leave her head. Neither could the feel of his lips on hers go away as she put her bag and documents together.

She changed into simple jeans and was buttoning up the long-sleeved shirt when she felt a hand on her shoulder.

Ajiri swirled around. The words died on her lips temporarily when her eyes came into contact with the blue man from her dreams.

"You're here?" she asked.

"I am," he said almost in a whisper as he wrapped his hands around her waist and held her firmly. "You can't seem to get him out of your head, can you?"

"I don't know what you're talking about."

"I'm talking about your driver. Rabin." He turned her to face him. "You love him?"

"I still don't know what you're talking about," she lied. Not because she was scared to admit the truth, but because the heartbreak she saw in his eyes wouldn't let her admit it.

"Okay. But you enjoyed being in his arms?"

"If you hadn't been in his room or somewhere around there fighting spirits, I wouldn't have been curious. I wouldn't have rushed down there to be sure he wasn't hurt, and then, whatever you saw wouldn't have happened."

"So was it wrong, that I was looking out for him and for you?"

Ajiri swallowed. This blue man loved her. The pain in his eyes and voice told her so. He looked out for her. He understood her. He fought her battles and pleasured her every night, begging for acceptance. What exactly did she see in Rabin that she couldn't find in this stranger, and even more?

"I'm not here to quarrel. You have a right to your choices. It wouldn't stop me from looking out for you." He leaned toward and planted a soft kiss on her lips.

Ajiri couldn't deny the rush of excitement she felt. It spread through her body. She wanted to say something. But before she could, he disappeared out of sight.

She closed her eyes. Somehow, she was sad she had hurt him.

CHAPTER FIVE

The drive to Eko Hotels and Suites was a quiet one. Rabin didn't, not even by mistake, look at her through his rear-view mirror. As much as she was determined to return their relationship to that of boss and employee, she couldn't help but feel he was pulling himself away from her by minding his business.

She tried not to care. Rabin was human, anyway.

The man who understood her and looked out for her? The one who made love to her every night? That was the man she should worry about.

She just needed to know exactly who he was first.

They got to the hotel just in time for her to have her bath and get dressed before heading downstairs for the event.

The conference room teemed as busy as a beehive. Dignitaries strolled about in their Halloween costumes, some still yet to arrive. Having put on her fish gown glittering all over with real diamonds, all eyes seemed to be on Ajiri. Adebayo smiled like a fool as he moved to introduce her to every one of his guests.

I wonder how he would feel or look when he eventually comes in contact with Irene.

And about Irene, Ajiri wondered where she was. Almost eight already, and the celebrity model was still nowhere to be found. This made her uneasy because Adebayo mostly hung around her, and she didn't like it.

The event started properly at eight-thirty p.m. on the dot, opened by the chairman of one of the new generation banks, Chief Osa Yandhi, and the topic of discussion focused on 'Best Strategies for Trading African Textile and Fashion Within and Outside the Shores of the Continent'.

Lucky for Ajiri, it was a topic she truly was interested in. However, she couldn't help but feel that her reason for inviting Rabin to act as her bodyguard or boyfriend to scare off Adebayo had almost been defeated, as she was yet to set eyes on him. Was he staying away from her due to what had transpired earlier?

The event ended two hours and forty-five minutes later. Drinks and food flowed freely afterwards. Everyone present moved to socialize and network with each other.

Thanks to Adebayo, he introduced Ajiri to all the top members in that event. And by the time she gave out the last business card and invitation for her next fashion show, she was sure business would triple in growth and income before the year ended.

She was having a nice time with one of the numerous guests, a very hilarious one at that, when Adebayo walked up to them and took an excuse to discuss something important with her.

Although she suspected his actions, she followed him quietly to a corner, away from all the noise. He turned and smiled at her sheepishly. She knew then exactly what he was up to.

"Mr. Adebayo, if you are thinking what I am thinking, then it is best to stop."

"Why? This event will soon be over. I just want to be sure that we can spend the night together, you know." He looked really confident in himself and his offer.

"I won't be able to spend the night with you, please. This event is strictly official for me. Not fun."

"Why can't it be fun? Why can't we have fun after the guests have gone? In the next hour or thirty minutes, this hall will be almost empty. Every meetup after that time is personal because I also make it a habit to keep personal stuff away from business."

"You are doing the opposite right now," she reminded him.

"No. I'm not doing the opposite. I am just making plans ahead for the night." He grinned.

"But you took me away from a conversation that meant something to me. I think you should have waited until the event was over—"

"Come on, Ajiri! You're a grown woman, a celebrity in the fashion world, a business mogul, and an exposed one, too. You're not a kid. Of course, I want to believe you understand where I'm coming from and where I'm going with this."

"I'm sorry, but I do not understand where you're coming from, nor do I understand where you're going. Can you kindly explain?"

He grinned. She knew he perceived her to be a gamer, and of course, he'd play her games with her.

"Okay, Ajiri. Here it is. I like you a lot, and I really would like us to get to know each other better."

Her brows shot up in a sly manner. "But earlier today, my friend and new brand model introduced you to me as her fiancé. Why would I want to date the fiancé of my brand ambassador?"

"Oh, please, don't let Irene deceive you. I really don't have anything with that girl."

"Really? So why didn't you counter her claim when she made it? Why did you need to wait until she's not here to say that?"

"You don't understand. Irene is like a baby. She gets glued to everything she thinks is fun. The minute you counter her claims to anyone or anything, she starts getting emotional. And before you know it, she's violent and causing trouble everywhere you go."

"Really?" a voice said from behind.

Adebayo turned to see Irene standing at the corner. Ajiri smiled triumphantly.

"You mean when you counter me, I go about making trouble? I get emotional? Really, Adebayo, this is what you have to say about me?" She was obviously sad.

He managed a smile. "Oh, baby, not you now. How can I say things like that about you? There are so many Irenes in this world, for crying out loud."

"And I'm supposed to believe you were talking about another Irene." She moved closer as she folded her arms in front of her.

"Yes, you really have to believe me. You can ask Ajiri. She's right here."

"Ade, I heard enough of your conversations to know you were referring to me. You didn't think I would be here because you didn't invite me. You didn't tell me you were having a fashion show, but you conveniently invited Ajiri. And to think I only introduced her to you this morning. She's right here, in your event, connecting with all the big people. I have been around long enough, watching you two. And I saw how you followed her around like fly after poop. But I know Ajiri is not into you. She is a true friend that can never betray me. You, on the other hand, I will deal with you so next time you think before messing up with me."

"Oh, shut up, Irene," a very irritated Adebayo spoke. "If you must know, yes, I purposely refused to invite you because I know the kind of person you are. Secondly, there is nothing you can do to me. I'll rubbish you first. And yes, I've got a strong interest in your friend. At least, from what I have seen so far, she is a hundred and one percent independent, a hundred and one percent creative, a hundred and one percent the kind of woman I should give my ring to, not you, a cry baby who does what exactly for a living? Nothing. You're a celebrity for showing your breasts and arse on TV and Instagram. There are wonderful movie producers in this country. But you keep acting in films that do not make any sense. So what exactly are you creative at? I'm trying to understand."

"So now, you are insulting me, right? Just watch me drag you at your own event. I will embarrass the Ade out of the Bayo. You're mad!"

"Irene, please, don't do this," Ajiri spoke as she thought it wise to step in. "The minute you go out there and start to raise your voice all in a bid to drag him down, everyone will turn on you. The media will carry it. They will talk about how you made noise over a boyfriend in a very important event like this. This wouldn't be good for you or me, because I have already distributed papers and invites for our fashion show, and I've already shown these people your photo as our brand ambassador. Your photo and your name are in the hands of almost every top client in this room. If you make that move, you will be killing our chance."

Irene sighed with pouty lips. "You see why I love you, Ajiri. You always think ahead. Thank you for helping me not to embarrass myself this night."

"No. You'd have gone ahead. Make noise and scream all you want, then you would have proved me right that all you know how to do is cause trouble and bring violence all because someone is no longer interested in you. Like I said before, Ajiri is a hundred and one percent boss. In less than two hours of this event, she has successfully marketed herself, her business, and even you, to the top bidders in this place. While she's going places, you stay there and scream blood just because a man is no longer interested in you."

He turned around to face Ajiri. "Ajiri, I know she's your friend, but think about it, please. I'd very much prefer to spend the rest of my life when a beautiful, smart woman like you than trash like her."

"Sir, you just called my business partner trash to my face. I'm sorry, but I cannot get married to a man who can call the woman he has been sleeping with trash. Now, if you'll kindly excuse me, I would like to remove myself from this drama."

Ajiri turned and walked away, leaving the couple to either patch up their sour relationship or end it.

She hadn't gone too far when she spotted Rabin at the far left of the conference room, looking intensely in her direction. Her breath caught. He was wearing the suit she'd picked for him, but without the Joker mask. And he really looked strikingly handsome in it. No one would ever guess he was her driver. He looked elegant.

She didn't miss the fact that several ladies had their eyes on him, even though his eyes remained focused on her, like she was the only one in the room. As weird as it was, she also felt he was the only one in the room.

"Ajiri, please, let's talk things over," Adebayo said, coming up from behind her.

Not wanting to say anything to him, she moved away.

Her heart slammed against her chest. Not because of Adebayo, but because Rabin wouldn't stop looking at her. His eyes followed her to every corner. And even when she stopped briefly to greet one of the guests, he still stared openly at her.

She stopped in front of the bar to take a drink as she really needed to calm her nerves. When she turned around again, she saw one of the celebrity ladies already engaging him in a discussion. She didn't know what they were talking about, but the celebrity looked like she was really into him. Rabin, on the other hand, stole occasional glances at Ajiri. And he looked like he couldn't wait to get away from the woman.

She chuckled at the realisation and ordered a drink while stealing glances at the duo.

She couldn't understand why she suddenly felt attracted to Rabin. She couldn't understand why his stares put butterflies in her belly.

She sighed and took a sip from her drink. She looked up afterwards to find Rabin wasn't listening to the celebrity lady any more. Instead, he was watching her intently. Their eyes met, and she was sure her heart skipped a beat, if not several.

She was getting attracted to her driver. He, in turn, was getting attracted to her. But then, there was the stranger— the man who dominated her dreams and her body. He could be the real deal for her, and she wouldn't be scared he'd die. Rabin, on the other hand, would die a few weeks after lovemaking that would give her thrills and orgasms, no doubt.

Ajiri turned back to the counter, and just then, Irene joined her.

"Thank you so much, Ajiri, for having my back."

"You're welcome," she replied, taking another sip from her drink.

"I can't believe I've been lying in bed with a man as stupid as Adebayo."

"I equally can't believe you have been dating a man who has no regard for you," Ajiri said. "Tell me something, Irene. Has he ever beaten you? Has he ever slapped you? Has he ever talked down on you in your presence? What about cheating? Have you ever caught him red-handed with another girl?

Irene sighed and waved lazily at the bartender. "I need a drink."

After she was served, she gulped down the content in one go and ordered another. She downed two more glasses of champagne before turning to face her friend. "Girl, he has done all of that, and worse."

"So why are you still with him? Why do you let him treat you like this?"

"Because he is the only man who hadn't used my past against me. A lot of the men I have dated in the past didn't want to have anything to do with me when they discovered I was once a stripper and a call girl for politicians. I don't blame them. This is Africa."

Ajiri felt sorry for her that moment. She could only understand that her brand ambassador was going through a very rough time. And from time immemorial, she knew relationship issues were never easy to just overlook or ignore.

"You need to try and walk away from him," she said. "You need to try to forget him. It is not going to be easy, but I assure you, you'll have peace of mind."

Irene laughed. "You want me to leave him so you can have him?"

"I can't even believe you think such. Why would I want you to leave an abuser so I can be with him? If I want, I can be with him even while you two are still together. But I'm not that kind. I told you earlier at the office this afternoon. So it's best if you think about your well-being and your health first. For me, I have other important things to do, and they do not include dragging men with my brand ambassador."

"I'm sorry, Ajiri. The whole thing really gets to me sometimes, and I find myself fighting with people who are actually supposed to be my friend."

"Think about it. Clear your head and make your decision. Okay?"

"Okay."

Irene reached for another glass of wine, and then another, and another, and another, until Ajiri had to stop her.

"You are going to get yourself wasted."

"It seems like the only way I can get my head clear." Irene laughed.

"Come, let me escort you to your room. Hope you are planning to spend the night here? Did you book a room?

"No. All the rooms were taken by the time I called to book one."

"Okay then, you're spending the night in my room."

Ajiri pulled her friend up and supported her to the room on the fifth floor. She opened the door and led Irene into the expensive suite.

"Now you try and get some sleep. You might have a headache when you wake up, though. But you'll be fine."

"Thank you, Ajiri. I wonder what I'll do without you."

"With the way you're looking now, nothing."

The ladies laughed.

"Goodnight, Irene. Please lock the door after me."

"Definitely."

Irene turned the key in the lock after Ajiri had stepped out of the room. But Ajiri's countenance changed when she saw Adebayo coming in her direction.

"You see what I've been talking about?" he asked. "She is so useless. She drank herself into a stupor. If not for you, she would have made a mess of herself right there. Can you now understand why I did not want to have anything to do with her?"

"And you, being her man, why were you not there to help her? If you didn't want anything to do with her, you shouldn't have taken her to bed. You shouldn't have continued dating her. You shouldn't have proposed marriage to her."

"I never proposed marriage to her. And like I said before, she is the one trying to tie me down with it."

"Okay, if you say so. But now, I have to go to my room. The event is over, the guests are leaving, the others are going up to their own rooms, and it's time I did the same."

She wasn't sure she'd sleep on the same bed with a drunk Irene. She wasn't even sure where she'd sleep for the night.

"Ajiri, as I said before, you're not a baby. You're not a kid. The grown-ups are still downstairs holding the place active. Why don't we join them, have a few drinks so we can get to know each other more?"

"I can't, actually. I need to be strong for tomorrow's activities. We have a lot going on at the office."

"Okay. What if I promise to introduce you to other clients that you haven't met yet?"

"Are you trying to bribe me?"

"If this is a bribe you will take, then yes."

"I really appreciate your help and connections, but now, I think I need to get to bed. Thank you so much, Mr. Adebayo, for inviting me to this wonderful event."

She started towards the elevator. She needed to head to the first floor to ask if there were any spare rooms. But she hadn't taken three steps when Adebayo grabbed her hand.

"Don't walk out on me, beautiful. It would be unfair after all I have done by inviting you to a life-changing program."

Ajiri frowned. She yanked her hand away from his.

"I don't know what you're insinuating, but you didn't make me, Mr. Adebayo. And your small clicks here can't make me. If I want to get to the top spot in the world and maintain it for years, I can. I'm not Irene that you mess around with. Ajiri is different. I can go down there and tell all your guests to hell with them. And they'd still—"

"Shut up! Even if nobody else knows who you are, I know exactly who you are, Princess."

Ajiri backed away from him. It was then she noticed his eyes had turned black. Definitely, he was not himself—one of the ways ghosts used humans to attack her.

Knowing full well that fighting an entity right there in the hotel hallway meant that the cameras would catch the fact that she was not human, she backed farther away and started hurriedly towards the elevator at the end of the passage. Adebayo went after her, yelling. However, a voice stopped both of them in their tracks.

Ajiri turned around to see Rabin at the other end of the passage. For a guy that always looked cool and collected, she was surprised to see him looking so unsure of himself.

He threw his room key at her.

"Go to my room," he said as she caught it.

Without a moment's delay, she was in the elevator. She typed in the floor number, and the door closed.

***

Rabin turned his eyes on Adebayo. He had long suspected something of this nature would happen; he just wasn't sure who would be used. He stepped out of his body, leaving it motionless as he started to take gentle steps towards Adebayo and stopped in front of him.

"Tell whoever sent you, he wouldn't touch her," he said.

"She is a target. You and I know that. Stay out of this."

"That she you so freely talk about is mine alone."

"She killed innocent men and ripped them apart from their families for life."

"Those innocent men wanted fun. She gave it. Now, I repeat, you don't touch her."

"How about we rape her endlessly befor—argh!"

A blue force picked the demon out of Adebayo's body and threw him backwards. He landed hard but quickly got to his feet again. A confused Adebayo, who couldn't really understand what was happening, ran past Rabin's motionless body and back to the conference room.

Rabin, still holding a fist glowing with blue light, walked toward the ghost. "Don't you dare touch her!"

"Argh!" The entity rushed at him.

He caught him with one hand and sent fists covered in a blue fireball to his middle. The spirit tried to retaliate but only found himself slammed against the floor and pinned to it. Rabin's arms, glowing with blue fire, circled around his neck.

"Stop!" he pleaded.

"You'll never go near her!" Rabin said, before sending his free hand, with glowing flames, into the entity's head.

It screamed viciously before exploding into a thousand pieces that got instantly consumed in the blue fire.

Rabin looked up at the camera in the passage. Definitely, it may have picked up some of his vibrations. He walked back into his body before heading for the elevator.

CHAPTER SIX

Ajiri sat on her bed. She normally had these sort of attacks at home or in her sleep where it was easy to fight back without dragging public eyes to herself. Now, it came as a regular daily occurrence, and she wasn't sure why.

She feared for herself, her business, and most importantly, her driver. Now she wished she hadn't run off. She wished she'd simply stepped out of her body and fought back. How would Rabin deal with something far stronger than him, and all alone? What would happen if she got called by the hotel staff, saying her driver had been killed in a fight?

She had lost one driver once to the entities. She wasn't going to lose another one.

Ajiri got to her feet, grabbed the room key, and headed for the door. She was only a few steps away from it when a soft knock from the other side startled her.

"Yes? Who is there?"

"Rabin," the familiar voice said.

"Rabin," she whispered before rushing to open the door.

Ajiri grabbed his hands and pulled him into the room. She started to examine his body when a light chuckle made her stop and look up.

"What's funny?" she enquired.

"I didn't think you cared." He let the smile remain on his lips.

"I'm not heartless. You helped me out there. The least I can do is ensure you're okay." She returned to inspecting his arm. "Please, I'll need you to take off your shirt."

She moved to the drawers to get a mini first-aid box before returning to the side of the bed where he sat. She unlocked the box, took out a balm and opened it.

Her breath caught when she turned around to see his shirt was unbuttoned, revealing a six pack and a chest that could make her lose her senses. The same chest she'd seen earlier in the evening.

She took a deep breath and swallowed before pretending not to care about the attraction she felt.

"Where exactly were you hurt?" She was no longer interested in searching his body for injuries or bruises, now at risk of ending up bruised if she went any further.

"I thought you were searching for it?" he teased.

She was more confused than angry. If Rabin was flirting with her, if he even liked her, he had never mentioned it to her, be it privately or publicly. Now, he was acting up and flirting.

"Rabin, I'm still your boss. You will show some respect, and if you keep up this way, I'll be forced to leave you to yourself. I'm guessing you can treat your own wounds?"

She left the balm beside him on the bed and retreated to the dressing table. As much as he was sexy—something she'd never really thought of before—he had no right to flirt or act all familiar with her.

If only that stupid ambassador of hers had rented a room, she'd have run to her own room and slept peacefully on her bed.

Ajiri pulled the pin out of her hair, letting it unwrap and fall to her shoulders. She placed the pin on a dressing table as a dark-skinned hand covered hers.

Not long afterwards, the colour of the skin started to change into a sea blue complexion. The tattoo of a dolphin rested on the arm, just below the elbow.

Ajiri's heart skipped. She pulled her hand away from under his and looked up in time to see the complete transformation from Rabin to the very man who had haunted her dreams for about a month.

"You," she whispered.

"Yes, sweetheart." He stepped forward.

But she moved backwards. "What do you want? And what did you do with Rabin?"

"I didn't do anything to him."

"What did you do to my driver?" she almost yelled.

He stopped in his tracks and eyed her closely. "You think I killed him?"

"For all I care, you could have."

"You don't remember me much, do you?"

"The man who has taken over my dreams. Yes, I remember you."

He started to move closer again. But Ajiri backed away. She reached for a wine bottle placed in a bucket of melting ice that had been delivered to his room much earlier. "Stay away from me."

"You love Rabin. But you can't even stand me."

He covered the distance, seized the bottle from her, and pulled her into his embrace. She struggled to free herself. But his hands were firm around her.

"We are married, my love. You ran away from home because you couldn't bear the thought of being married off to a stranger. But the ceremony went on anyway. You know how it is with our people."

"I am not your wife. I did not get married to anyone." She was yelling now.

"I'm not some imposter, Jenali."

Ajiri stopped struggling and looked sternly at him. "What did you call me?"

She needed to ask, because only someone who knew her from her home in the river world knew that name. Her birth name.

"I am your husband. It took me almost one whole year to find you."

"Where is Rabin?" she yelled.

"Rabin is right here. Holding you."

"If you're truly him, you've been in my employ for a whole month. All you do is stare at me like a fool and harass me in my dreams. So why didn't you come clean from the start?"

"Would you have accepted me? In the dream, as your seductor, you haven't accepted me. As your driver, coming clean with you now, you can't even accept me. Why would you have accepted or believed me at our first contact?"

He lifted her chin with one hand.

"Why should I believe you now?"

She slapped his hand off and tried fruitlessly to wriggle out of his grip.

"Because you know I'm saying the truth, and because you witnessed a bit of me downstairs with that Adebayo guy. Who accurately throws a key to a person at the end of a hallway? If you'll calm down, I'll explain. I can show you the records. You can even run it yourself. We're from the same world. Separate kingdoms. Your father rules the north of the Nile. My father rules the south. Both houses pledged to come together by marriage between their children."

She had stopped struggling now.

He raised her face to look at him. "I've known you since we were kids, Jenali. And I have loved you since the first time I set eyes on you. Do you remember the little boy who came with his father one morning? Your mother told you to go out and play. You did and even went farther than you were allowed to go. I followed you secretly."

He rubbed the back of his hand against her cheek. "And then, you got attacked by men from the human world who saw you sunbathing on the shore. I fought them off and got you back into the water."

Ajiri frowned. At the same time, she felt confused and totally speechless as she looked up at the man talking.

"On our way back to the palace," he continued, "we ran into sharks and octopi. We fought our way through—"

"And we got home that day with your arms bleeding," she completed and stepped back a bit to look at him.

Now, she could place his features. It was truly him.

"Yunad?"

She whispered the name she had known him by. Her heart skipped several beats. She was excited, but unsure until a smile curved his lips.

"You even remember my name."

"Yunad!"

She rushed in for a tight hug as emotions overwhelmed her. All this while, how could she not have known it was him? How could she not have seen through? And to think she had stopped to think about or wish for him? To think she cleared him out of her mind, concluding that he must be married to another already.

"Oh, Yunad," she whispered as she let her mind drift back to her childhood, and to the announcement of her marriage to Prince Ago.

She'd never thought she'd be this close to the man she loved. She'd never thought they could be together. And she'd been sure she would not love again.

But here he was. Flesh and blood. In her embrace. His heart beating against hers in unison. And his features? She pulled back to look at him again.

His eyes were watery. Hers weren't dry, either. This was her man; the one she had longed for. The only one she would live for. His perfect features and lovemaking skills were the cherry on top.

"You really did get more handsome."

They chuckled, still staring at each other. His hand moved to push back strands of her hair. "And your beauty is out of this world."

"You were brave in that fight, you know. I didn't forget you. I told my father every day that if I ever got married, it would have to be to you. I think we only saw each other twice. The second time was when you were leaving with your father. And then I received all your funny letters. I really loved them. But it's been years. We were only kids. I was eight or nine, there about. I held on to your name and our friendship. But when my father announced my wedding, out of the blue, I was given the impression I was to marry your elder brother. I wasn't buying that. It's why I ran away."

"You don't need to explain, my love. Your mother told me everything during the wedding. But we hadn't seen each other in years and there was a lot of gap between us."

He pulled her into his embrace, patting her hair lovingly. "I guess your father misunderstood my dad's request at the time. It was the eve of the ceremony, the same night you ran away, that my father clarified that it was me he wanted you for. I had told him several times that I was in love with you."

Her grip tightened around him. "But I sent letters to you after the announcement was made. I never got a response."

Yunad pulled back to look at her with all seriousness. "I never got your letters, sweetheart. If I did, I would have responded. And perhaps that would have saved us all the headaches and pains we've gone through."

"It would have." She smiled, nodding. "But what about your brother?"

"My elder brother has since run off with a beautiful human he rescued from drowning. He comes home once in a while. But he is married to her."

"How come she didn't die from his lovemaking?" This perplexed her.

"An elixir. He came home to tell us what had happened with his wife. My mom got the physician to prepare an elixir. The substance saved her, but it heightened her senses and made her almost like us."

"Wow! If I had known such existed, I wouldn't have had entities aiming for my life."

"Well, I'm glad you didn't have it. You would have married someone else by now and even had kids." He grinned.

Ajiri chuckled.

They spent another minute staring at each other. There were no words, just understanding, love, and trust. When he moved in to take her lips, she didn't resist. She kissed him back, throwing her hands around his neck.

The kiss deepened, and moans escaped their mouths. Her hand ran the length of his chest; the chest that had claimed her senses earlier. He reached for the zip at her back, pulled it down gently, and slid the gown off her shoulders, to her waist. And then, he let it fall to the floor.

Ajiri stepped out of the dress while still locked lip to lip with him. She completely took off his shirt and reached for his belt. Her bra fell off. One hand gently grabbed her soft mould of flesh and caressed it, before slipping the nipple into his mouth.

She moaned as she patted his head. She let her free hand reach inside his pants and caress his hardness.

Yunad sighed as a soft groan escaped his lips.

"May you not be the death of me, woman," he said and kissed her.

"I hope not. You can't even die now when we're only just getting started."

He grinned.

Ajiri pushed him slightly away from her and got on her knees. She pulled down his pants and got it out from under his feet before taking him into her mouth. His sigh and the way he patted her head as she took him in and out spelled her satisfaction.

A while later, he pulled her to her feet and carried her to the big bed. He kissed her, passionately, as one hand caressed the length of her body and finally moved to cup her breast, squeezing gently.

His lips moved from her mouth to her neck, then the space between her breasts, her stomach, and then the V of her thighs. Ajiri's hips shot upward, asking for more. Her hand caressed his head and seemed to hold it firmly between her legs.

When he finally moved back up, he paused and looked into her eyes. "How did you manage to resist me before, even though you knew you wanted it?"

"I didn't know who you were. I like to know who I'm giving myself to."

"So who am I now?"

She smiled, not missing the passion burning in his eyes. "You're my husband. You're my friend. You're my king. You're the only man I ever want. The only man I can trust. The one I'll ever live for. The man—"

He covered her lips with his. A passionate kiss followed, and when he pulled back, he didn't miss the longing in her eyes. "You're my queen, the love of my life, the only woman I've always wanted. We can go back home together. Or stay here. Whichever you want."

He cupped her face.

"You have a kingdom to rule."

"The throne will be passed down to my elder brother."

"But he'll need you as his right-hand man. We can alternate between this world and ours."

Yunad kissed her. His hands travelled down further to raise one of her legs. He slid into her wetness, and a soft sigh escaped both their lips. A groan followed as his thrust came gently and then in quick strokes.

This was it. The moment she had dreamed of since as far back as she could remember. She had wanted him; a man who would be hers for life. And when he'd first started to visit her dreams, she had known she wanted him. As her driver, she'd wanted him more. But she hadn't been sure.

Now, there was nothing she was more sure of. As they reached an earth-shattering orgasm, one she'd never had with her human lovers, she knew this was her man. He would always be her man.

Yunad collapsed on top of her.

She kissed his forehead and then his nose. "I love you, sweetheart."

He smiled at her. "I love more, my queen."

THE END

ABOUT THE AUTHOR

Karo Oforofuo is a Nigerian author who started writing for fun at an early age. In 2013, she started writing professionally for her old blog and several clients.

She's the owner and editor at Pelleura; she's also the blogger at PelleuraLife, where she entertains readers with interesting fiction stories, real-life experiences and hacks, health tips, fashion, relationships, and business articles.

She's a story blogger with a difference, online business consultant, writing and content creation coach. Karo is also a professional freelance writer and editor.

Connect with her on https://pelleura.top

Haunted

KIRU TAYE

BLURB

In life, he loved her. In death, he craved her. Somma is heartbroken when husband David is killed in a tragic accident. After a year she is struggling to move on, especially since she swears he haunts her dreams and does sexy stuff to her every night. When friends convince her to perform an exorcism, things take a turn she doesn't expect.

CHAPTER ONE

"This isn't living."

Omolade's cautionary words made Somma exhale a heavy sigh, well aware of the state of her existence.

Her life had ended a year ago when her husband, David, died in a catastrophic plane crash.

"I know," Somma replied in a quiet voice and reached for the glass of white wine on the dark-wood side-table to her right.

Omolade, Molade or just Lade, known in their circle as the wine connoisseur, had brought the South African Pinot Grigio while Efe, the foodie, ensured they had a selection of sweet and savoury nibbles spread out on the coffee table. Her two besties orchestrated this girls' night in to cheer her up and keep her company because it was the anniversary of David's death.

Somma took a sip of the crisp drink but didn't taste the usual flavour of delicious tropical fruits. Instead, an acidic tang filled her mouth, and she swallowed, forcing the alcohol down. She placed the glass back on the table with trembling hands as she relived the day her husband died as if it had just happened.

"You know how I read the breaking news of the plane crash on Twitter," she continued.

Sweat beads popped along her hairline although the standing fan circulated cold gusts of air. She clutched her arms to her chest, body rocking slightly.

"I remember the tightness in my chest, the dread making my stomach roll as I rushed to turn on the TV so I could watch the news programme and confirm details about the flight. Remember the way I panicked and called you?" She glanced at her friends.

Lade shifted forward, reached out and covered Somma's hand with both of hers. "I do remember, and I rushed over here to be with you and called Efe on the way."

"Yes," Efe said, her wrinkled brows and watery eyes mirrored her concerned words. "We were all worried. It was an awful day."

Awful didn't seem like a strong enough word to describe the agonising and frantic search for information, the number of times she had called David's phone, praying he would pick up but never got connected. The anxious text messages she'd sent, asking him to call her as soon as he got them but with no reply.

"And when we finally got confirmation from the airline that David had been on the flight and that there had been no survivors..." A whimper escaped Somma's lips, and she swallowed excessively. She closed her eyes to stem the rush of tears. An ache bloomed in the back of her throat as the severe emotional shrapnel that had pierced her heart a year ago twisted.

The old mental sore ripped open. The pain renewed, raw and bitter. Torturous.

Her shoulders curled in on themselves as she swayed back and forth.

Arms circled her, drawing her to a soft body. Efe. She recognised her friend's heady floral perfume. She was the hugger of the group. Omolade, not so much.

But they'd both been here for her whenever she'd needed her friends.

Efe didn't say anything just held her while she sobbed. Lade joined their group hug.

There were no words that would take away her pain. Her friends knew this about her. The physical contact was more effective than empty phrases.

She'd heard all the platitudes before—"Sorry for your loss";

"He is resting in peace";

"The Lord is your strength";

"It is well"—that last one had to be one of the most insensitive things to tell a woman who'd just lost her husband.

Never mind the people who told her "Time heals everything."

Three hundred and sixty-five days on, she wasn't any more 'healed' than she'd been at hour-zero. She still had moments when her despair made her want to lay in bed and never get up.

She didn't have a family. David had been her family.

Of course, David had relatives. They had also lost a son and a brother. They had been devastated.

"One hundred and twelve people died that day," she muttered against Efe's shoulder.

One hundred and twelve members of family and friends who had grieved for their loved ones. One year on, had they all moved on? Had the pain gotten less?

Not for her. Her heart still ached each time she thought about David. Every night she dreamt about him.

As quiet tears rolled down her face, someone shoved tissues into her hand. She dabbed her face before lifting her head.

"The wine is making me weepy," she tried for a joke. They spent the evening here to cheer her up not for her to drag them down into her gloom.

"Yeah, lightweight." Lade made a mock face. "You never could hold your drink."

Somma smiled. "I blame you. Your blood must be one-quarter alcohol. No one can keep up with you."

Efe laughed. "Molade is pretty hardcore but Somma you're definitely a lightweight. Every time we went clubbing, you would end up falling asleep on the dance floor."

Somma burst out laughing. "OMG! I was terrible, wasn't I?"

"You were hilarious," Lade chimed in as both of her friends joined in the giggling.

"We had to practically dance around you just to make sure you didn't tip over or something," Efe said between chuckles.

"I can't believe what we got up to in those days." Somma shook her head as she remembered the days just after they'd left university. "Working all day and partying all night. Something had to give."

"Yeah, you." Both her friends chorused.

"It's not my fault alcohol made me sleepy." And weepy, it seemed. "It's been forever since we did anything like that."

"Yes, that's because you refuse to leave the house. You practically live like a hermit."

"Yeah, a hermit with mod-cons."

"But even so. I don't think I could go partying all night like we used to. Anyway, all that is for young people."

"Young people, *ke*? Please speak for yourself." Lade preened, tugging at her sleeves and lifting her shoulders. "Some of us are still very young."

Efe lifted her hand and covered the side of her mouth as if about to share a secret, but her voice stayed loud enough for Omolade to hear. "She's only feeling young because she picked up a toyboy. You should see her new beau."

"Is that so?" Somma glanced from one friend to the other. "Lade, You didn't tell me you were dating anyone?"

"I won't call the thing they are doing dating," Efe cut in.

Omolade grinned. "Who asked you?"

"Dating or not, I want to hear the gist of this man." Somma was happy to forget her troubles and immerse herself in her friends' love lives. "Who is he? What is his name? Where did you meet him?"

"His name is Jaiyesimi. I met him at Fola's wedding."

"Fola's wedding?" Somma asked with a frown on her friend. Fola was another mutual friend from University days but not as close as Efe or Lade.

"She got married months ago. Remember? You didn't go because you were still in mourning."

"Yes." Somma grimaced. The memory returned. She'd been invited to the wedding but had politely refused, citing her mourning period although she had officially been released by her in-laws. She hadn't felt up to celebrating, not when it hadn't been long since she'd lost her husband.

Her chest constricted. Not wanting to wallow in self-pity again, she diverted attention to her friend. "So you've been dating him for months, and you never said anything to me?"

"We weren't exactly dating."

"I told you," Efe chimed in and laughed when Lade swatted her thigh.

"Shush. I'm the one telling the story," Lade said, raising her brow in a mock glare and resting her left hand on her hip. "Where was I, *jare*?"

Somma giggled. Her friends were crazy, but she loved them just as much as they loved her. "You weren't exactly dating Jaiyesimi?"

"Oh, yes. After a lousy marriage, I have a lot of catching up to do. So Jaiye and I were doing everything but dating at the beginning."

"Basically you were bonking like rabbits at every opportunity," Efe joked.

"We're still bonking like rabbits, but we try and do other things as well." Lade didn't even blink.

"Like what?" Somma asked.

"Like eat food." Lade grinned like the cat that got the cream.

"Oh, my goodness." Somma bent over with laughter.

"Stopping to eat food in between a sex marathon isn't a dinner date," Efe quipped.

"It's an improvement from waking up hungry the next morning," Lade replied.

The three of them practically broke down with laughter.

Somma held her hurting ribs. She hadn't laughed so much in a long time. "Seriously though, how old is your young man?"

"He's twenty-eight," Lade replied.

"She's now a cougar," Efe added.

Somma laughed. "Doesn't there have to be at least a ten-year gap for her to be classified as a cougar? Plus she's not even forty."

They were all in their mid-thirties, although Omolade was the oldest at thirty-six.

"She's getting there," Efe said.

"So are you," Lade replied.

"Exactly," Efe said. "I still wonder how you have the energy to keep up with him. These days I'm happy to curl up with a good book and a glass of wine."

"Are you serious?" Somma said. "I would rather curl up with David any day."

A pang hit her chest. There were so many things she still wanted to do with her late husband. She couldn't understand why anyone would prefer to miss out on the opportunity.

"My dear, that's because you don't have four children running you ragged on top of everything else. Where is the energy to *do* at the end of the day? Plus I don't want to get pregnant again."

"Use contraceptive then," Lade said, always quick off the mark.

"Was I not on contraceptive when I got pregnant with the last two? Enofe's sperms are just way too active, and he refuses to have a vasectomy. I'm not taking the chance. Abstinence, *abeg*."

"Men and their aversion to surgical procedures." Lade shook her head. "After four children, hasn't he had enough?"

"That's why I've told him to go and retire his loaded weapon." Efe lifted her fingers in the sign of a gun. "Bang and you're pregnant. No. *I don tire*."

The ladies burst out laughing again.

CHAPTER TWO

"I'll call you tomorrow and see how you're doing," Efe said as she climbed into the back seat of the charcoal BMW SUV.

"I'll be fine," Somma replied, waving her hand in a 'don't worry' gesture.

"We know you'll be fine," Lade said through the open window beside Efe. "But you know she'll still worry if she doesn't check in with you."

"Okay. I'll talk to you tomorrow," Somma conceded. "Goodnight."

Efe was the mother of the group, always checking to see how everyone was doing, especially since David's passing.

"Bye," Lade said. "We'll talk soon."

"Bye," Efe said.

Somma watched as the chauffeur drove the car through the open gateway, glad she didn't have to worry about her friend drinking alcohol and driving. The red taillights blinked in the night before the car disappeared after turning right into the road.

She swivelled and headed indoors as the security man pulled the metal barrier back in place.

The complex was made up of two duplexes. She and David had bought theirs outright, partly with the money she'd inherited after her parents' deaths and partly from David's investments portfolio. One of the best decisions they'd made because now she didn't have to worry about paying rent. No matter what else happened, she had a roof over her head.

Inside, she shut and double-locked the steel-reinforced sand-coloured front door. In the silence of the night, the sounds echoed, an indication of the ample space within.

And of her loneliness.

This house hadn't been designed for a single person. It had been built as a family home, to accommodate a couple and children.

The frost-coloured foyer led to a dining area to her immediate right. The living room stood opposite, and the kitchen lay to her left.

Efe and Omolade had helped her wash up the crockery they'd used for dinner and drinks, so she didn't have to worry about tidying up. She didn't have live-in domestic staff, although a woman came once a week to clean the house.

She turned left, flicked on the light switch for the landing and climbed the stairs. A little tipsy, she held onto the cold metal balustrade with her left hand and bunched her long skirt with her right one to stop from tripping. Her leather flip-flops slapped against the concrete.

At the top, she flicked off the lights for downstairs in her nightly ritual before walking into the master bedroom. The other two rooms stood on the opposite side of the corridor, along with the main bathroom.

Not stopping, she stepped into the master bathroom to wash her face and brush her teeth.

The phone beeped, and she pulled it out of the pocket of her A-line cotton maxi skirt. An SMS from Efe read: *It was really great seeing you laugh so much today, Hun. We should do it again soon.*

She typed out a reply: Yes, I felt fantastic today. Still do. You and Lade are the best friends a girl can have. Of course, we'll do it again soon.

She tossed the phone on the counter. In the mirror, she caught the smile on her face. Her friends' visit had done wonders for her spirit, lifting the gloom hovering over her with their wacky conversations.

None of them had a perfect life. But they'd been there for each other, showing solidarity, no matter what happened.

They had all gotten married within two years of each other.

Efe had been the first to get married in a shotgun wedding of sorts. She'd been engaged to Enofe, but when they found out she was pregnant, they had to rush the wedding preparations so that the pregnancy didn't show on the wedding date. Ten years on, she was the only one in the group still married. She was also the only one with kids.

Omolade had been the last to marry and the first to break up. She'd been through a violent marriage which had ended in a vicious divorce. She had always been the backbone of the group. So when she'd revealed that her ex-husband had been abusive, they had rallied to provide whatever support she needed, even as far as having David and Enofe present when they'd helped Lade move out of her matrimonial home so that Kunle wouldn't try to hurt her like he'd threatened.

In the end, Lade had to take out a restraining order against the man to keep him at bay. After the divorce, Kunle seemed to have focused his hot air on other things.

After completing her ablutions, Somma entered the walk-in closet and opened a drawer. She was about to pick up one of her casual nightwears when she changed her mind and opened the drawer beneath.

This one stored exclusive lingerie—the ones she reserved for her times with David. He had loved sexy lingerie and had bought plenty, more than she'd ever needed. Satin babydoll sets, mesh teddy sets, silk camisole sets, and lace chemise sets filled the drawer in various shades—reds, pinks, whites, and blacks mainly.

Letting out a shallow exhale, she traced fingertips over the soft fabrics. She hadn't worn these since her husband died. It had felt like disrespecting him to wear them previously.

Now nostalgia made excitement flutter in her belly as she remembered how they'd loved and played in the outfits.

Would it be so wrong to experience the intimacy of the luxurious fabrics against her flesh one more time?

Her skin prickled with heat and her pulse rate increased.

Perhaps it was the alcohol in her veins that extinguished her inhibitions. Without further thought, she quickly pulled off her clothes, tossing them aside until she was completely naked.

Her hands shook a little as she pulled the first one she could reach out—a black babydoll with a padded pink satin bra that always made her boobs appear larger and mesh lace skirt that barely covered her bum. It came with matching thong-knickers which she always skipped on. No point in wearing panties when David was around. They were the first things he removed.

"David, I hope this is okay," she said in a quiet voice, feeling as if she needed his permission to wear these again.

As if in response, a chill went through the air and Goosebumps rose on her arms. Strange, because the air-con wasn't on. She didn't use the AC in this room as she'd opted for an electricity meter and didn't want to rack up extra high bills now she lived by herself.

She pulled the lingerie over her head and secured the clasp to her back. Then she pulled the knickers on. She picked up the discarded clothes and hung them over the upholstered armchair in the corner.

Remembering the phone she left in the bathroom, she grabbed it and headed for the king-size bed in the middle of the room covered in white cotton sheets, and an auburn patterned duvet cover folded at the foot of the mattress that matched the window drapes.

She lay on the fresh sheet, head on the pillow and stared at David's picture in a frame on the bedside table. Another nightly ritual which soothed her sometimes when she was inconsolable.

Tonight, she didn't have the weighted heart of previous evenings.

In the picture, her husband smiled as warmly as the first time she'd met him.

She hadn't been a believer in love at first sight when she'd met David. In fact, the first time she'd met him, she'd been annoyed at him because he'd been trying to wiggle his way past her in a queue.

She'd been in her favourite eatery where she'd popped in to grab a late lunch. As usual, the place had been packed, and she'd been in the queue, waiting for her turn to be served. She'd been on her phone exchanging messages with Efe when someone bumped into her and then cut into the line before her.

Shocked, she'd glanced up from her phone to find broad shoulders spread across a navy suit in front of her. He hadn't been there before.

"Excuse me." She'd tapped his back.

He didn't move or respond to her but seemed to be talking to the girl at the counter.

Bristling and not deterred by his lack of response, she stepped around and stood beside him before pulling the sleeve of his jacket. "It's my turn."

He turned to her then, dark eyes narrowed in annoyance. "You were preoccupied with your phone. I'm in a hurry."

With a hitch of her breath, she caught herself staring at the firm features of his face and wondering why God made insanely handsome men arrogant or was it that He made proud men crazily attractive.

Handsome or not, she wasn't about to let him railroad her out of her spot. "You're just grasping for an excuse to behave like an uncouth lout. Everyone here has behaved themselves and waited their turn except you. Step back and join the queue."

His eyes narrowed, and his jaw tensed.

The man she challenged was bigger and taller than her. If he didn't move, she couldn't shift him without someone else's intervention. No one else had challenged him.

Usually, she would let things like that slide if the man had apologised when she'd first tapped him. But blaming her had only riled her and made her dig her heels in.

Then his hard face melted into a smile, and he turned to the girl at the counter, "Can you add whatever she's having to my bill." He glanced back at Somma. "What would you like?"

"I can buy my own lunch." She didn't take kindly to his bribe.

"I know you can. But you're in a hurry. I'm in a hurry. This is a compromise. I'll pay for whatever you're having, and we'll call it even."

"Fine," she said and ordered her usual grilled chicken and Caesar salad. Not wanting to get sucked into the compelling presence that Mr Uncouth Lout oozed, she took the ticket and went to find a free table to wait for the food.

As she sat down, her eyes still searched and picked him out of the crowd. The place was full of professionals who worked in the business district, so being in a suit wasn't unusual.

However, Mr Uncouth carried himself with a commanding air of self-confidence that made every woman look at him, including Somma.

She couldn't look away or shake the heat that skittered down her skin when he turned and headed in her direction. His movements were swift, full of grace and virility.

He wasn't bulky in terms of muscles from what she could see in the fit of his suit. He was more athletic—tight, lean and sinewy.

The lines etched on his face made him appear older than her, maybe in his mid-thirties.

He stopped by her, a bone-melting smile on his face as he placed a takeaway pack on the table. "My name is David Orji. The lady at the counter told me your name is Somma and that you come here frequently."

"Yes. And?" She wasn't ready to be charmed by him.

His grin widened. "And you had me at 'uncouth lout' back there. I would love to have lunch with you tomorrow."

Her heart raced at the idea of meeting him again. But she couldn't give in. Men like him were trouble.

"I wouldn't," she managed to say in a bored voice.

"Come on. Give me a chance to redeem myself."

"We called it even, remember? You paid for my lunch already."

"But I want the chance to show you that I can be a gentleman." He glanced at his watch and pulled out a thick business card from the inside of his jacket, which he passed to her.

A tingle of excitement raced through her as his long fingers grazed hers. "I've really got to go now. I'll see you tomorrow."

Before she could respond, he grabbed his food-to-go, swivelled and strode out of the restaurant.

CHAPTER THREE

David stood in the shaded corner of the room and watched his wife drift off to sleep. Even if he had wanted to be somewhere else, she had inadvertently summoned him when she'd spoken his name in a sensuous voice and asked if she could wear the satin lingerie.

He was never far from her anyway. Wherever he existed all it would take for him to be beside her would be for her to whisper his name. As it was, he felt her every emotion, in all its extremities, magnified a thousandfold.

In the past months, she'd been in a state of depression, a desperate expression of her grief. He hadn't known she would be as devastated as she'd been at losing him. Her heartbreak had tormented him for the past year. He had been in Hell, physically wrenched and torn to shreds by her cries and despair.

The only way to soothe her had been through her dreams, which had healed him in turn. Only for the whole cycle to repeat itself when she fell into a depression again.

Each time her friends visited, her spirits had lifted only for her to sink back into darkness after they left.

Today had been a good day for her. Different.

It seemed she had turned a corner. Perhaps it was reaching one annual cycle since the plane crash.

His spirit had lifted as hers had done, soaring and rejuvenating him. His energy had been boosted to almost its peak.

There was only one thing that would make his power complete. And as he stared at her sleeping form, his craving swelled.

Heat flared from his skin, radiating into the room.

Unable to keep away, he stepped closer. With a flick of the switch in his mind, the whole house descended into darkness.

While he remained at less than peak strength, the artificial lighting stole his form and blurred his sight.

His vision became magnified in the dark, and his body took shape.

He tugged the sheet she'd used to cover up, all the way down until he revealed the sexy lace nightwear that barely covered her flawless cinnamon skin.

The sight snatched his breath away. His fingers tingled with the need to caress her smooth skin and his mouth moistened from wanting to taste her essence.

From the moment he'd met her, as she'd spewed blistering words at him for jumping the queue, she had captured his heart.

He attracted women. It was in his nature to charm and seduce.

Yet, none of them had ever captivated him. Until Somma.

The afternoon he'd met her, he'd been in a hurry to get to a meeting about a contract his company had bid to execute. Otherwise, he would've cancelled and stayed with her for lunch so he could find out more about her. The best he could do at the time had been to ask her to meet him for lunch the next day.

After his meeting had concluded, he'd called his mother to break the news that he had found *the one*.

"Mum, I found her," he'd said as soon as his mother had answered the call.

He hadn't even bothered with pleasantries. That was how important it had been to share the piece of news.

"Who?" she'd asked, her surprise carrying through the telephone connection.

"The one. The woman I'm going to marry," he replied as he sat in the back seat of the car being driven by his chauffeur.

"Who is she? Where is she from?"

"I met her briefly today. All I know is her name, Somma, and what she looks like. But I know she's the one."

"How do you know she's the one based on one encounter? She might not be suitable."

"Oh, mum. You won't understand it. As she stood there raining down a tirade on me for cutting into her place in the line, a bolt of lightning hit me and everything became clear at that moment. I just knew in my heart."

It was a strange thing to explain to someone who hadn't experienced something similar, knowing with one glance that Somma was meant for him and him for her.

"David, I do understand. Your father was the same way with me. He told me he would marry me the first day he met me."

"He did? And what did you say to him."

"I told him he was crazy." His mother's soft laughter filled his ear.

He smiled. "You did?"

"Yes. I liked him, but I thought he had to be insane to make that kind of declaration when he didn't even know me. But weeks later, he showed up at my parents' house with his uncles to introduce himself."

"Wow. I didn't know this story."

"Well—" in his mind's eye, he saw his mother's shoulders lift in a shrug. "—it hasn't been important to tell it before. But if you're sure that you've met your future wife, then I can't wait to meet her."

"Yeah. I can't wait for you to meet her too. First, I have to find her again. I invited her to lunch tomorrow, but she initially turned me down. I hope she'll show up."

More tinkling laughter filled his ear. "She sounds like she will give you a hard time."

"She already gave me a hard time this afternoon." He smiled as he remembered Somma's brown eyes blazing with fury as she glared at him.

"Then she sounds perfect for you. Bring her to see me soon."

"Okay, I will."

"Bye, David."

"Bye, Mum."

Of course, his mother had been correct about Somma giving him a hard time. She didn't show up for their lunchtime date. Neither the next day nor the rest of the week.

Every day he'd shown up at the restaurant and asked them if she'd turned up. They'd said no. He would sit there for most of the afternoon break until he had to go back to his office.

Two weeks later, he'd taken his search online and eventually tracked her down through her Facebook profile. He'd found out she was a co-host for a literary radio show at a local station and staked out the building.

Luckily, he caught her as she left to go home one evening.

She looked stunning in her yellow and blue bolero-style jacket and high-waist wide-legged navy trousers matched with Ankara and cork platform sandals. Her long braided hair was packed in a crown-like bun.

"You do know that it's rude to not show up for an appointment without any call or messages," he said as he strode up beside Somma.

She glanced at him, eyes wide, and lips apart. Her mouth opened and closed a few times before she spoke. "Mr Un—David, what are you doing here?"

He smiled, knowing she'd been about to call him Mr Uncouth Lout. "I came to see you. As I said, we had a date, and you didn't show up. Not a very nice thing for a well-mannered woman to do."

"I didn't agree to any date." She stiffened and bit the corner of her bottom lip.

The early evening light showed the pulse at the base of her neck beating fast.

"I asked you to meet me for lunch, and you didn't say no. I gave you my card. You could've called to cancel if you didn't want to meet."

She glanced away and kicked a pebble. "I'm sorry. I should've called, but I didn't want you getting an even bigger head than you've already got."

She might have been speaking metaphorically, but a real head was swelling in his groin from just watching and listening to her. He was naturally a highly sexual being, and he struggled to keep his mind clear of intimate thoughts.

He diverted his mind to mundane things. "If you really want to apologise, you can come to dinner with me tonight."

She shook her head and walked across the car park. "I'm not going to dinner with you. I don't know you."

He kept pace with her. "You would've known me better by now if you'd come to lunch. If you come to dinner with me, you can ask me any questions you want to ask."

"No."

"Okay. Not dinner. Do you have a car?"

She shook her head.

"Then let me take you home," he said.

She opened her mouth to speak, and he raised his hand.

"And before you say no, would you be satisfied if someone you know vouches for me, so you know that I'm not a murderer or a psycho?"

"I guess so." She shrugged.

He raised his hand in the direction of one the radio station staff he saw approaching. "Mike, hello."

"David." The man glanced in his direction before pressing the fob in his hand, and the lights on a red Nissan Almera flashed. "How are you? It's been a while."

"I'm doing great. And how are you?"

"You know, same old, same old. What are you doing here?" Mike pointed at the building which housed the radio station and other businesses.

"I came to see Somma." David brushed his fingertips on her shoulder and tingles shot up his arm. Being near her was like being exposed to a live wire, and he loved how she made him feel.

"Okay. Well, I have to go now. Have a good evening," Mike said and opened his car door in a hurry.

"Same to you, Mike." David turned back to Somma, who had watched the exchange silently. "So now there is someone who can say they saw me with you if anything happens. But I promise you nothing will harm you tonight." or any other night if he could help it.

"Look, you're a charming man, and you might be genuine. But I don't know how you know Mike, the station manager. The two of you could be in collusion, and he could cover up for you. The only people I trust fully are my friends so if you don't mind I'm going to take a picture of you and your car and send it to them, so they know who I'm with."

Clever girl. His admiration for her grew tenfold at her quick thinking and not accepting his words. Although he had good intentions, he remained a stranger, and she should be wary.

"Of course you can." He beamed a charming smile as she lifted her phone from her tote and took snaps of him.

She then typed something on her phone. Afterwards, she followed him to the car and got into the back seat with him. The enclosed space enhanced her feminine scent, and deep longing for her gnawed at his gut.

He wanted to spend more time with her this evening. "Now that your friends know who you're with, is it okay if we go to dinner before I take you home?"

"You really are persistent." She shook her head and smiled. "Yes, you can take me out to dinner—"

The phone in her hand played a musical tune from Fela's Shakara, cutting off her words. She lifted the gadget to her ear, and he couldn't help smiling at the irony of the song.

"Lade, hi," she said into the phone.

Although he could hear the tinny sound of someone on the other end of the conversation, he focused on Somma's words, enjoying the sweet tone of her voice.

"I'm in the car with David."

"Yes, he's the same guy that I told about. Mr-You-Know." She glanced at him and looked away as if blushing.

"He's actually taking me out to dinner so I won't be home early."

"You want to speak to him? ... Hold on." She turned to him and held out her phone. "My friend, Omolade, wants to talk to you."

He took the phone and pressed the speaker button. "Hello, this is David."

"Hello, David. My name is Omolade Sawyer. I'm sure you know what that means because my father is the Chief Justice of this country. Somma is my best friend. So if anything happens to her. If she doesn't come home in one piece tonight, there's nowhere you can hide in this country. As I'm talking, your picture has been forwarded to the Secret Services liaison so you can be sure that they will track you down."

David's breath hitched, and he suppressed a bark of laughter, not wanting to make light of the threat. "You can be certain that I won't let your friend come to harm. I'll bring her home in one piece after dinner."

"Good," Omolade said. "The two of you should enjoy your evening."

"Same to you."

The line went dead. He grinned as he handed the phone back to Somma who watched him with head cocked to the side and eyes narrowed in a wary gaze.

"Is she for real?" he asked, still amused by the phone conversation.

"Yes. You don't mind her brashness?"

"No. I think it's wonderful that you have friends who care enough to protect you from danger. But I'm curious about your choice of ringtone. I guess you're a Fela fan."

"I am. I never got to watch him perform live, but I love his music. I match his tracks as the ringtone to my friends. So Omolade is 'Shakara' because she really is the queen of Shakara and my other friend Efe is 'Lady.'"

"Oh, I see. So what track would you match with me?"

"Zombie," she said, quick fire.

"Oh, come on!" he raised his brow.

She laughed, the tinkling sound sending arousing signals down his spine.

"Okay. What about 'Mr. Follow-Follow'?" She gave him a devious smile.

He chuckled. "You can't be serious."

She giggled again. "Okay. On a serious note, I think 'Trouble Sleep Yanga Wake Am' is more you. But for now, I'll go with 'Who're You?'"

He nodded slowly as he thought about it. "That makes sense. But I'm hoping the track you choose for me eventually will be 'Lover.'"

CHAPTER FOUR

Somma dreamt about David. It wasn't the first she'd imagined him since his death.

Usually, their encounters in dreams were brief and hazy, and the overwhelming emotions would be of sorrow.

Tonight was different.

Her sorrow diminished, overwhelmed by a different energy wave—vibrant and sexual. It radiated around the room and seeped into her pores.

Heat flushed her skin and sweat coated her skin. She writhed and tangled in the sheets.

"Oh, David. I wish you were here," she murmured, craving his touch to make the fever burn bright and give her ultimate satisfaction.

"I know you do, my sweet. That's why I'm right here," a deep voice whispered back.

Her eyelids fluttered open.

Silver moonlight peeked through the gap in the drapes covering the window. A shadow stood at the foot of the bed. Her husband. It wasn't the first time she'd conjured him into her dream. This was another illusion of her mind.

"David," her voice choked as her throat tightened. "I miss you so much."

"I miss you, too, my sweet." He shifted to the left-hand side. His side of the bed.

The air undulated around her in a rhythm that made her body writhe, heat flushing through her. Tingles spread on her body. Her breast became heavy, and her nipples chafed against the satin negligee.

"Oh," she moaned and kicked off the bed cover making her hot.

"Somma," he said her name in a sexy drawl. "You're wearing undies. Naughty girl."

Her cheeks heated at his chiding tone. He never liked her wearing panties when she was in sexy lingerie.

"I thought it would be okay since you weren't here. I'm sorry," she replied.

"Now, I'm going to have to take it off, and you know what that means." Hands grabbed her thighs, yanking them apart.

Her insides clutched in expectation, and she gasped for air when his face hovered above her crotch. Electrified warm air fanned her skin, making it sensitive.

Her heart raced and desire coursed through her veins.

He grabbed the edge of the panties with his teeth and tugged. Her hips seemed to lift by their own volition, and the underwear slid down her legs and off.

One minute David stood by her bed with her pink knickers between his lips. Next, he wore them over his groin.

Her breath hitched. But she reminded herself that this was a dream, and all kinds of weird things happened in dreams.

Still, watching her hunk of a husband dressed in nothing but her undies sent her pulse rate into overdrive. In the dimness, the contrast between his dark skin and the pink lace was even more apparent. The counterpoint of powerful lean muscles against delicate feminine underwear was one of the most erotic things she'd ever seen.

Her husband became even more turned on when he wore her knickers as proven by the fat bulge now looking like it would burst through the fragile fabric.

"Lift your hands up," he said in a husky voice.

She didn't hesitate to obey, and in the blink of an eye, her wrists were bound to the wooden slats at the headboard with silk ties.

She loved this whole fantasy sex thing. Time seemed irrelevant.

Perhaps if she focused, she could get David to suck her pussy and blow her mind the way only he could.

But her husband seemed to have other plans. He appeared on the bed, above her, his knees either side of her chest while his groin hovered over her face.

She could do this too. Focus on his pleasure.

She lifted her head and nuzzled his bulge through the soft fabric. She breathed in the unique scent of him—musky and woody notes of bergamot and baked earth.

His smell intoxicated and gave a heady high.

"Mmhmm," she moaned, rubbing him over and over.

His breathing quickened, and his hips gyrated as he held her head to him.

"You're going to make me come in your panties," his voice was guttural, showing how close to the edge he was.

David loved being in command. Sometimes, when they made love, he gave her the reins. Not often.

"Is that such a bad thing?" she asked before she tongued the damp patch on the lace smudged with his precum. She tasted the salty flavour and proceeded to mouth the ridged head of his cock.

"No," he sounded croaky. "But I want to feel the inside of your mouth first."

He pushed the edge of the knickers down. His dick sprang free and smacked her face.

Her eyes went wide. He had expanded more than she remembered.

"Open your mouth for me."

"You're too big." She glanced up at his face that remained in the dark. She could only see his eyes and the side of his face.

"Trust me." The pad of his fingers grazed her right cheek. "You'll be fine."

She trusted him. Granted, this was a fantasy David. But he was still her husband, and he had never hurt her before. He wouldn't hurt her now.

She parted her lips, and the beefy crown of his cock slid past them. She rolled her tongue around the smooth flesh and veiny underside before opening wide to let him ram home.

"Yes," he breathed, pulling out and gliding back in. "You feel so good. So warm and wet and welcoming. It's been too long."

Each time he nudged the back of her mouth, his balls encased in the satin rubbed her chin. He loved to fuck her this way. The restraint of the fabric on his scrotum drew out his pleasure and made him last longer than without them. He'd told her once that his orgasms when he wore her underwear were exponentially more fulfilling than without them.

"Hang on," he said and pulled out. "I need to taste you."

He turned around and positioned himself so that his head hovered over her pussy and his groin over her face.

Her body trembled, and adrenaline surged through her. Her husband did cunnilingus like it was an Olympic Sport. He was her number-one star athlete every time. Her Olympic Champion.

She opened her mouth and took his crown back just as his fingers parted her labia and exposed her engorged clitoris.

"Do you know you have a scent and taste just before you climax, which is different from you just being turned on?" he asked, his breath warm on her sensitive flesh.

Her mouth was full of him, so she didn't answer. He was right. Her body was primed and ready, although he hadn't done anything to her. Yet.

The flow of the energized air around her felt like many caresses on her skin. Her nipples tightened, her body twisted as he held her down. Her pulse rate skyrocketed, and her channel clenched again and again.

His question seemed rhetorical, anyway. He didn't wait for a response and pressed his tongue down on the swollen bundle of nerves.

She came apart, thrashing around and letting out a long moan which was stifled by his shaft still in her mouth. Her first orgasm in a year, it washed over her in waves.

"That's my girl," David murmured as he covered her body with his and held onto her.

His cock popped out of her mouth, and he turned around. He stroked her neck, making her skin tingle.

She sighed and tilted her head on the pillow to watch him. She still couldn't see all of him, just the mass of rippling muscles when the light caught them.

He kissed a path to her breast while stroking her belly and reigniting her desire. He palmed her breasts, weighing and squeezing them.

"Oh," a moan escaped her lips and pleasure zinged around her body.

Hot tongue rolled over her right nipple while he tugged the other with thumb and forefinger until it hardened into a bullet.

An electric arc made her clit throb and her core clenched with need.

"Please, David," she couldn't help begging as the restlessness returned.

"What do you want?" he asked after lifting his head from her breast.

"I need you inside me," she said in a breathless voice, not getting enough air into her lungs.

He leaned back and stared at her body. "Open your legs. Let me see you."

He loved to admire her body, especially when she wasn't wearing panties. Luckily she'd trimmed her pubic hairs into clean lines. He preferred her to be totally smooth. But she hadn't seen the point of shaving everything after his demise. No one was going to see it but her.

"Next time, I want you to shave it all off," he said as he trailed a finger to her opening, making her shiver.

"Next time?" she asked in a confused voice. As much as she loved his presence, this was still a dream.

"Yes, next time. Or don't you want me here?" There was an urgency to his question as if so much depended on her answer.

"Of course, I want you here. I miss you when you're not here."

"Good." He opened her up. "You're so beautiful. Your clit is begging for my tongue again."

He flicked his tongue in a circle around her nub.

A thrill coursed through her body. She panted, fever rushing through her body.

"I need to be inside you now. Is that okay, my sweet?" He thrust a finger into her wet channel.

"Oh, David. Yes, please."

He nudged her thighs apart and settled between them as his cock pressed against her slit. She tilted her hips, and slowly he pushed in an inch at a time, filling her up.

It felt so good having him inside her. Tears pricked the back of her eyes. She really had missed him and the intimacy they had shared amongst other aspects. David had been highly sexual, and they'd made love in one form or the other at least once a day when he'd been alive except when she'd been on her cycle.

Now he rammed all the way in, tilted his head back and let out a long groan that bounced off the walls. The whole room pulsated, and her body trembled as fever rushed through her, and she climaxed again.

He gripped her hips and slammed into her again and again, reawakening her body only to send her into more bliss before she came down from the last.

She felt him in every pore, and every part of her body became an erogenous area. The slapping sound of flesh against flesh, as well as their groans, matched the whoosh of blood in her ears.

His body glowed. It was a weird thing like a flickering bulb during an electricity low current, not quite bright enough to light up the room but still visible.

Before she could process why that was happening another throe of orgasm hit and exhaustion took over.

As she drifted off, he cocooned her with his body and whispered in her ear. "Thank you, my sweet."

***

Somma stirred slowly, her body weighed down, languid. She lifted her eyelids and blinked a few times.

Sunlight streamed in through the embroidered navy blue heavy curtains. The scent of bergamot, burnt earth and sex lingered in the air. Perspiration made her body cling to the sheets.

It must have been a hot night for her to be so sweaty. She swung her legs out of bed and realized that she wasn't wearing panties. Just the babydoll outfit she'd put on last night.

Had she taken the underwear off?

She frowned and glanced around. The knickers were on the bedside table along with one of David's silk ties. How did those get there?

The dream from last night replayed in her mind. David had been with her. But that had been a dream. Fantasy didn't make physical objects move.

Had she removed the undies last night before she'd slept off and placed the ties next to her bed? Maybe that's what happened which would explain the dream.

Shaking her head, she walked to the bathroom and took the lingerie off. Her thighs felt sticky. Out of curiosity, she slid her fingers into her pussy. It was soaked with her juice and what looked like semen.

Her heart thudded in her chest, and she sat on the cover of the WC with a thud as her legs gave way.

Had she really had sex last night with David?

Don't be ridiculous, she chided herself.

Dead men don't have sex, do they?

CHAPTER FIVE

"You're looking so amazing," Efe commented as they sat on low leather sofas in a quiet corner of a bar six weeks later.

Somma went out to dinner with Lade and Efe for Lade's thirty-seventh birthday. They had a meal at a restaurant and transferred to a jazz lounge for drinks. Afro beats music played in the background, and it wasn't loud enough to drown out conversations.

"Thank you," Somma replied. She felt amazing. She'd even started socializing again.

She'd shoved aside the ridiculous idea that fantasy sex with David had somehow become real intercourse in her bedroom.

She'd read all kinds of articles about the brain as a wondrous organ and only doing a fraction of what it could potentially do. So perhaps somehow her mind had become overactive and sent signals to her body that she'd really had sex. There had to be an entirely logical explanation other than she'd had sex with a ghost which was impossible anyway.

But the David dreams hadn't stopped.

In fact, she looked forward to falling asleep and waking sated. She had even started shaving all the hair off from her nether regions just to keep him happy. Every night she would wear a different sexy negligee and leave the knickers out for him.

Every morning she would wake up with the languidness of someone who had been thoroughly loved.

One remarkable result was that her depression waned and gradually she was back to the energy levels she'd had when David had been alive.

The draft manuscript for a novel she'd been struggling with for eight months, she had completed in four weeks as David became her muse. The story flowed, and her fingers flew over the keyboard every time she sat with her laptop.

"Yes, you look fabulous," Fola who sat to Somma's right on the sofa said, drawing Somma out of her thoughts. "I was saying at dinner that you are glowing."

"Thank you," Somma replied as her cheeks heated.

"You have to tell us your beauty secret." Lade grinned at her. "Is it a fresh diet or a new makeup technique?"

Somma laughed and shifted in her seat. Usually, she would be happy to tell all about her love life. But she hesitated and took a sip of the refreshing non-alcoholic cocktail.

"If I didn't know better, I'd say she was pregnant." Fola had a weird smile on her face.

Somma nearly choked on her drink as it went down the wrong way. She broke into a coughing fit. Efe patted her back as the ladies expressed their concerns.

She eventually calmed down.

"I'm not pregnant, although I wish I were." She lowered her voice. "Actually I've been feeling amazing the past few weeks. It's like David is with me and he's telling me to get on with my life. So I am."

Omolade nodded. "Makes sense."

Efe tilted her head to the side in a confused look. "What do you mean by David is with you?"

"He's been visiting me in dreams." She couldn't possibly tell them that the dreams were becoming more vivid and she was struggling to differentiate between reality and illusions.

"You mean he's haunting you," Fola said with a frown.

"He's not haunting me. He doesn't do anything bad." Not unless they classified sex as bad. "And it's just dreaming."

"So what exactly does he do when he visits your dream?" Lade now looked more interested.

Somma's cheeks flamed, and she picked up her drink and took a sip. "You know."

"You're having sex with a ghost!" Fola said with a shocked gasp.

"Lower your voice!" Efe hissed. "We don't need everyone hearing this."

"Sorry," Fola lowered her voice and leaned forward. "But if your dead husband is having sex with you, then you're being haunted, and you will need an exorcism."

"*Exor-kini*?" Lade glanced at Fola, brows raised.

"I'm serious," Fola said. "I know someone very good at those sorts of things."

"You're mad," Somma said. "I'm perfectly fine. I don't need an exor-whatever."

"Somma, she has a point though. What if there's something else going on?" Efe said.

"Oh, come on. Not you as well, Efe." Somma stared at her friend, wide-eyed. "Then again I suppose you have a thing against sex anyway, Mrs Loaded Weapon."

Efe laughed. "Yes. Maybe I'm biased. But I can't help worrying."

"What's there to worry about? You all said I look amazing, *and* I feel amazing. So there's nothing wrong."

"I'm with Somma. There's no point swallowing Panadol when there is no headache. She looks fab to me, and there's nothing wrong with sexy dreams. It's just her imagination. She's a writer, after all."

"Maybe I'm wrong, *sha*," Fola said and shrugged. "Maybe it's just her imagination going wild. But if things start happening around you that don't look normal, you have to ask for help. That kind of thing can lead to madness. I've seen it happen."

"Oh," Somma gasped and fidgeted with her necklace at Fola's mention of strange things. Her mind went to all the objects that have moved around her house recently that she could swear she didn't move, especially the sex objects.

One morning she'd woken to find the armchair in her bedroom had relocated from the foot of the bed to the window after she'd made love with David on it in her dream. It and David had appeared by the window where he'd instructed her to climb onto his rigid shaft and ride him while he bucked like a bronco. She'd woken up achy from the physical exertion.

"What is it?" Efe asked, pulling her out of the memory. The woman didn't miss anything.

"It's nothing." Somma didn't want to entertain where this conversation headed. The fact that they sat as professional women didn't elude her. Efe was head of a children's charity. Lade was a top lawyer, and Fola was a physiotherapist. Yet they all sat here talking about ghosts and exorcisms.

"I don't believe you," Efe insisted. "Something has happened that isn't in a dream. Am I right?"

"Yes, but it is not serious," Somma tried to appease her friend's concern. "Just some items have been moved around in the house. There has to be a simple explanation. I could've forgotten that I moved the objects."

They all stared at her with bulging eyes and open mouths as if she'd just revealed the most horrific thing. Even skeptical Lade appeared alarmed.

She leaned back in her seat and let out a heavy sigh. For the first time this evening she wished she hadn't told them anything. Her belly tied in knots.

"Honey." Efe took her hand. "It sounds like there's a little more going on. But as you say it could be nothing. Having someone who knows what to do to check it out and give you the all-clear is a good idea."

Somma shook her head. "I don't know."

"Please do it for me. You know I'm not going to sleep because I'm going to worry about you."

"That's blackmail, Efe."

"I know. Please."

"Okay. Fine," Somma grumbled. "I'll go and see Fola's pastor." She assumed she would have to attend church service with Fola to be able to see the man.

"It's probably best if I speak to her and she comes to your house," Fola said with a pensive expression. "It's usually the house that is haunted, and that's what she needs to see."

"How the hell do you know all these about ghosts and haunting?" Lade asked.

"One of my relatives had the same problem, and we had to get help for her," Fola replied.

"So your pastor is a woman?" Somma asked.

"Yes and she's mighty." Fola pulled her phone from her purse. "Let me call her." She stood up and walked towards the exit to make the phone call.

"Gosh. I need another drink," Lade said and stood up. "Anyone want anything?"

"Same for me," Efe said and stood up as well. "I'm going to call the nanny and make sure the kids are okay."

"Just get me lemonade," Somma said. She could use something substantial, but she needed to keep her wits about her tonight with all the talk about exorcisms.

As soon as she was left alone, Somma heard a Fela tune playing. The sound was so familiar that she smiled and swayed to the music. At first, she thought it was from the speakers in the venue until she realized her phone was buzzing in her bag. She pulled it out and saw that it was ringing and playing Lover by Fela Kuti, the track that she'd set as her ringtone for David.

David was calling her.

No! She dropped the phone back into her bag like it had bitten her and jumped from the sofa just as Efe returned.

"What's the matter?"

"My ... phone ..." Somma's body trembled, and she could barely get the words out. She wrapped her arms around her midriff and swallowed. "My phone was ringing, and the caller ID said it was David."

Efe's eyes bulged. "David? Are you sure?"

"Yes. Have a look." Somma pointed at the bag.

Efe picked it up tentatively and pulled out the phone. It had stopped ringing.

"There's a missed call notification on here, but it says the number is unknown."

Somma grabbed the phone and swiped the screen. True enough, the notification showed 'unknown number.'

"I swear to you it said 'David' when it rang."

"But it could be another David."

"No, it's not. You know how I set the ringtones for my close friends and family."

"Yes, and which song was it playing?"

"Lover by Fela. You know the only person on my phone with that ring tone was David."

"But that number could've been reassigned to someone else, and they called you by mistake."

"No. Because I paid to have that number exclusively. I have the number on a SIM card at home. So unless someone just broke into my house tonight, then no one else used it."

This left only one other option.

She really was being haunted by her husband.

A dizzy spell swept through her, and she sat slowly on the chair, staring blankly at her phone.

Efe came and sat beside her. "This is serious, Somma."

She nodded her head and swallowed again but couldn't speak. What was there to say?

Omolade returned with the drinks. "What's going on?" she asked when she saw their glum expressions.

Efe explained the situation, and they all sat silently, sipping their drinks, the mood now changed from one of fun to seriousness.

Fola returned and announced, "I have good news. She says she can come to yours tonight."

It seemed there would be an exorcism, after all.

CHAPTER SIX

Somma paced her living room floor as her friends sat around on the sofa. They'd arrived at her house about fifteen minutes earlier and awaited the arrival of Fola's pastor.

She fiddled with the necklace on her collar as her stomach churned. A sense of foreboding hung in the air, and she couldn't shake the feeling that something terrible would happen.

Now that she'd gotten home, she wished she hadn't agreed to an exorcism. Was it awful to have David's ghost visit her occasionally? Why were humans so afraid of the dead?

Granted, he had been in her dreams every night for the past six weeks. But he hadn't done anything horrific to her. He hadn't hurt her or caused her illness.

She was energetic and full of life. For the first time in months, she looked forward to each day with a sense of peace.

What would happen after David's ghost was exorcised? Would she go back to being depressed and wanting to join him in death?

She turned to her friends. "I have a bad feeling about this."

"Don't worry. Everything will be sorted out soon," Fola said.

"I don't know. Where is your pastor anyway?" Somma's gaze darted to the door.

"She'll be here any minute now. Just be patient." Fola leaned forward and picked her phone from the table to check it.

Patience didn't cut it at the moment. Somma's chest tightened, and her legs just wouldn't stay still. "I'm going to get a drink."

She left them and walked through the archway into the kitchen. As soon as she entered, the door shut behind her as if someone had pushed it. She startled, her gaze bounced around the space. Goosebumps rose on her bare arms, and the hairs on nape stood erect.

The scent of bergamot and baked earth floated in the air.

David was here.

Even without seeing him, she knew it. She felt none of the fear that had gripped her when her phone had rung while they'd been at the bar. Perhaps it was all the things her friends had said about ghosts and exorcisms that had put the fright into her.

Here and now, in her home, she didn't feel threatened by the thought of her dead husband visiting her. He had never hurt her while he was alive. And he hadn't hurt her in the past six weeks. She didn't think he ever would.

But she needed to understand what was going on and why he was visiting her.

"David, I know you're here," she whispered into the hot air. The temperature in the room seemed to be nearing the boiling point. Perspiration dripped down her neck and between the breasts and her dress clung to her clammy skin.

She glanced around the place and saw nothing except the usual kitchen equipment. She didn't know what to expect. Whether he would just appear to her. She'd only ever seen him while she'd been asleep. Even then he remained in shadows, and she never saw him illuminated, although sometimes he glowed while they made love.

Her mouth dried out and she strode to the fridge and withdrew a cold bottle of water. She found glass from the cupboard above and poured some liquid into it. After she drank some, she left the glass and bottle on the table.

"I need to know what's going on, David. You should be resting in peace not stalking me," she said in a loud voice as frustration took hold of her. At the moment, she felt as if she was going insane.

"Stalking you?"

A strong gust of air buffeted her, making her sway and she had to grip the kitchen counter so as not to fall over.

"Have you forgotten so soon? All those days and nights you cried because I wasn't here? Your heartbreak tormented me over and over. Now you're accusing me of stalking you?"

The back of her throat hurt and tears welled in her eyes. She struggled to keep upright. He was correct. She had wailed at his loss regularly. Perhaps he hadn't been able to rest in peace because she hadn't let him.

"You were my father, my brother, my best friend and my lover. You were my life. Losing you was devastating. I couldn't imagine life without you. I'm sorry." She crumpled on the floor tiles and burst into sobs.

"Don't cry, my sweet." Arms wrapped around her body, encasing her in the firm, warm skin.

She jerked back and wiped her eyes with her palms. Her mouth dropped open at the man sitting beside her on the kitchen floor.

David. He looked like she remembered him—handsome and fit, in the sky blue button-up shirt, navy jeans and tan leather boots. His head was cocked to the side and his brow furrowed in a wary expression.

Why wasn't she freaking out? A ghost sat next to her.

The sight of him was familiar and comforting. She'd enjoyed his company every night for the past six weeks. It felt natural to see him like this now. Her heart raced, and her breaths came quickly. But there wasn't an ounce of fear, just excitement.

She placed her hand on his chest, exploring. He was firm and warm. Beneath her palm, his heart thumped regularly.

"David, is this really you?" she asked, staring up at his face.

The high cheekbones, the prominent broad nose, the twinkle in his onyx eyes and the sensual lips looked the same as she remembered. She trailed her palm up to his chin, and the short hair bristled against her skin.

"Yes, it's me," he replied, the husky edge that she knew so well sending tingles down her spine.

"But how come? You don't look dead. Aren't ghosts supposed to be hollow and cold?" She leaned into him as if pulled by an invisible string. There was something about him, an aura that captivated her.

"I—" He didn't finish.

"Somma, are you okay?" Someone knocked at the door. Efe.

Shit. She'd forgotten about her friends and the exorcism.

She stood up and spoke in a clear voice. "Efe, I'm fine."

"The door is locked," her friend said and rattled the handle.

Somma glanced at David, who stayed beside her. She hadn't seen him get up.

"Did you lock the door?" she asked in a low voice.

"Yes. I didn't want someone barging in," he said, not moving from her side. He didn't appear concerned of discovery. Would anyone else see him, or was he just visible to her?

"Somma?" Efe called out again.

"Yes, I locked the door," she replied. "I needed a quiet moment. I'll be out in a minute."

"Is there someone there with you?" Efe asked again.

Somma glanced at David. But he just stared at her as if waiting for her response.

"No," she answered, still holding David's gaze. A calmness settled over her mind. She couldn't tell her friends that he was here in the flesh, especially since she didn't fully understand what was going on. "Just give me a moment."

"Okay," her friend said.

She waited a few seconds to make sure Efe had left before she spoke to David. "They are here for an exorcism."

"I know," he said.

"You know? How?"

"I was at the bar with you. I heard your discussions."

She took a step back from him. "You've been following me around and spying on me?"

"No." His hands clenched into fists. "I don't follow you. You summon me, especially when you're in distress. I felt your stress, and I had to go to you."

"I summon you?" Her mind spun at that revelation. How was that possible?

"Yes." He took a step to her. "That's how I got to the bar and heard your friends talking about an exorcism. Don't let them do it?"

She shook her head and shifted from one foot to the other. A part of her didn't want him gone. But it didn't change that fact that he was dead and shouldn't be here. If she was the one summoning him, then she needed to let go and set him free so he could rest in peace. Not to mention that people would never understand his presence.

"Surely you know that you being here like this isn't right?"

"Who says?"

"You're dead, remember?"

"I've never felt more alive."

"Same here, but—"

"She's here." David tilted his head as if listening for something.

"Who's here?" she asked, picking up on his tension. The air around them thickened, and she struggled to breathe. Her heart slowed down and her mouth soured. The dread she'd felt earlier returned. Something dark and oppressive hovered around them.

He grabbed her arm. "There are things I need to explain to you. But you need to get rid of everyone else, especially the woman who's just arrived."

Before she could reply, someone knocked at the door.

"Somma!" Efe called out. "You need to come out now."

CHAPTER SEVEN

As soon as Somma stepped out of the kitchen, the air thickened. As if she waded through sludge, her footsteps slowed.

"There you are." Efe stood beside her. "Are you okay?"

"Yes, I'm fine. What's going on?" Somma asked, glancing from Efe to Omolade who stood from where she sat on the sofa.

"Fola's pastor is here. She's gone to let her in," Lade said.

Just that minute, the air around them shifted. From where she stood, Somma could see the hallway and the entrance to the house.

A woman she didn't recognize stepped into the foyer, dressed in a white flowing silk boo-boo, straight long dark extensions cascading down her back and a face that shimmered with makeup. The woman walked with the poise of a beauty pageant contestant, her heels clicking on the tiled floor.

"Is that Fola's pastor?" Lade whispered, now standing on Somma's left side.

"I guess so," Efe answered from her right side in an equally low voice.

They all seemed to be gawking at the woman who had just arrived with the same shock that ran through Somma. What kind of pastor looked like that?

Fola shut the front door and followed the woman until they entered the living room.

"This is Prophetess Omosun," Fola announced.

The woman beamed a smile at them before directing her gaze at Somma.

Cold fingers skittered down Somma's spine. Her mind became fuzzy. Something wasn't right.

Shaking her head, she stepped forward. "My name is Somma. Thank you for coming at such short notice,

Prophetess. But I'm afraid you've wasted your time. There's no need for you to be here."

"There's a need for cleansing, my child," the woman's voice boomed in the room as she came towards Somma. "Your house is possessed by an evil spirit."

What was the woman talking about? David didn't have an evil bone in him. "No. David is not evil."

"Your husband is dead. Any apparition that visits you is a spirit. The one I feel here is evil, here to torment and destroy. He will drive you insane."

Somma burst out laughing. This was so ridiculous.

The women stared at her as if she'd gone insane. She should never have allowed them to convince her to let the prophetess or whatever she was to come here.

"If David is evil, then I'm the fucking Queen of England." Her voice rose as she suddenly had a flare of annoyance.

Lade gasped and covered her mouth, her eyes bugged out.

"Somma, what are you saying?" Efe said in an incredulous voice.

Her friends would be shocked at her outburst, especially to someone who was supposed to be a holy person.

"I'm saying that this woman Fola brought here is the evil one. Look at the way she's dressed. Does she look like a Christian, let alone a pastor or prophet or whatever?"

"I'm afraid this is worse than I thought. Your friend is already possessed by the evil spirit. It dwells in her." The woman flicked her manicured right hand.

Something slammed into Somma and sent her careening into a sofa. Her mind became hazy again, and her vision blurred. Somma tried to get up, but her weak limbs didn't move.

"Hold her down," the prophetess ordered.

Hands descended on her, pinning her to the sofa. She blinked several times until her sight cleared. Lade held her left arm, Efe her right hand while Fola held her feet.

She tried shaking her head. "Don't do this. I don't want this."

"I'm sorry," Efe said with tears in her eyes. "She's going to make you better."

"No. She's not." Somma wriggled but didn't have enough energy to escape.

Prophetess loomed over her and placed her palm over Somma's stomach. She reeled back and closed her eyes. "You're pregnant."

Somma struggled again. "You see what I mean. The woman is crazy. How can I be pregnant?"

As she said the words, in her mind's eye, she saw the developing embryo in her womb and heard the tiny patter of the heart pumping blood. Although from the size it would be too early to tell the gender, she knew it was male instinctively. She carried a male child in her womb.

"It's true!" Somma cried. "I'm pregnant."

"How is that possible?" Lade asked, staring from Somma to the prophetess.

"She carries a demon child in her womb," the woman replied and lowered her hand again. "She needs to be delivered from its clutches."

"No, you don't!" David's voice echoed.

Something yanked the woman off Somma, and she shrieked. Everyone else released her and shrank away.

Somma's strength returned, and she sat up as David reached for her. She placed her hand on his, and he tugged her up.

"I won't let them hurt you," he said and shielded her with his body.

She wasn't afraid. Her muscles relaxed, and her chest lightened. She felt confident and bold, stepping to his side. This was where she was meant to be, by his side. Not cowering behind him.

"And I won't let them hurt our baby." She looked up at his face with a stern expression. "You have a lot of explaining to do once we get rid of them."

"Yes, my sweet. I will explain everything later," he replied with a wink.

Omosun seemed to regain herself and straightened, facing them. Lade, Efe, and Fola stood behind the woman, their fear evident.

Somma didn't blame her friends for being frightened by David's presence. Humans were conditioned to believe that the dead didn't exist in this realm and shouldn't walk amongst the living.

"Somma, come to me," the prophetess stretched out her hands.

Invisible hands grabbed Somma's shoulders and tugged. David still held her hand, and she was suddenly in the middle of a tug of war.

David struck his hand in the air, and the woman jerked back as if she'd been hit. But her invisible grip on Somma didn't lessen.

"Fight her," David said to Somma. "Open your mind and see the witch for what she really is. Do it."

Somma closed her eyes and images bombarded her. She saw her friend's auras, pinks and browns surrounding Efe and Lade while black surrounded Fola and the prophetess. Focusing her mind, Somma broke through the cloak around the woman. She saw her real being, a wrinkled hag.

Another image slammed into her, from the plane crash. The prophetess walked among the dead and drank the blood of the young.

"It was you!" Somma screamed as she opened her eyes. "You caused the plane crash and killed them."

The witch's eyes glowed black, and she cackled. "So, you know. I was there to kill him. Everyone else was a bonus."

"Why?" Somma reared back. The evil woman had killed David? She glanced at her husband, who stood beside her, holding her hand.

"Hasn't he told you yet?" the witch chortled. "He's a warlock, and I hate warlocks."

Lade and Efe collapsed on the floor. Somma jerked her hand free from David. "What?"

"Don't let go—" Before he could finish, he flew off the ground and slammed into the wall. He slumped to the floor, unmoving.

"No!" Somma ran to him and knelt beside him. His body was cold to the touch. "David, don't you dare die on me again."

"Now, your turn." The witch loomed over her. "I want that baby in your womb."

Rage boiled in Somma. Blood pounded in her ears, and her breathing came out in quick pants. She straightened to her full height. "Over my dead body. You are not getting your wrinkly hands on my baby."

Omosun bared a row of sharp teeth. "That can be arranged."

The witch wrapped her hand around Somma's neck.

A bolt of energy went through Somma, and she slammed both palms against the woman's chest and sent her flying across the room. How the hell did she do that? What had possessed her?

She turned to David, who lay on the floor, but his eyes were now opened as he smiled at her.

"You sure can kick ass," he said with a grin.

She reached for his hand. "Get your ass off that floor and tell me how to kill this bitch. She is not getting my baby."

Somma had waited years to have a child, and now that she was finally pregnant, she wasn't going to let anyone rob her of this gift.

"I thought you'd say that." His smile widened as he put his hand back in hers. When they were connected, it seemed their strengths were multiplied. She'd figured that out already.

The witch leapt into the air at them. They both lifted their hands and balls of fire shot into the woman.

"How am I doing that?" Somma asked, wanting to understand what was going on.

"It's our son. You're tapping into his powers."

She didn't have time to absorb the full implications of his words when something knocked them both back. The witch jumped onto Somma, her claws digging into the skin as her razor-like teeth descended.

David chanted something and rammed his hand into the woman's chest. She gave a blood-curdling shriek, eyes bulging, as David pulled his hand out along with a beating organ. He held the woman's heart in his hand and squeezed it.

Omosun crumpled to the floor. Slowly her body changed from that of a young woman, ageing gradually until she was skeletal and then turned to ashes, all in a few seconds. Even the organ in David's hand blacked and turned to ash.

Somma scrambled back against the wall, shocked at what she'd just witnessed.

David reached for her and helped her to stand up. "Are you okay?"

"Yes, I'm fine." She glanced around the room.

Fola had disappeared. Lade and Efe still lay on the floor. Heart-thumping, she rushed over to them and checked for signs of life. She couldn't bear it if they were hurt or dead.

"They're alive," David said as he waved his hand over the ashes on the floor. "Don't wake them yet until I clear this place up."

As he moved his hands, the soot vanished from the floor.

"How are we going to explain this to them?" Somma asked. She still wasn't entirely sure what had happened.

"I have to wipe their memories," David said in a conversational voice.

"What? You can't do that?" She stood and glared at him.

"Nobody can know what I am."

"And what are you?"

He held her gaze. "I'm a warlock."

Her heart thumped hard. "What is that? Like a male witch?"

"No. A warlock is a hybrid sired by a guardian spirit and a human."

"Oh, my goodness. I really am carrying a demon child." Her pulse skyrocketed, and she backed away, clutching her stomach.

He grabbed her arm and pulled her into a chair. "Listen to me. You have to hear the full story before you jump to a conclusion."

"Start explaining." She turned sideways on the sofa to stare at him with a little suspicion.

He sighed and scrubbed his face.

"A long time ago, guardian spirits were assigned to guard the humans. They were not permitted to mate with humans. The only humans they could mate with were sorceresses. Unfortunately, one guardian spirit, Offurum, fell in love with a human and mated her. Omosun was the sorceress to whom he'd been betrothed. She cursed him and his future lineage."

Somma gasped. "What?"

"She did. The first was that every child in his lineage would lose their powers when born. Also, they would only ever marry a human and they would die at a young age."

He puffed out a breath. "So for thousands of years, my ancestors have fallen in love with a human woman, married her, sired a son and died young. Omosun had been responsible for each death, and the cycle has been repeating itself."

She frowned. "So what was different this time?"

He glanced at her and sighed again. "The difference this time was that I didn't sire a son as a human. So when I died as a human, the spell was partially broken. I got some of my powers back as a warlock. That's how I could feel you and your anguish. And then when you called to me, I came to life."

"So that's how you got me pregnant?" She still needed to understand that bit.

"Yes. Our child is a hybrid with powers because I had regained some strength, so I passed them on to him. He will be a gifted child."

"Goodness." She covered her stomach with her hands. "So, what happens now?"

"It's up to you. Would you rather not have our baby?" He stared at her in a wary expression.

"Of course I want to have our baby. I just need to get used to the idea." She raised her hands. "How am I going to explain it to people, to my friends?"

She glanced at Efe and Lade.

"I have a plan." David took her hands. "I just need to know that you want me to stay."

"You can stay?" Her mouth dropped open.

"Yes, I can. If you want me here," he replied with a smile.

Her heart raced at the possibility of having her husband back in her life. She'd grieved him for months. What if this was her second chance? Could she turn it down just because she was worried about what people would think?

She reached for his face and caressed his stubbly cheek. "I want you to stay."

"That's what I wanted to hear." His smile widened, and he pulled her into his arms and sealed their lips together.

EPILOGUE

One Year Later

Somma pulled out a short champagne silk nightdress from the drawer. Across the bedroom, David tucked sleeping baby Jude into the beech wood-framed cot.

A smile tugged at her lips as she watched her virile and athletic husband handle their infant with such gentility. She'd witnessed his sheer power in action and knew his inherent capabilities. Yet he never displayed any force towards her or their son.

She pulled the T-shirt over her head and tossed it into the clothes bin in the closet before pushing the linen trousers and panties down her hips and kicking them off.

As if sensing her state of undress, David glanced in her direction, a killer smile on his face. Her insides quaked the way they always did when he turned his attention to her.

Two years ago she had neither a husband nor a son after David had been killed in a plane crash. In the years following their marriage and leading up to his death, she'd been unable to conceive a child. David had never lost faith in her, even when she'd despaired because her friend Efe had been getting pregnant every other year.

Efe had seemed like the standard of a fruitful marriage while Somma felt like the flag bearer of infertility. Efe had never rubbed it in her face. Somma had been the one beating herself up and racing from one doctor to the other to find answers. Each one had given her the all-clear, saying there was nothing wrong with her.

Then David had died, and she'd had a double whammy of loss. She'd lost her husband and any possibility of ever having a child. She'd known she would never remarry. David had been her all. No other man would've ever compared.

Then last year, everything changed.

Her husband came back from the dead—a supercharged version of David.

And she'd conceived, finally, their beautiful baby boy everything she'd ever wanted in a child and more.

"What are you thinking about?" David stood behind her, his breath whispered on her bare nape before his fingers tangled in her braids.

Her heart stuttered, and she swallowed before she spoke. "I'm just thinking about the past two years and everything that happened. I'm so grateful to have you and Jude. I didn't think it was ever going to happen."

"You made it happen," he said as he nibbled her earlobe.

She tilted her head as tingles skittered over her flesh. "Actually Omosun made it happen. If she hadn't killed you, I wouldn't have grieved, and we wouldn't have Jude."

"Maybe." He kissed the side of her neck. "But your love and grief brought me back to life. You allowed me to make love to you, which restored my powers. You gave us a second chance."

True. Apparently, if she hadn't grieved him and held on to the memory of him as intensely and as much as she'd done, he might never have come back to life.

When he'd started visiting her at night, her friends had thought he'd been haunting her and had convinced her to undertake an exorcism.

Unfortunately, the woman Fola had invited had been an ancient sorceress bent on revenge.

"Do you think anyone would ever find out what really happened?" she asked as niggles of doubt entered her mind.

David had wiped her friends' memories of what happened on the night of Lade's thirty-seventh birthday. Neither Efe nor Lade could recall any talk of exorcism or what happened after they'd left the wine bar. They assumed they'd gone to their respective homes straight afterwards.

"The event is blocked from your friends' minds, and Fola is dead. There are no other witnesses to worry about."

His words eased her concern.

They had told everyone that David had been in a coma after the crash. Someone had found him and taken him to hospital. When he'd eventually woken up, he'd had no memories so couldn't return home until the memories came back.

Everyone had bought the story, and there had been a big celebration. Only his mother knew the truth, and she had been overjoyed to have her son back and a grandchild on the way.

Unfortunately, Fola had died in her sleep one night due to heart failure. Well, that's what the doctor concluded when she'd failed to wake up.

David had told Somma that she'd been killed during a raid on her coven by guardian spirits who'd been ordered to kill off Omosun's coven members. Apparently, the coven fed on the blood of children to stay young. Omosun had been the power protecting them, but after the witch's demise, the Spirit Council voted to execute the coven members.

Somma had felt no sorrow at Fola's death. The woman whom she'd once called a friend had sensed Somma's early pregnancy and had invited Omosun to harvest the fetus under the guise of an exorcism.

Unfortunately for Fola and Omosun, they hadn't reckoned on the combined magical strength of Somma, David, and their unborn son. They'd fought the sorceress and killed her.

Now, David pressed his chest against her back, his hard erection rubbed against the curve of her bum. His left hand trailed to her breasts, and his right palm tilted her head so that his mouth hovered above hers for a moment.

His actions brought her out of her thoughts and focused her on the here and now and the possibilities for the future.

His mouth crashed on hers, his tongue flicking in a hard and smooth slide over hers. The passion that always lay under the surface ignited. A moan rose from her belly.

Their love for each other had always been expressed physically. It was in everything they did. The way they cared for each other and protected each other.

Lust was a big part of it. Passion came to life with one look, one touch or one taste.

Now she burned as their bodies melded together, her backside to his front, her naked, him fully clothed.

He released her face, and she breathed just as he breathed her in before he kissed her neck and shoulder as his left hand cupped her breasts and squeezed. She arched with the sensation while his right palm travelled to the smooth, shaved sensitive skin between her legs.

As soon as he parted her plump flesh, her intense arousal became evident. The scent floated in the air as his fingers circled her throbbing clit.

"Do you know what you do to me when you respond so fervently?" his gravelly voice only heightened her stimulation.

"Mm-mm," she replied, shaking her head. She parted her thighs, inviting him to explore.

"You make me insatiable. I can never get enough of you."

She felt voracious, hungry for everything he could do to her. With his mouth sucking on the delicate skin of her neck, one hand playing her erogenous breasts and turning her nipples into tight, aching buds and the other caressing her pussy and making her wetter than Kainji Dam, she still longed for more.

As if reading her mind, he swept her off her feet and onto the bed without carrying her. That was one thing about being married to a warlock, magic and reality melded together.

He pulled a pair of black Brazilian lace knickers from the drawer. "This will do for tonight."

One minute he was fully clothed, the next he wore just the panties and a sexy grin tipped his lips.

Her heart raced, and her mouth watered at the sight of him. He was the sexiest man alive, and he made lace lingerie look fantastic. Her body responded as if he touched her and Goosebumps lifted her skin.

He crawled onto the bed and with deliberate slowness, kissed his way up from her legs. With every inch he covered, her skin came alive with tingles. The air around them heated. She clutched the sheets, twisted and writhed until she neared combustion.

"David, please. You're driving me insane." She reached down to cover his head with her hand.

He looked up from where his mouth sucked her breast. "Just the way you drive me crazy, my sweet."

He lifted himself and pressed his hips against hers, the bulge of his erection ground against her pussy, her cream rubbing all over the lace fabric. The friction alone sent her panting and flushing. In a blink, a wave of orgasm crashed over her.

"Oh ... oh ... oh," she cried, thrashing around.

Powerful arms lifted her thighs and his released cockhead pressed against her opening. There was always something intense about having him slam inside her while she was in the middle of a climax. It still sent her into multiples rippling over her skin and mind in wave after wave as he withdrew and slammed in, riding the extreme surge with her.

"You are perfect," he said in a sandpaper and silk voice before he kissed her, snatching the rest of her breath away.

With his strong arms wrapped around her, he made love to her, their hot, slick bodies sliding against each other. Her nerve-endings came alive, and she wrapped her legs around his hips, her fingernails digging into his back.

When she thought she couldn't possibly come apart again, she splintered, crying out his name and clamping around him again and again. She pulled him to a climax, and his hips snapped a couple of times before he went still.

Afterwards, he rolled onto his side and pulled her body flush to his. He pressed his mouth to her shoulder and whispered. "I love you."

In these moments, when her big powerful magical husband opened himself up to her, she knew he needed her, just as much as she needed him. Without her, he wouldn't be, and without him, she wouldn't have survived.

"I love you, too," she said in a choked voice.

Soon she heard his gentle snores as he slept, her body cocooned by his, while their son lay a few feet away, in his cot.

This was their life, their reality, their love. No one else would understand it. But she didn't care. She would fight to protect her family with every ounce of breath she had left. Even if it meant she would remain haunted.

THE END.

ABOUT THE AUTHOR

As a lover of romance novels, Kiru wanted to read stories about Africans falling in love. When she couldn't find those books, she decided to write the stories she wanted to read.

Kiru writes passionate romance and sensual erotica stories featuring African characters whether on the continent or in the Diaspora. When she's not writing you can find her either immersed in a good book or catching up with friends and family. She currently lives in the South of England with her husband and three children.

Kiru is a founding member of Romance Writers of West Africa. In 2011, her debut romance novella, His Treasure, won the Book of the Year at the Love Romances Café Awards. She is the 2015 Romance Writer of the Year at the Nigerian Writers Awards.

Connect with Kiru http://www.kirutaye.com/

EXCERPT FROM DAWSK BY ERHU KOME YELLOW

PROLOGUE

The western region, Nigeria
1875

The warm rays of the evening sun disappeared in the horizon.

The incantations began.

Maa bo pelu iji!

Mo pe agbara ti orun!

Mo pe ironse merin; tin se aye, omi, inan, ati afefe!

Fun emi ti o se dà wà ati eyi ton bo!

Gbo ebe wa!

Wa pelu wa ni ajo ti ale ji!

Lati ti ibi ro nitori ko ma ba le si lekun!

Ma se se wa ni ijamba mo!

Emi pe o wa!

From the east, the wind rose and whipped the trees, bending the branches and leaves. Dark clouds hovered over the Meje clan gathered in the forest clearing. The powers of the spirits they evoked with resonant voices surged in their midst.

The air reeked of a foul presence. Gusts of wind screamed, making the animals scamper in fright.

The hunters of Ori clan remained still and silent, hidden in the long grass, undeterred by the bloodcurdling sounds.

They had waited for this moment all their lives. This mission was the reason they existed, the reason they had been fiercely trained for years.

As devout worshippers of Yemaja, the earth goddess had imbued them with the strength to rid the earth of the abomination that tarnished her order.

The demon hunters with their bodies painted black and white, the symbol of impending war, had in their hands, daggers with long thick horns for handles.

These daggers had been forged from the rocks in the hidden cave beneath *Yemaja's* waterfall—the only weapons capable of slaying the beasts short of taking their heads off from their bodies, which proved to be an almost impossible task.

The hunters waited for the opportune moment to strike, their bodies primed for action, eager for the victory to come.

The Meje clan folk held hands firmly by the edge of the lake and chanted after their leader whose head was adorned with cowries and raffia palm.

Emi pe o wa!

Emi pe o wa!

A great whirlwind rose, startling everyone, including the hunters. It halted after a few heart-thumping moments.

A woman dressed in luminous white cloth materialised and settled gracefully on the surface of the water.

Her white eyes struck fear into the hearts of the Meje people, but their voices only became louder as they chanted without stop.

Thunder clapped in the distance.

The woman did not appear surprised by the events happening around her. She did not even try to escape when a cocoon-like substance began to envelop her body.

This worried the leader of the Meje clan, but they had to continue. There was no stopping now. They had risked their lives coming out of their sanctuary. They were already halfway to their goal of sealing the witch, and that was incentive enough.

As the chanting went on, the Meje people began changing to their true nature, a transformation which brought gasps from the hunters. Astonishingly, their bodies gradually transformed into beast-like forms.

At last, the cocoon swallowed up the woman and then it was slowly lowered into the water.

"It is done!" the leader of the clan, who had not transformed, spoke out in a loud trembling voice.

There were growls and high-pitched howling from the creatures.

A signal went up among the hunters. The time had come to fulfil the wish of their deity. The resonance of their war cries rent the air as the Hunters went out of their hiding places and laid waste to the people of the Meje clan who at that moment tried to salvage any strength they had left to fight back. The ritual had taken quite a toll on them

The stench of death hung heavy in the air as blood was spilt on both sides. One by one, the mark of the hunters, which linked them to the beasts, began to fade, which signified their task was at the verge of completion. The abominations would soon be wiped out from mother earth, and once again balance and order would be restored.

One of the creatures who found a path to escape ran off into the forest guided by the light of the silvery moon. It growled in pain as blood dripped from its side.

"Whatever is out there show yourself, be you spirit or man." A traveller who had found an abandoned hut and settled there for the night came out of it.

The noise among the bushes brought great fear into his heart. He picked a piece of burning firewood and moved forward.

The creature leapt out of the bushes and bounded for the man. It dug its fangs into his shoulders, and at the same time, they both fell to the ground.

The man shocked and injured remained on the ground. He was afraid the beast would come at him again and prayed to the gods of his fathers to save him. He waited for the final blow from the creature, but when none was forthcoming, he turned to his side. His eyes could not believe what he saw.

In place of the beast was a severely wounded woman.

CHAPTER ONE

Orient City, Creek State, Nigeria
2025

For the third time this week, I stayed back to work a shift I hadn't bargained for.

Okay. Maybe I had.

Sure the doctors were bossy and the patients even bossier. Still, being a nurse at St. Cloud, one of the best if not the best hospital in the capital city, was very rewarding.

I loved my job. Maybe too much.

It was my most significant flaw and my greatest strength.

I stepped out of the elevator on the first floor and made my way to the lab. A voice stopped me when I turned right, heading down the chilly corridor.

"Nurse Simi." The attending paediatrician, Dr Izuchukwu, stood at the threshold of the door to a private room. The white patient chart in his hand looked like a cloud against his sky blue scrubs. "I need you to get the MRI results for Latifah Peters. Her mother wants to make sure she's not in any danger. I already told her it's just a bump and nothing more, but you know parents."

Yes, I did. I had to deal with them every day, answering their questions and listening to their complaints. Getting an MRI meant taking the elevator back to the fifth floor to wake up the attending radiologist, Dr Ezeogu.

"I'll get you the results soon," I told him.

"Thanks," he said and hurried off without looking back.

I took the elevator down to the floor, which held the MRI machine.

The patient was already in Radiology with her mother. The older woman held onto her daughter's arms as if the little girl would melt away any moment. I offered her a reassuring smile and waited for Dr Ezeogu to begin.

Begging the five-year-old girl to keep still so we could get a clear picture of her head was a task of its own. She kept squirming inside the MRI machine while her mother sang her a lullaby. Her mother offered her ice cream as a bribe if she remained still, but that did not work either. In the end, I had to administer a sedative.

Thirty minutes later, the radiologist handed me the results just in time for him to get back to sleep. I found the paediatrician and gave him the file.

My next stop was the nurse's station, where I had left my bag. I was ready to catch up on some needed sleep. I took the bag into the changing room and removed my scrubs, changing into a pair of jeans, a wrap top and sneakers. Casual chic and an off-and-on relationship with bohemian was my go-to style. I put my straightened hair into a ponytail and stared at the mirror right above the baby-changing table. I touched my jaw and groaned. Any skinnier and I would have to sign up with a modelling agency.

"I need food," I said to myself and made a mental note not to immediately lie on any flat surface when I got home.

Joshua waited for me at the nurses' station when I got out. I had completely forgotten about him. He was talking to Nadia, my colleague and best friend.

Joshua and I had been dating for three months, and he seemed to have understood precisely what my job entailed. He always did his best not to get angry when I had to cancel any plans we had. But he could only understand for so long.

With a pleading expression on my face, I walked up to him,

"I'm so sorry, Josh," I said and gave him a peck on the cheek, hoping it would ease his anger. "I know we were supposed to go out tonight."

"Three hours ago, Simi. Three hours ago. I had to leave the restaurant in shame and come here."

"I'm so sorry. I promise I'll make it up to you."

"When?" he asked with a scowl.

"How about tomorrow night?"

He shook his head and sighed. "I need to talk to you alone."

My heart sank. I glanced at Nadia who had one hand under her chin elbow on the desk, her ears perked up to catch every word we were about to say.

"Yes, we definitely need some privacy," I agreed, leading him by the arm to the main stairway.

"What do you want to tell me?" I asked when we were in the clear.

"Listen..."

"Oh no..." I said, my throat slowly closing up.

"I'm so sorry, Simi, but I think we should end this. I see no future for us."

When did a noose get around my neck? I could barely breathe.

"You're a gorgeous woman. I'm sure you'll find someone else. Or you could change your job."

I balled my sweaty hands and swallowed, hoping the boulder in my throat would go down smoothly. It didn't.

"I think you should stop putting work before men. Do you want to be an old spinster?"

I wanted to tell him to drop dead. Instead, with an icy smile, I said, "Thank you, Joshua."

"I hope ..." he began to say, but I was well on my way back to the nurse's station.

Nadia pretended to be buried in paperwork.

My body felt like jelly. My fists were still balled up, and my stomach knotted. I slowly looked up at Nadia.

"You can stop pretending," I told her.

"What happened? Tell me," she asked without hesitation.

I loosened my fists. "Nothing. Don't you have a job to do?"

She hissed and said "I don't care about that right now. Start talking, Oladeji."

"Like I said, nothing."

"Then why are you so sad? And look, Joshua is leaving."

I glanced back in time to see him push the glass door open and walk out.

"Did you guys have a quarrel? What did you say to him, he looked pissed?"

"We broke up, okay? He broke up with me. Are you satisfied, huh? Are you?" I meant to sound unfazed, but my voice betrayed me. My words came out like a child who just lost her favourite toy.

Her eyes suddenly went dim, and she gave me that 'what a pity' look I hated so much.

"I'm so sorry," She said, coming around to give me a hug.

"Why?" I sobbed against her chest. "I'm okay, right? I'm dateable, right?"

"Shhhh," Nadia's soothing voice tried to calm me down. "You're a hottie, you know that. Any man would be lucky to have you."

"But not Joshua," I said, spite rife in my tone.

"Not Joshua. Someone else."

"I don't want to be an old spinster."

"You won't be."

"I'm going home," I said, not wanting to draw any more attention to myself. I picked up my bag and slung it over my slouched shoulder.

"Yes, you should go home, dear. I'll call you."

I strode out into the cold night and walked down the street full of people going in and out of St. Cloud. I stopped at the T-junction, waiting for the tramcar.

Orient city was the first place in the country that had begun the use of tramcars. All thanks to Governor Ebeye, most of these streetcars operated in the shopping district. It was the best way for me to get from A to B.

I took the car at the T-junction and headed west for Darcy Avenue before taking a cab to Ugbe Boulevard where I lived in a sub-urban type cul-de-sac.

By the time I got home, my appetite and need to sleep had disappeared.

I spent hours sitting on the worn out couch, staring at pictures of Joshua and me on my phone. My heart pounded with every swipe. I noticed the delete button and started deleting in a rush. My hands were wound so tight around the phone, it switched off. I flung it, but it landed on the armchair across me unharmed. Even my phone gave up on me. I hadn't planned on crying, but I found myself bawling my eyes out until I fell asleep.

By the next morning, word had gone around St. Cloud that I had been dumped and was single and searching. I definitely was not.

I swear I could kill Nadia with my bare hands, but it was her default setting. She thought going around telling every male available I was single would make them respond like the predators they were, and that would boost my confidence.

Each time I walked past male nurses or doctors, they greeted me with stares. My face and ears burned with embarrassment. I wanted to hide, but I had to work, so I held my head up high and went about my business.

Halfway through my shift, I was making my way out of the coma ward when I was accosted by Dr Nicholas. He was one of three resident gynaecologists. His hands were in his pockets as he approached me. His long thin legs reminded me of a spider's.

"Simi."

My mouth fell open as I jerked my head, taken aback because he had never spoken to me. And now he was addressing me by my first name.

"Yes, Doctor Nicholas."

"You can drop the formalities, Simi. I heard about your recent breakup."

Of course. Nadia's gossip communication's system went wide, indeed.

"It's quite unfortunate."

"Yes, it is." The noose was back, and my palms itched.

"How are you holding up?"

"I am fine, thank you." The situation was becoming awkward with him standing in front of me and saying nothing.

"Do you need my help with something, Dr Nicholas?" Other than to talk about my damaged love life?

He hesitated before asking. "I was wondering if we could have dinner sometime. Tonight perhaps?"

Another awkward moment I had been hoping to avoid.

"Um..."

"It's just dinner," he persuaded. "What harm can be done?"

"I don't know, Dr Nicholas."

He took a step backwards and raised an eyebrow. "Call me, Nicholas."

"Right."

"I know you're not working late tonight."

That was true.

"So?"

"Okay." I forced a smile. "We can have dinner."

"I'll pick you up by eight."

"I'll be at the nurse's station."

He sauntered away and exchanged greetings with one of the orderlies.

It was fifteen minutes past eight when Nicholas reached the nurse's station. He was dressed in a casual long-sleeved shirt and black cotton trousers. He said hello and led the way to his car. I wore the knee-length kimono dress I got for myself on my last birthday tucked in the back of my locker and the sneakers I had planned on wearing home I regretted not taking the knitted sweater I had put out that morning. I hated the sight of Goosebumps all over my hands and legs.

"Cold night," I said, trying to start a conversation.

"Yes, indeed," was his input to my observation.

"Last year's Harmattan season wasn't as terrible as this year's. The night keeps getting colder and the day hotter."

"I imagine it wasn't. I was not in the country this time last year. I hate this weather; the extreme heat and the extreme cold." He frowned as he fumbled with his key.

We arrived at the restaurant at Bayside, a commercial district, after he drove for ten minutes. It was one of those old restaurants that had made a name for themselves when Creek state was formed. He ordered red wine to start, and we drank slowly.

"What happened to end your relationship so quickly?" he began.

"Work."

"Ha, I see. The great excuse."

"Yes."

"I'll get straight to the point, Simisola. I know it's too soon for you with your breakup and all, but we could have a good time."

I smiled at him if only to ease the increasing awkwardness of the situation.

"You're a lovely woman, Simi, any man—" He was cut short by the waiter.

"Are you ready to order?" He looked at me and then at Nicholas, who already picked up the menu from the table.

I stared down at the menu on my side of the table, not wanting to touch the darn thing. I let him order for both of us.

"We'll have the snail thing you have here. Is that good for you, Simi?"

I nodded.

The waiter left after Nicholas asked him to bring another bottle of red wine.

"As I was saying, you are..."

"You disgraceful adulterer!"

A woman in a blue blouse and pleated skirt shouted from the entrance of the restaurant. Everyone turned to stare at her. I wondered who she was and who she was referring to. And then I saw the fear in Nicholas' eyes and the way he tried to avert the gaze of the woman who was now strolling with determined steps towards us.

"Oh heavens, no..."" I muttered with my head down. "You're married?"

I had neither seen a ring on his finger nor heard anything about him being a husband.

He said nothing.

"Well, that's just fantastic."

The woman reached our table and gave him a slap that could be heard at the end of the room. "So the rumours were true. You seduce tramps like this one over here and have your way with them."

My hands trembled as she rained down insults on her adulterous husband and me. Was this a sign for me to give up on men?

"Eghe, I can explain," Dr Nicolas began.

"Explain what? Explain what, you bastard?" She gripped him by the collar of his shirt and spat in his face. That was not enough for her. She picked up the wine glass and emptied the contents on his head.

I could not hold back a slight chuckle. I laughed at the wimp of a man on bended knees, and at myself. How did I end up there? My eyes watered. I bit my lower lip to hold back the tears.

"We've only been married for two months, and you've already become a chronic adulterer. You have me. What else do you want?"

Dr Nicholas cleaned his face and said "I'm sorry. Let me explain."

"I want a divorce," was the last thing the crazed woman said before stomping away. Nicholas went after her, pleading woefully.

There was total silence in the restaurant.

I was too scared to look around. I could already feel the judgmental stares from the other customers burning uncountable holes in my body.

"Who's going to pay for the drinks?" The waiter was back.

"I'll... I'll pay. But just for the opened bottle." I gave him the money. I was ready to go when I heard someone say 'whore'. I called the waiter back. "On second thought I would like to have the second bottle."

I drank my wine at the bar, hoping it would drown out the voice that called me a whore. Whore? Really? Damn. I poured the drink down my throat to keep myself from retching. I finished the bottle and ordered another.

The person by my side who had been drinking slowly from a tall glass cleared his throat. I turned my attention to him. He was wearing a hooded sweater and jean trousers. He pulled down his baseball cap to conceal his face even though the dim light in the room was already helping him.

"Did you see what happened over there?"

I pointed in the direction of the restaurant. I was highly tipsy.

"I was disgraced, that's what happened. Embarrassed is the word."

He angled his body toward me, his face still hidden.

"A hard man is good to find. Wait, or is it the other way around?"

He appeared to be listening to me blab because he responded with a smile.

"I know I just met you, but I feel you should know these things. I am sad, stranger. I love my job, and it's constantly affecting my relationships. I'm never going to settle down. Maybe I should just concentrate on my job, you know? But my sister won't like to hear that. No, she won't. She's a crazy one, my sister, but she wants the best for me. No, I'll concentrate on my job."

He nodded slowly.

"I should. Yes, I should. I should have another drink."

I looked into my purse to find out I had no money on me and remembered I had left my phone charging in the nurses changing room. I laughed.

"Wow, no way to get home. No more money, no way to call for a ride. Aren't I just the unluckiest woman on earth?"

"I'll give you a ride home, Miss..." It was the first time I heard him speak, and I wanted to see the face behind such a soothing voice.

"Miss Simi, no," I waved my arms around sluggishly.

"Ice Queen." Hiccup. "Ice Queen is my name. My sister gave me the name, and it really is more befitting with the way I seem to put my job before my lovers."

I laughed and hiccupped loudly. "It's my superhero name. Shush, don't tell anyone."

"Can you write down your address?"

He gave me a pen and paper, and I managed to scribble down my address in handwriting that did not belong to me.

"Let's go," he said, getting out of his chair. I made to stand up, but my legs did a lousy job of supporting my drunken weight. The man was by my side, holding me up.

Big strong arms which could only be from so many sessions in a gym, half dragged me all the way to his car and put me in the passenger's seat. When he got in, he adjusted the cap on his head, and a stream of lustrous jet black hair partially spilt down his forehead. His hands reached for my body.

"What are you doing? What are you doing you, pervert?" I was ready to use my teeth on him if he tried to take advantage of the situation.

"I'm strapping you in, Ice Queen."

"Oh."

A sigh escaped from his full lips as he started his car.

"Where are you from?"

His eyes were focused on the road.

"What?"

"What country are you from, stranger?"

"Here, Nigeria."

The moving car and strawberry scent most likely from an air freshener made me sick.

"But…"

"My mother's German." His answer came out in a forced manner.

"I see."

He helped me out of the car when we arrived in front of my bungalow, the last house in the quiet cul-de-sac.

"Take care of yourself," he told me. I fumbled with my bag for a few minutes and finally found my keys.

"Thank you..." I turned around, but he was already gone.

***

It seemed like another lifetime when I found myself walking down this strange, lonely road, darkness closing behind me. The night seemed to be conjured out of the fog, clouding my senses and making me numb.

I did not recognise where I was or why I kept on moving forward. Soon I appeared in a forest. Falling leaves floated across to me and danced around the tall trees. I walked in and out of them baffled by how green and bright everything seemed. Behind a tree, about twenty feet from me was an outline of a person who hid as if afraid to get out.

"Who's there?" I asked, my voice shaky.

No answer.

I moved towards the shape, but it floated to the trees on my right. I turned sharply to find it gliding toward me.

It was a woman clad in white, holding a staff. She had a smile on her dark blue lips.

Trembling all over, I fell to my knees.

The sight of her terrifyingly white pupils should have sent me running, but my legs didn't move.

She came close, ever so gracefully and said, "Daughter of Ireti. The time is almost upon us."

"What ... what ... what ...?" I couldn't form words, and I blinked so fast I could barely see.

"When the time comes, you'll know," she answered. Her white eyes became black. "You'll certainly know."

She disappeared through the trees.

***

My body jerked as I woke to find my curtains on fire. I scrambled for the bottle of water on my bedside table and threw the contents on the flames. It went out with a searing sound.

As I stared at my charred curtains, my heart raced uncontrollably. I recalled the dream clearly. I knew not what to make of it other than a drunken delusion, but there was no explanation for the fire.

Thank you for reading Enchanted: Volume Two.
If you enjoyed the stories please leave a review.

OTHER BOOKS BY LOVE AFRICA PRESS

Enchanted: Volume One features stories by:
Emem Bassey, Lauri Kubuitsile, Michele Sims and Obinna
Obioma

Dawsk by Erhu Kome Yellow

Scar's Redemption by Kiru Taye

Twisted by Stanley Umezulike

Pharaoh's Bed by Mukami Ngari

Find out more:
www.loveafricapress.com

www.ingramcontent.com/pod-product-compliance
Lightning Source LLC
Chambersburg PA
CBHW050843190726
48286CB00007B/2203